In the Shadow of the Throne

IN THE SHADOW OF THE THRONE

David Tudor

Aureus

First Published 1997

Printed in Great Britain.

A catalogue record for this book is available from the British Library.

Aureus Publishing 144 Marlborough Road Cardiff CF2 5BZ.

ISBN 1 899750 01 0

To Diana, Princess of Wales

Prologue

'All the world's a stage
And all men and women merely players.'
Shakespeare

She had learned how to paint her own face, and now as she sat before the mirror - a thing she endured only when she had to - the hands of the queen busied themselves with an agility that belied her age. Gradually the face before her, flushed at the moment by the warmth of her thoughts, turned lighter and lighter with applications of ceruse until it looked as chalky-white as the visage of a statue.

This substance, a mixture of lead and vinegar, turned women's skin so calcimine in colour they sometimes pencilled in false veins on their breasts to make the unearthly shade look natural, and with time it had a tendency to harden the flesh like the surface of an old painting. Yet she among all her subjects would least have questioned this torturing of God's creation: fairness of skin dominated all other aspects of style, followed by golden hair, thin brows, and lean features.

In a word, every woman in the kingdom wanted to look like her, and the English standard of beauty had taken her name: Elizabethan. Few people, men or women, had ever lived to see the appellation their parents gave them at their birth become an adjective. But then no woman ever - not Cleopatra, not Joan of Arc, not the mother of Christ herself - had ever commanded such power.

She ruled the world's greatest empire, a realm that exceeded Rome in its might and rivalled Greece for its achievement. At her bidding, armies and navies waged war or brought peace on the continent of Europe, at the fringes of India, and on the shores of the distant American colony named for her, the second and last woman in history known by the title of Virgin. Her sword had dubbed knights, and her words had raised men to honour before the whole nation; so also her orders had brought the most promising careers to an end in the grisly knighthood of the axe.

And now in the seventh decade of her life, Elizabeth faced the mirror for one rare moment. In the glass, a critical counsellor whose wisdom she most often avoided, she saw the creeping certitude of aging that with time catches up to all mere mortals.

Her ancient predecessor to the throne, Canute, had tried to stop the waves from splashing on the shore, but she'd never been so vain. In spite of courtiers' praise - that ever-rising tide of words through the years, words that might have swallowed her in their lulling surf if she'd allowed them - she'd kept her wits (and her counsel) close about her. She had always known, and now as the vastness of eternity lapped at the latter years of her life she knew better than ever, how small her own image loomed before the great King on high.

Yet had not even He found Himself alone, and out of His solitude created man with all his folly just so that He might have a companion? He could create a man, she thought now at her dressing table, and yet it is not my fortune even to have one as a husband.

Before her she saw the mask of her face, and without the application of rouge it looked white as death. She would never have left her chambers like this, never have received the kings and princes and dukes who paid her honour; the mask had to appear natural, and for that a little reddening was required. She took a vial of fucus and began to put it on, and just as the ceruse had covered her wrinkles and lines, now this gave her the sanguine aspect so prized by men and women alike.

With each year, she'd had to work a little harder to look like herself, to conform to the standard she had set. But then 'Queen Elizabeth' had always been a creation, a property owned by the crown and the people of England. She had simply played a role written for her by destiny, and played it with such skill that only the closest of her intimates would ever have guessed that she and it were not one and the same.

And yet in a jewelled casket beside her bed she kept another face, another image of herself, and when she turned from the mirror she lifted the lid on the box and looked down into the life of Elizabeth Tudor.

First out came a locket that held a portrait of her mother. She never mentioned Anne Boleyn in public, and indeed she had only the dimmest recollection of this woman from whom she'd inherited the slender neck around which she now placed the locket on a chain. No doubt her celebrated courage had likewise come from Anne, who had gone to her death in order to ensure that she, Elizabeth, might rise to become sovereign over all England.

Anne herself had reigned as queen consort for a thousand days; then her husband, in a time of grief for the death of his first wife, let his eye fall on Anne's comely maid, Jane Seymour. Accused of adultery, sent to the dreaded Tower of London, and condemned to die, Anne had been given the choice of life if she would only renounce her 'bastard' daughter's claims to the throne. She had refused, and her grace as she faced her execution - joking that her little neck would make her death at the axe easier, and begging the crowd to pray for the king - had proven her a queen in spirit.

Next Elizabeth took a large ring from the casket and slid it onto her slender index finger, where it rolled around like a grown man's hat on the head of a boy. It had belonged to her father, Henry VIII, and she had given it to her friend Lord Essex with the vow that if ever he needed a favour, whatever it might be, he need only send it back to her.

He'd been an ambitious young man - she'd known so many of those in her time! - and his vainglory had brought him to trial for treason, whereupon he'd sought to call in the favour long postponed. But the lady-in-waiting who received the ring, not knowing its significance, had failed to give it to her queen, and Essex too went to his death in the Tower. In private Elizabeth had wept for Essex, though not before she exclaimed with vehemence to the errant maid, 'God may forgive you, but I never will!'

Beneath the locket and the ring inside the casket she found a yellowed sheet of paper on which she'd written in her own hand three mournful words. She unfolded it and read once again the last lines she'd ever received from the only man she had loved enough to marry.

Robert Dudley, Earl of Leicester, had accrued no shortage of scorn from the queen's other admirers, and she had found herself angry enough with him to embarrass him in public more than once; but her affection for him had been no secret, and she'd shown it sometimes in surreptitious ways. (No doubt Essex had first won her favour for being Dudley's stepson.) And then in the year of her navy's glorious victory over the Armada, Dudley had passed from her, leaving only the letter. When she received it, she'd read it without any sign of emotion; then she'd folded it, written His Last Letter across the front, and put it away among her dearest treasures.

In spite of many proposals, she'd refused to marry for fear that her people might perceive that her husband, whoever he might be, had usurped the throne. Yet though she would let no man rule her, she lived her life almost entirely among men. She'd lost her mother in the dark years of her early childhood, and her one sister had almost had her killed, so experience had not taught her to count on the constancy of other women. Instead she surrounded herself with close admirers like Dudley and Essex, and distant ones among the crowned heads of Europe; wise men such as Francis Bacon and Philip Sydney, and adventurous ones like Walter Raleigh and Francis Drake.

Within these concentric circles, she had consigned herself to her solitude, knowing that in spite of (or perhaps because of) the many men seeking her favour, she could repose her confidence in no man. Once again, she had her own painful memories as a guide. Her father had betrayed her when he turned against her mother, and her one legitimate half-brother, who ruled to the age of sixteen as Edward VI, had died fifty years before. She'd had two 'natural' half-brothers (which meant that her father had not married their mothers): Henry Fitzroy, Duke of Richmond, who died when she was three; and Henry Carey, Lord Hunsdon. Her father had never acknowledged his paternity to the latter; therefore she and Hunsdon did not recognise one another as brother and sister, but rather as cousins.

But there had been one other natural son, one other half-brother, and he had a secret place at the bottom of her jewelled casket. There among the dust of years she found a sheet older by three decades than Leicester's final missive. It bore a poem, but no one's hand had signed it, and she alone of those alive knew the identity of its author.

Her sister Mary still reigned when that poem was new, and Elizabeth had only shortly before had her life spared from the Tower. She had stopped to pray at St. Botolph's, to thank God for her reprieve, and there in the twilight of the quiet church she had met with a man whose relation to her no one else could know. Before they parted, aware as they were that they could speak as intimates only in the rarest and most secret moments, he had slipped his anonymous verse to her.

Sitting now alone in her room, recognising that in not too distant a time death would join her to her brother, she remembered the young girl she had been and the young man who so gallantly had pledged to protect her. And he had indeed, standing beside her (far, far back in the shadows) to provide counsel and comfort. When she had needed him most, in those days that followed when she assumed the throne, he'd proven himself the closest thing to a friend she would ever know.

Perhaps there had been one love in her life even greater than that which she'd felt for Leicester...

This man too had had his ambitions, hoping as he did to become England's greatest poet and playwright. But he had died young, and a lifetime had passed since then. Another man had taken the title to which he'd aspired, and would likely hold it for all time; just two years old when Richard died, he had quoted a song by him in his play *Romeo and Juliet.*

But in her eyes, Richard had done something greater. It was one thing to stand at the centre of attention, as she had for most of her life; it was quite another to serve without glory. She had ruled plenty long enough to know that a monarch is a symbol, an identity half fictional, composed both of the person who holds the title and the sum total of the wisdom (or lack of it) she receives from those around her. Even these many years later, she hated to imagine what her early reign would have been like without Richard.

She had loved him as she had no other member of her family, yet custom had prevented them from acknowledging this before the world. Now, though, sitting alone in her chambers, she said the words she never could while he lived: 'Yes, dear Richard, you were my greatest friend, and I love thee dearly still.' She stopped for fear that a tear would mar her royal visage, then she went on, her voice cracked with the feelings long unspoken. 'Your secret has been guarded well, but you and I can take comfort in knowing that the Tudor name will live when I, like you, am dust.'

She shut the lid on her private treasures, locking away once more the unsigned poem whose meaning to her constituted more than the sum of its words - the poem which would go with her to her grave, unread by any eyes other than her own. 'The legacy will live,' she said again, 'thanks to you.'

I

The rain ran in rivulets down the leaded glass panes of the window to Richard Edwardes's room. Outside through the mists loomed the gray Gothic buildings of Oxford, already old in 1545, and he glimpsed a few solitary figures here and there hurrying through the cold drizzle. He got up from his books, stirred the fire in the great hearth, put on a kettle of tea, then sat back down at his desk. Later that day he would teach a class in logic for the younger men, lads of fifteen just beginning their studies here at the university, but he had several hours to prepare. Glorious solitude stretched before him, an afternoon spent warm and dry while the world without the window shivered.

Richard looked into the fire burning briskly, and his thoughts wandered for a moment to the strange but happy events that had placed him here. A mere country lad, he'd been selected to sing in the choir of the Chapel Royal, a glorious experience that had exposed him to languages and other undiscovered worlds. He had performed in theatrical productions, sung for the royal family, and played a part in His Majesty's own special church services. In those disciplined years, he had grown and matured as a thinker; but alas, as a boy matures his voice does too, and when his vocal chords could no longer bring forth the dulcet tones so prized by the choirmaster and the royal ears, he might have expected an early retirement to his home in the west of England.

But then the king himself had granted him a scholarship to the great Oxford University at the age of fifteen. After four years of hard study in theology, music, and the ancient Greek and Hebrew languages, he received his bachelor's degree, and soon afterward had been appointed the first professor at the newly created Christ Church College. Just last month he had received the university's highest degree and been ordained a priest, or 'clerk,' but more importantly to him, his poetry had of late begun gaining recognition among his peers in the academic world.

The academic world... His studies called, and he knew he'd best apply himself to his books anon if he would have anything to tell his lads that afternoon. A man might be born with a notion of God in his spirit, as St. Augustine taught, but knowledge of Aristotle and Zeno could only be achieved by hard work.

Just then a knock came at the heavy wooden door, and Richard looked up, startled. Perhaps it's a student, he thought, closing his book. The knocking continued, louder and insistent. 'I'm coming,' he said, reaching for the door, but the sight he saw when he opened it shocked him so much he knew not what to say next.

It was the Dean of Oxford himself, standing stern and imperious before him in his robes. For him, the humblest of professors, to receive a visit from that exalted don was as improbable as the most minor baron in the furthest-flung shire of the realm entertaining King Henry himself. The fact that the dean, John Edwardes, was his uncle made no difference at all: in Richard's five years at the university, the man had acknowledged his existence only on a handful of occasions, and even then he'd treated him as a subordinate and not a nephew.

For a moment Richard stared speechless into his uncle's fierce, hawk-like eyes, then he regained a measure of poise and said, 'Please come in, sir.' He had never dared call him 'Uncle John', almost as though their relation to one another were a secret.

The dean brushed past him and with a single sweeping glance took in Richard's room. Even by the standards of Oxford, John Edwardes had a stuffy, indeed chilly, demeanour; no one would have guessed, witnessing the magisterial way in which he carried himself now, that he had not entered the university as a student until the age of twenty-two. By that point in their lives, most scholars were expected to have moved on to their professions, and yet he had commenced his studies and from that late start emerged to the exalted position he now held.

But in spite of this most prestigious office, and in spite of his dedication to it - as well as his considerable intellect - the Dean of Oxford had lately demonstrated an inability to conform to the changes afoot in the kingdom. Like many of his generation, John Edwardes had grown up and been educated and later ordained believing without deviation in the infallibility of the Church of Rome and its Supreme Pontiff. Now King Henry had severed England's ties with the Vicar of Christ and his church, sundering the fixed world John knew, and had made known his disfavour with any cleric who could not adapt to the times. Just two years before, the Archbishop of Canterbury had rebuked the dean for 'keeping the students from the true Word,' and though John had ever since tried to appear reconciled to the changes, he could not hide his ingrained rejection of the new Church of England.

The dean stood for a moment in lordly silence, but before Richard could guess a reason for his visit or even offer him a chair, he announced, 'I have come that you may know the truth of a secret long hidden.'

The man stood there a moment longer, and Richard started to speak, but the dean spoke again: 'I have been dismissed from the university because your true father believes himself above God!'

'My father...'

'Have respect for your elders, boy!' The dean's high, reedy voice seemed inappropriate to his appearance, perhaps the reason why he spoke so seldom. 'Pray remain silent until I have finished what I am here to say. Your position at this university is not at all what you think. Let this visit serve as a warning of what ills you too may taste before King Henry's wrath is assuaged.'

Having finished this prologue, the dean seemed to relax ever so slightly, and he accepted both the chair and the cup of tea Richard offered him. As the younger man watched the steam rising off the cup in a spiral before his uncle's face, he saw in the other man's expression - what? Was it anger or fear or grief?

'Your father,' the dean now continued, 'is not the man you think him to be. In plain words, your father is not my brother, Master Will Edwardes, at all.' He paused dramatically. 'Your father, boy, is none other than the king.'

Richard stared at the bearer of the these strange words. The king? King Henry? But -

'How do you think you came to be trained in the choir of the Chapel Royal,' the uncle asked rhetorically, 'and then suddenly chosen for a scholarship to this university? Do you imagine such happens to all young men, or even to all young men of talent?'

'But sir,' Richard said, his voice feeble from shock, 'how can this be true?'

A thin, almost imperceptible smile of spite rippled the dean's face. 'To find the answer to that question, I suggest you ask your mother.' He took a sip of tea. 'Mayhap you are wondering why now, in the twenty-first year of your life,

I have chosen to reveal this secret to you. A fair question.' He seemed to slacken his stiffness just a bit more, as though the telling of this tale had unfettered a tension long held within him. 'Your father - your true father, that is, the king - has seen fit to dismiss me from my office because I dare question aspects of his reform, nay his revolt against, the Holy Catholic Church.'

John stopped for some moments to sip reflectively on his tea, and for want of other words Richard asked, 'What will you do now, sir?'

The dean lifted a finger. 'That is none of your concern, nor have I come here to speak of myself. The message I give you, beside that which I have already said, is this: God alone knows what the king may do next. No doubt he guesses that I may retaliate by revealing this secret of your birth, as I have, and you must be prepared that he may require an interview with you, though whether for good or for ill is not mine to say. Forewarned is forearmed!'

And then he relaxed even more, so much that he appeared exhausted from his mission and the words he'd had to speak. In a voice that sounded near spent, he said, 'Seek no more answers from me. I have acquitted my conscience, and am done with this place and this secret. Now I must ready myself to leave.'

He stood up, and Richard stood too. 'Forgive me, sir,' Richard managed to say, 'if I am so stunned by this news you bring that I lack words to speak of it. I am certainly sorry for your misfortune, and can only pray that...'

'Think not of me, boy,' the uncle said in a grim but also strangely kind tone. 'You'll have matters enough with which to concern yourself in the future.' With that, he bade his nephew good-bye and disappeared into the dim light of the hallway beyond the door.

2

The moment his uncle had gone, Richard sat back heavily on his chair. The rain continued, spangling the panes with jewelled droplets, but now everything in his world looked different to him. Could this sombre room, once his castle but now revealed in its unadorned simplicity, contain one of royal blood? Who, he asked himself, was Richard Edwardes?

At the age of twenty, Richard possessed all the features that qualified a man as handsome in 1545: tall and lean, he had strong features and large, expressive blue eyes, with a fair complexion and hair and beard of a deep auburn shade. At this moment something new in his appearance struck him - did not his face conform to the likeness of the ruler? And not just his face. Like King Henry, he was a sportsman, and he loved hunting, horsemanship, and any other activity that required the use of his natural agility and dexterity. So too he had a piercing intelligence and appetite for scholarship, as well as a talent for writing and composing music, which he guessed now might have come from - his father?

The son of Will Edwardes and Agnes Blewitt Edwardes had entered the world on March 21, 1525, in the quiet parish of North Petherton in Somersetshire, and was christened there in the Church of St. Mary the Virgin. Nestled in the glorious rolling foothills of the Cotswold Mountains, his home lay among a patchwork of emerald farms stretching as far as the eye could see in three directions; to the north, across the Bristol Channel, lay the ancient land of Wales, and on a clear day he could glimpse its craggy coast from the rooftop of the house where he first saw light.

The man he'd known as his father, whose great physical stature he'd always assumed to be the source of his own considerable height, had come from the other side of Bristol Channel. He'd been called, after the traditional Welsh manner, William ap Robert ap John, the 'ap' signifying son-ship not unlike the 'ben' or 'ibn' common in the Levant, but though Richard had been the first son 'ap William', that name fell instead to his younger brother, born a year later.

His parents had four boys in all, and Will Edwardes, as most people knew the father, became a friend and a hero to all his sons. A year ago he had died, and Richard had missed him dearly, nor would the bittersweet news his uncle had brought him do anything to lessen his love for that kind and gentle man.

Richard had left his family early. At the age of seven, his parents had called him into the parlour for a special meeting, and there had told him that he'd been chosen to sing in the Boys' Choir at the Chapel Royal. Of course he'd been overjoyed at this news, but though he showed wisdom in excess of what one might expect from a seven-year-old, he was a child still, and did not relish the thought of leaving his home, his parents, and his brothers to go off to London. He and his brother William were especially close, comrades in play and adventure, and it sorrowed him to think he should leave his friend behind.

Nor again because of his years - did it occur to him to ask how the son of a family with modest means and name had been invited to such a great honour. But as he reflected on it now, from the vantage point of time and his uncle's revelations, he saw a clue in a strange interchange he'd had not long after he learned of his acceptance to the Chapel.

King Henry often came to his Huntworth lodge at North Petherton, a special occasion for the parish, with banqueting and celebrations every day. In the spring of the year Richard turned eight, the monarch came as always, and the boy had watched with wonder the manner in which His Highness conducted himself at the commencement of the hunt.

Henry VIII, as Holbein would later so faithfully capture in his famous portrait, was an imposing figure, and he strutted about majestically on the first morning of the hunt as the beaters and huntsmen began to assemble. He mounted his horse with the ease of an expert, and even had he been clad in sackcloth everyone present would have known him for the king he was, so regal was his bearing. The crowd waited for his signal to begin, and when once he gave his grand gesture, the air was pierced with the baying of the hounds and the thump of horses' hooves resounding across the countryside. Truly it must be an awesome thing to be a king, Richard had thought to himself. Never have I seen a man more grand, not even - it had frightened him to admit it then - my father himself.

At the end of the day, King Henry and his retinue had returned with the prizes of the hunt, which his men delivered to the kitchen. He'd dismounted close to where Richard was standing, and when he got down he looked at the lad for a moment. The king had eyes as gray and as sharp as the blade of a sword, and standing there without a smile, he had that fierce expression he must have shown Cardinal Wolsey and other men unfortunate enough to earn his disfavour. Richard trembled, wondering what ill he could have done, and at the sight of this the king broke into a giant smile and then a hearty laugh. 'Why,' he exclaimed in a jovial and even familiar tone, 'this must be Richard Edwardes, son of Will and Agnes!'

With all the dignity his frightened young heart could muster, Richard said, 'Yes, Your Majesty, I am Richard Edwardes.' Tardily, remembering the instructions of his mother in the event such a terrifying encounter should occur, he bowed.

Even with his head down, Richard could still feel the knife-blade of the sovereign's eyes on him, but when he looked up again he saw that the gaze was kindly. 'And how, Master Richard,' asked Henry, 'are your studies? I understand you are an apt student.'

'My studies go well, Your Majesty,' Richard answered, letting his eyes fall once again. He feared sounding boastful, but it seemed peremptory to reply in so laconic a fashion, so he added, 'In fact, sire, I have been chosen for the choir of His Majesty's own Chapel Royal.'

'Have you, now?' The king smiled. 'Only a truly good student could earn such an honour as that.'

'Your Highness speaks rightly, if I may say so. Your subject was surprised but pleased to have been so chosen.'

'I suppose,' said the king, watching as his servants took his horse away to the stable, 'that we shall be seeing each other more often when you join the choir, shan't we?'

Again the words sounded oddly familiar, not what a mere boy would expect to hear from the king of all the English. 'Yes, Your Majesty,' he replied, 'no doubt that is so.'

'Very well, then,' said Henry. 'Go on and play now.'

'Thank you, sire.'

The king's words gave him assurance, and when finally it came time to leave for London he did so with an excited heart. He had much to look forward to: singing in the choir of the king's very own chapel, seeing London with all its fine buildings, and delving into the studies which would first inspire in him the dream of becoming a poet and dramatist. Like many other young boys, he'd read Malory's tales of *King Arthur*, and in the pageantry and splendour of palaces and royalty around him in the capital he saw that the spirit of the storied king and his knights lived on.

These were to be years of rigid discipline as well, with a monk-like commitment to learning and few of the joys to which a country lad had become accustomed. He acquired knowledge in strange languages, learned to play musical instruments, and gained his first exposure to the theatre and the art of performing and play-acting. In short, he became an accomplished gentleman, and when at fifteen he won a scholarship to Oxford, it had seemed only proper that he should move on to the greatest university in the English-speaking realms.

Now, however, he realised that just as with the Chapel Royal, the fact of that scholarship raised questions as to its ultimate source. As his uncle had implied, there existed many young men of talent and intellect, most of whom would live their entire lives without the opportunity to plumb the depths of their abilities. Why had he been chosen?

He had always thought the dean to be his benefactor, yet just as some among the ancients had speculated that the world rested on the back of a turtle (whereupon others had asked what held up the turtle), so now Richard glimpsed a power underlying both his uncle and himself. Apparently John Edwardes's knowledge of the secret behind his nephew's birth had gained his own entrance to Oxford, and perhaps also the uncle's prodigious success there owed more than a little to his leverage on the king.

Still, Richard found this scenario lacking in logical symmetry. King Henry was hardly one to succumb to the extortion of a commoner, and would sooner have a man's head than cower before one of his subjects. Besides that, everyone in the realm knew of their monarch's lusty ways. Had not his reformation of the English church resulted from his desire to put away his wife, Catherine of Aragon, in favour of Anne Boleyn? And when Anne too failed to give him a son, had he not moved on first to Jane Seymour, then to Anne of Cleves, then to Catherine Howard, and finally to Catherine Parr? And these were only the women he'd honoured with the sacrament of marriage; no one spoke it aloud out of doors, but anyone could guess that those six represented but a fraction of the king's conquests.

So if his uncle's tale were true, whose reputation had the king sought to protect these twenty years? With a rush of emotion, Richard realised that it was for him - and for one other. She alone would have all the answers to the questions now rampaging in his mind.

3

The next days passed slowly, and Richard went through his routines at Oxford rather like a moving mannequin of wood, waiting only for the day when he could visit his mother in Somersetshire. The night following his uncle's visit, after a distracted lesson to the youths under his tutelage, he had written to her and announced his plans to journey homeward without giving any particular reason for it. He didn't need to, of course: Richard and she had always been close, and ever since the death of Will Edwardes, he'd been particularly solicitous of her well-being. He hadn't gone home, however, since the funeral, and to her his impending visit must have seemed well nigh due.

Finally the time came for him to start out in a carriage, which would wind its way through the gorgeous green countryside to the hills and coast he loved best. The sojourn would take many days, for roads were crude affairs paved with little more than the ruts made by the wagons that had gone before. Often the rains would mire a carriage in the mud, and the best progress any traveller could hope for was fifteen miles in one long, long day.

But though the roughness of the roads taxed the endurance of even one as young and strong as Richard, the trip had the beneficial effect of giving him time to think, away from his responsibilities at the college. There were several overnight stops at friendly inns in towns along the road, and Richard found it pleasant to share food and drink with the hospitable country folk they met along the way.

As he rode and reflected, it occurred to him that though his life had been a pleasant one as far as he could judge, its phases each seemed sharply and abruptly divided. Instead of rolling like a serene river, a poetic conceit already ancient in his day, the stream of his own existence had periodic rapids which made returning to the past impossible. First there had been the shift from the country life to London, and then (though it had appeared natural enough at the time) from the known world of the capital to the unknown world of the university - and now this latest and greatest shock.

Unless his mother proved his uncle false - and he doubted she would - he could never be the same knowing as he did of his identity. He'd felt comfortable with his assigned place in the world until he learned it had not been the only one possible, and now he found inside himself a growing dissatisfaction with the roles assigned to him: scholar and priest, a man rigidly controlled and conformed to his office. Everything in his education had prepared him to be just that, and from the time he entered the Chapel Royal, he'd accustomed himself to a constant regimen of *do's* and *don'ts.* Yet from the beginning he had glimpsed within himself other stirrings, other urgings.

This second side of his being, which forever asserted itself in spite of starvation and neglect, wanted to write poetry and plays, to imagine and dream, to cause people to laugh and see beauty in new ways. It did him no good to recognise the value of his priestly and pedantic duties; the denial of his gentler self had daily added another pebble to the heap of uncertainty that darkened his unexplored world.

Likewise he wanted to share his life with a woman, for he'd cherished a single love since childhood and she remained unmarried, but that dream too had fallen to necessity. King Henry's reforms might have permitted him to divorce, but surely it would be a thousand years before the church allowed priests to take wives.

As he thought of these things, he felt a trace of envy toward the many folk for whom destiny had not chosen to take such a path as his. Was he never to know their contentment, or did they simply fail to see things as deeply as he saw them?

At that moment the carriage passed what appeared to be the ruins of an ancient monastery, and even as the vehicle lurched on the rutted road, the sight recalled to him the memory of Glastonbury Abbey. At the age of six, his mother had related to him the legend of the Abbey and its famed thornbush, a story first recorded in the early twelfth century by William of Malmesbury. According to Malmesbury, in the year 166 the Pope sent missionaries to the heathen of England, but when they arrived at the spot where Glastonbury would later stand, they found to their surprise the remains of a wattle structure that had housed a Christian church.

It had been established, they were told, by St. Philip the Disciple and

Joseph of Arimathea, the man who had given up his own burial crypt in order that the crucified Saviour might be entombed there for his three days and nights. Another historical tale, which also placed Joseph in England at the latter part of his life, had him catching Christ's blood in the bowl from which Jesus had drunk on the night of the Last Supper, and thus began the legend of the Holy Grail; the Grail, of course, would become a part of Arthurian legend, and some said that Glastonbury was the site of the graves of King Arthur and Queen Guinevere.

Given the stories that linked it to kings both heavenly and earthly, one might have expected the Glastonbury Thorn to look as lovely as the Tree of Life depicted in St. John's Revelation at the end of the Bible, or as tempting as the Tree of the Knowledge of Good and Evil at its beginning. But the plant was rightly named the Thorn, and no imagination could have dubbed its gnarled limbs and cruelly sharp nettles beautiful. Yet twice (and sometimes thrice) a year it did indeed shine forth in splendour: as though it knew its dual origins, the bush bloomed with gorgeous flowers at Christmas and again at Easter - and on the occasion of a visit to it by one of royal blood.

This legend had made an impression on Richard as a boy, and he'd insisted on seeing the Abbey and the famed thornbush for himself. His family went on Palm Sunday, and just as the legend had foretold, the shrub had flowered. He had wondered then, and he wondered now, by what means its mystic memory caused its flourishing on those two spiritual holidays - and whether indeed it bloomed in the presence of royalty. Would it bloom now if he visited it?

In time the coach had wound its way through the countryside, placing them well within the boundaries of Somerset. In the distance he could see the fine estates of Wolmersdon and Fairfield, and beyond them the manor of North Petherton. Fairfield was by far the grandest house in the shire, with its great hall, its leaded stained glass windows, its staircase of heroic proportions, and its chandeliers fashioned from the most exquisite crystal in Europe. But the manor of North Petherton, half a mile beyond the spot where his parents' home nestled in a small grove of trees, was much dearer to his heart.

William the Conqueror had bequeathed that glorious house to one of his trusted lords from Normandy, and over the centuries it had passed to the Beaupine family. Then came a generation of Beaupines without a male heir, and when Agnes Beaupine married John Blewitt, the manor became a part of his family's holdings. Richard knew well of Lady Agnes, a woman of such great beauty and character that her memory had passed down the ages along with her name, which his grandparents gave to his mother.

Agnes Blewitt's branch of the family had not inherited North Petherton, but had lived instead in a house not nearly so grand. As long as the Blewitts owned the estate, her parents had lived in their less magnificent home rent-free; however, once the manor had passed through marriage to a family of another name, it became necessary to pay the leaseholder every month. Thus her people had lived as dispossessed tenants on land that had once belonged to them.

And then their fortunes changed yet again. Soon after Agnes's parents moved from North Petherton, at about the time of Richard's birth, they became heirs to a very large estate in Ireland, and they moved there while Agnes and her new husband Will Edwardes settled in the parish. No one at the time had understood exactly how this providential gift had befallen the family, but Richard could scarcely help but wonder now whether it had something to do with the great unseen benefactor in his life, King Henry.

In the distance loomed the outline of Huntworth, the royal hunting lodge, another Norman-built estate granted to a loyal lord by the great William I. Unlike Fairfield, this one was simple in design and even rugged in appearance, a place made for a warrior race still unsettled in their new land. Beside the grand palaces of the king in London it would have looked like a chambermaid in the presence of princesses, but it had reverted to the crown as well, and on his sporting holidays in Somerset, King Henry took himself here.

A jolt of the coach brought Richard suddenly and squarely back to the moment and the final approach to his family home, his personal Eden, his place from which he drew strength and refreshment for his soul. Having passed North Petherton itself, the carriage thundered down a tiny lane flanked by hedgerows and barely wide enough to pass. They rode under ancient oaks whose branches nearly blocked out the sun, then turned at the grand gate of Halswell Hall.

It was not to the grand hall he was returning, but to a humble structure on its lands, and as they climbed the winding hill toward the great manor, his eyes searched the grove of trees beside it to find the tiled roof of the place he loved. The cottage lay with others to the left and behind Halswell, and together with the farm buildings and stables, these houses formed a large and rustic courtyard for the great house. Further on and out of sight lay a large sunken garden, and beyond it more and more majestic trees.

His heart rejoiced - and likewise he felt a rising lump in his throat - as he glimpsed his home and the familiar scenes all around it. The carriage drew near to the house, and the driver blew a long brass horn to alert the family of his arrival; now they spilled out onto the front steps and stood eagerly awaiting his emergence from the coach.

There stood his brothers, William, Henry, and Christopher, William a man like him and the other two all but grown - and in the midst of them he glimpsed his mother. Agnes Blewitt Edwardes had been from her youth an extraordinarily beautiful woman, her hair a deep shiny black and her eyes as blue as the flowers that bloomed on the mountainsides of Scotland. Time had not diminished this beauty, only mellowed it, and she remained as lovely as ever.

As he alighted from the carriage, her eyes sparkled with tears of joy, and once more she held her son in her arms. 'Oh, dear boy, it is so wonderful to have you home again,' she cried, pressing him to her, 'even if only for a few days.'

Richard could say nothing, caught up in the emotion of the moment as he was, and he reached a hand out to grab that of William. 'We have missed you so,' his mother said, drawing back and surveying her four sons together once again. 'There is so much to tell - William has decided to move to London and go into the wine trade, and Christopher and Henry...' She caught her breath, and everyone laughed with joy. 'Everything is happening so fast these days!' she exclaimed, holding Richard at arm's length and looking him up and down. 'At least you appear well, my son, and that is one less thing I need worry about.'

With that Richard greeted his brothers, who immediately got his luggage from the coach and preceded him and his mother into the house. Agnes had prepared a large feast in celebration of Richard's visit, and the evening passed quickly as the family reminisced over the past and speculated on the future. By the time his brothers retired for the evening and he found himself alone with his mother, the clock had struck ten.

He didn't want to embarrass her or approach things too abruptly, and throughout the evening he had rehearsed many times just what he might say to her. Several times he'd noticed her staring at him as though she knew what he had come to ask, and the look had disconcerted him. Now as he sat chatting with her of this or that, avoiding the real reason for his visit, he saw her again gazing at him with that look mothers have when they know very well that what is being discussed is not at all true topic of concern.

Finally she reached for his hand and said gently, 'You've been working gallantly, my dear son, at talking of inconsequential things, but you needn't try any longer. I know what a long way it is to come here from Oxford, and how busy you must be with your work there, so when I received your letter I guessed that you must have more on your mind than a mere visit to your mother and brothers.' She smiled. 'Just what is it of which you truly wish to speak?'

Richard paused for a moment, looking tenderly at his mother, then he drew in a breath and related all of what his uncle had told him. 'I have since learned,' he concluded, 'that Uncle John has been appointed Vicar of Bishopstone in Wiltshire, which everyone reckons as a form of exile, being as far removed as it is from Oxford. I suspect that anger overtook him, and he lost his usual restraint; he said he spoke to me in order to protect my position in the event it was likewise threatened, but in my mind he spoke rashly. If what he has said is true, then he has betrayed a trust to the Crown, and what's more' - here he rubbed his forehead - 'he has cast doubt on everything I believed of myself and my origins.'

He turned to her. 'So I have come to you, Mother, as the one person who can set the story right.' He paused again, drawing up his courage, then put the question baldly: 'Mother, is King Henry my natural father?'

Agnes had listened in silence, a soft sad smile drawing across her face, and now she studied her hands. 'You are right, Richard, when you say that your uncle spoke rashly.' She raised her eyes to meet those of her son and answered in a small and trembling voice, 'But not untruly: yes, you are the king's son.'

4

She paused again for a short time, as though struggling with emotions long before tucked away in a secret place and brought out for discussion. When at last she had regained her composure, she commenced speaking with great control, but Richard could see plainly enough that even now the telling of the story caused her pain.

'It all happened,' she began, 'a very, very long time ago, when I was very young. Then, just as the king still does today, he would make at least one and sometimes two visits a year to the royal lodge at Huntworth. All our families would join in the feasts, as you remember from your own childhood, and the women would help in the preparation of the food. Although I was quite young, I too served, and King Henry was always jovial at such occasions.'

She looked away. 'Quite often, he became very friendly with those who served him, and I at the age of sixteen was often complimented on my beauty.' She did not say, though it was true, that she'd been considered the prettiest young woman in the whole shire. 'At that time the king's attentions became even more acute, and my heart being pure and inexperienced, I was not at all offended by his interest - to the contrary, I found myself rather flattered to be worthy of the king's notice at all.'

She recalled to Richard the fact that at that time the king was still married to Princess Catherine, and as a learned man well-versed in recent events, that did plenty to describe King Henry's state of affairs to him. Henry had been the second son of Henry VII, first Tudor monarch, and in 1501 his older brother Arthur had wed Catherine of Aragon, daughter of King Ferdinand and Queen Isabella of Spain. Catherine was fifteen years old then, a pretty and educated young lady gifted both as a horsewoman and dancer, and the match had been seen by all as a propitious one.

But within a few months of the wedding, Prince Arthur died of the sweating sickness (what a later age would call influenza), and for a time no one seemed to know what to do about Princess Catherine. Should she be returned to Spain? If so, her dowry would be forfeited, and all the gains England made by the match would be lost. King Ferdinand demanded either her return, along with her dowry, or her betrothal to Prince Henry, the new heir.

Although Prince Arthur had once coarsely boasted he'd gone 'six miles into Spain,' Princess Catherine protested that she remained a virgin after her husband's death. Some might have been inclined to dispute this improbable claim, but they kept their mouths shut once was it learned that a special dispensation from Rome would permit her to marry Henry. Virgin or not, a Biblical precedent existed for this plan: in the Book of Genesis, Judah's son Er had died without issue, and his younger brother Onan married Er's wife Tamar.

The marriage of Onan and Tamar had ended in disgrace, with Onan spilling his seed over the side of the bed rather than impregnating his former sister-in-law, but since Rome as well as London and Madrid wanted this union, everyone ignored the omen offered by the patriarchs, and Henry and Catherine were formally betrothed five days before the groom's twelfth birthday. In April 1509 his father died, and seven weeks later Henry, now crowned King Henry VIII of England, married Catherine.

At first it was a happy marriage, but as the years went by, frustration and anger took the place of love in Henry's heart. Though she went through confinements enough and produced plenty of sons, they were all either stillborn or died shortly after birth; finally in 1518 she produced a child who lived - a daughter, whom they named Mary. All men wanted sons, but King Henry, student of history that he was, desired an heir most of all: his own father and the House of Tudor had come to power in the wake of the War of the Roses, a series of conflicts over succession that had rocked England in the latter years of the preceding century, and when he died he wanted a son who could take the throne naturally without the shedding of blood.

Divorce was out of the question for the man who'd been proclaimed *Defensor Fidei* ('Defender of the Faith') by the Pope for his attacks on the seditious German rebel Martin Luther, and the matter of his successor tormented Henry to distraction. In time he would persuade the Archbishop of Canterbury to nullify his union with Catherine, opening the way for his marriage to Anne Boleyn. But Anne likewise gave him another daughter, this one called Elizabeth. Soon he would put her aside for Jane Seymour, who died giving birth to a son, Edward.

But by the time all these things came to pass, the necessity of fathering an heir had given license to the lust in the king's heart, and Henry took on the traits of another patriarch. Just as Abraham had gone to his wife's maid Hagar to produce the son Jehovah had promised him through his barren wife Sarah, Henry fathered two sons through separate mistresses.

The first came from Bessie Blount, who although not of the peerage was a beautiful, provocative, and voluptuous court favourite, and she named her son Henry Fitzroy. Henry acknowledged the boy's lineage by elevating him first to Duke of Beaufort and then to Duke of Richmond in preparation for his assumption of the throne should the king die without a legitimate male heir. With this came into being the royal House of Richmond, whose official residence became St. James Palace.

After her confinement, Bessie Blount returned to Court and was given the title 'Mother of the King's Son'. There was no stigma attached to the king's affair with her, and she remained a respected lady; the same fate would not meet the mother of Henry's second natural son, Henry Carey. Mary Boleyn, sister of Anne, had in earlier days been a favourite of the King of France, and perhaps for this reason, Henry banished her from the English Court and married her off to a minor courtier, William Carey. Their firstborn took the name Henry Carey (later Lord Hunsdon), and the king never openly acknowledged him as his son.

Richard, Agnes explained to him now, was the third and last of what were euphemistically called Henry VIII's 'natural sons'. He had known the formal history of the king's life, some of it sordid but most of it heroic, yet now he heard his mother describe King Henry in terms no one else had ever used.

'When the king was young,' she continued, 'being the second son and not expected to inherit the throne, he was trained for the church.' She smiled. 'As you would later be; thus you know all the disciplines required of him. He grew up to be brilliant, and he wrote poetry and composed songs. Likewise he was a great athlete, he loved jousting and wrestling, and he was a gifted dancer. I remember him as tall, handsome and very, very charming...' Her eyes drifted away for a moment, then she came to herself and said, 'You wouldn't know it to look at him now, but he was slender in those days, and to us young women of the country he seemed a virtual Adonis. He was much gentler, too, and more thoughtful in those days, but all that was to end.

'Besides the problems in his home, another thing happened that seemed to change the king. He loved to joust, and sometimes he sustained injuries. Though most of these were inconsequential, on one occasion he received a heavy blow to the head and was knocked into a stupor. Bleeding him did not help, and he lay many days as though asleep. Those nearest him did not know if he would live, and when he finally awoke, his memory seemed unimpaired, but he became a different man. Many of those finer qualities of his younger years vanished, and he became coarser, more...' - she hesitated before using the word - '...crude. And that was the Henry I knew in the autumn of my sixteenth year.'

She paused, as though waiting for a question from Richard, but he said nothing, and the only sound in the little room was the flickering of the fire and the ticking of the clock. She resumed her tale: 'When the king made his usual visit to Huntworth, many of us remarked that his temperament had changed. He seemed moody, irritable, and yet his attentions to the young ladies increased rather than diminished.' She folded her hands. 'Particularly in my case. At the first of the feasts, he consumed a great deal of wine and as he did so, he became louder and more difficult to serve. I came to his side to offer him more, for such was my duty. He took the wine, and when he did, he looked with kindness on me; after that I noticed that he seemed to calm himself for the rest of the evening.

'Presently he called for more wine, and I went to fetch it in the lodge. I did not know, however, that he had followed me.' Here she blushed and bit her lip, and Richard knew that from thenceforth the tale would be more difficult for her to tell. 'By now he'd become quite intoxicated, and he began to... to force himself on me, all the while making professions of undying love. Young as I was, I recognised the folly of his protestations, for I was but a country girl and he a king, but likewise I knew not what to do. Had I screamed, I might have faced the rebuke of those who would say I had invited his attentions. And so I...' Again she let her voice drift off, and she looked away from Richard.

'Mother?'

'You are a learned man, Richard,' she said, her voice for a moment strangely cold. 'You shall have to surmise the rest, for it is beyond my ability to recount.'

They were silent for a moment, then she gazed back at him again, this time with her accustomed warmth, and continued after this rupture in the continuity of the tale. 'Afterward, I left the lodge by a side entry, for I could not possibly face anyone feeling as I did. I ran until I could run no longer, and then turned homeward to await the arrival of my parents. I might have wished to hide my emotions, but I was too tender, and a moment after my father and mother entered the room, I broke into sobs and related all that had happened.

'My father was furious, but he was wise enough to know that he must proceed with caution. His immediate solution was to say nothing, and he removed the family from the celebrations for the rest of that season on account of illness. Presently he sent a note to the king stating simply that his daughter had told him all and that in time he would like an audience with him.

'King Henry, as I have said, was not an unkind man, and he had known and respected the Blewitts for years. Thus he could well understand how the family did not want a scandal, and before he left Somerset, he wrote a note announcing that he would be ready to talk whenever Father was. Meanwhile it became known for a certainty that I was with child, and the king was so informed, whereupon he sent a message that my father should present himself to him at Huntworth within the month.

'As you can guess, it was a difficult and awkward meeting between them. The king was no more anxious than Father that the secret be told, and in some way to make up for the damage he had caused, he offered him a rich estate in Ireland.' So my guess was true, Richard said to himself, but his face showed no sign of his thoughts. 'He persuaded Will Edwardes, the man you have always known as your father, to marry me and give our child a legitimate home and family.'

She smiled when she thought of her late husband. 'Will had always admired me at a distance, and he was a fine and honourable man. Though the Edwardes family were not wealthy people, they had a long history of gallantry and service to the Crown, and Will was happy to oblige the king, even knowing as he did that I was with child. In return, as your uncle told you, the king agreed to make arrangements for Will's brother John to attend Oxford.

'As for the child, if it were a boy, he would be trained at the Chapel Royal and ultimately sent to Oxford for his education; regardless of the sex, the king would keep the secret, and at the same time would see to it that the family and the child never wanted for anything.' She looked at her son. 'I say 'the child', but of course I mean you, Richard. Little did we know what a blessing would come into our lives...

'And so it was all done as promised and agreed. Will became a wonderful husband and father not only to your brothers, his true sons, but also to you. I suspect that you never sensed the slightest difference between you as children, for there was none. For my part, I grew to love Will with all my heart, and our lives proceeded as though nothing had ever happened. I never saw the king again, and the matter was never discussed; only King Henry, Will,

John, my parents, and I knew the secret of your birth.' She paused, then concluded: 'In all honesty, the matter seemed to have faded to a mere memory - nay, a dream - until your uncle betrayed the trust, but now that it is done I am glad I could tell you the truth of your lineage.'

Richard reached for his mother's hand and held it firmly but gently. 'These things you have told me, Mother, they are of no consequence: I love you and the father I always knew - nothing can change that - and indeed I love you all the more for keeping this trust as you have all these years. You need never feel shame for events you could not control, and I admire you for finding it in your heart to forgive the king. But then as you said, not forgiving would have harmed you more than helped.'

For the first time that night, Agnes began to weep as though releasing all she'd suppressed, not just in the hour that had passed since she began her story, but in all the years that had gone by since that troubled evening in the king's lodge. Then she regained her composure and said, 'I am glad that your father was spared this moment - truly I am, for he loved you as though you were his own. He dreaded the day you learned the truth, and feared you might change in your opinion toward him and toward me.' She placed her other hand on top of Richard's. 'He did not understand you as I do. But I fear you speak rashly when you say this secret will change nothing for you - how can it be so? What will you do now?'

Richard thought for a moment, but even as the facts went through his mind yet another time, the result remained: 'I will do nothing different than I always have. No one need know - no one at all. I will go on as I have, and soon I doubt I will even give thought to these things.'

'You are indeed wise for your years,' Agnes replied, brushing away a tear. She sat up straighter. 'But I feel it only right that the king should be told that you know the truth now. He may one day want to see you, and you may bring him comfort. He is changed a great deal from those earlier days, and I believe he suffers much.'

'But what of Uncle John?'

'What of him? The king will harm him no further.' Agnes spoke with resolve. 'I will break the silence! I will go to see the king in secret! Arrangements were made many years ago for just such a meeting if it became necessary, and perhaps this has all happened as it was meant to be. Surely to be king is not the happiest state that can befall a man.' Richard thought of his foolish observation as a child when he witnessed the splendour of King Henry, and now as a man he guessed that she spoke rightly. 'Perhaps it is the will of God - perhaps you are meant to be by the king's side in his troubled times and help in ways no other could.' She stood up. 'And now, my beloved son, we must rest and pray for guidance in the days to come.'

Richard kissed his mother tenderly, then they blew out the candles and made their way to their rooms, but Richard's mind was far too full of thought for sleep to come quickly. Now he saw both his parents and the king in a different light than he'd ever seen them before. He had never thought it possible to love and respect his father more than he already did, yet as he lay in bed, he thanked God to have been raised by such a man.

What an odd circumstance had befallen Will Edwardes at his marriage to Richard's mother! He'd found himself in the thankless position of assuming fatherhood when the king, like Zeus impregnating the earthly women Io and Europa, had dallied with a commoner and produced a child. The situation recalled to Richard's mind another story, this one from the Scriptures and not the myths. Joseph, future husband of Mary, had become the least of men even as his bride became the greatest of women: she carried within her the child not merely of a king but *The King*, and he'd accepted the responsibility of caring for a boy who had not come from his own loins. Likewise had Will shown fathomless love not only for his wife, neither blaming nor faulting her, but for the unborn child she'd brought to their marriage.

And Agnes - she had lived through a tragic experience not of her own design, and yet had found within herself compassion and forgiveness for the man who had injured her. Richard blessed her for her dignity and grace. She had the qualities some attributed to queens, but in his mind she was more than a queen: a saint.

As for the king, Richard saw him through his mother's eyes, understanding him as he truly was, with his troubled spirit and his heavy burden in guiding his country forward. He was a man after all, a mere man as subject to faults as anyone. Had he marred his son's life? Not at all! Richard had grown up in the most wonderful family anyone could had hoped for, and on top of that he carried within him a special kingly legacy.

God, he believed, permitted circumstances to befall men in order that they might profit from them and rise higher than they might otherwise have done. More than anything, Richard now wished to do as his mother had said, to stand by the king when he needed him. Perhaps the ambitions that had tugged at him all these years had come to him through his royal bloodline, and perhaps likewise his natural father could help him to make those grand desires come true...

5

The next morning Agnes awoke early, knowing in her heart what she must now do. She went immediately to a hiding place where she kept a ring given to her by King Henry through her father many years before. If ever the child discovers his true identity, the king had said then, and if she needed the king's council, she need only send him the ring and within two weeks he would receive her in secret at the royal lodge at Huntworth.

The month was October, and there could be no better timing for such a meeting, because the season would likely call the king to the hunt in any event. Agnes took great pains over her letter, composing it in such a way that its meaning would be abundantly clear to Henry himself but opaque to any third party. Then she made a small package containing the letter and ring, and dispatched it on the next coach to London.

When Richard appeared in the kitchen for breakfast, he gave his mother a special hug and shared in a whisper all the thoughts he'd had that night before he finally fell asleep. 'I have been given a special gift,' he concluded, 'a rare and beautiful, not an ugly thing - as at first it might have seemed to be.'

She squeezed his hand and looked into his eyes. All that she had hoped for her son had come true, she thought: not only had he grown up a gifted and talented soul, but he was wise, and no harm had touched him at all from the learning of the secret. Now for the first time she felt completely free of the burden she'd carried these past twenty-one years.

The next few days passed all too quickly for Richard, and he enjoyed his time at North Petherton as he never had before. Soon the day arrived for his return to Oxford, and with sad farewells he began the journey back. He left a different man than the one he'd been just a few days before: his identity was clear now, and he had his peace with it. Perhaps, as Agnes had said, all this had happened for a reason, and now he had only to look toward the unfolding of his life's purpose.

Two weeks to the day after Agnes sent the letter to King Henry, a footman arrived from Huntworth with a sealed message inviting her to a great banquet given by the king in celebration of the hunt. She was to arrive early, the letter said, and enter by a special door where she would find His Highness waiting for her; then when they had completed their discussion, she would leave again by that same passage and arrive at the main entrance as one of the guests.

She well remembered that door: she had used it for her escape on that fateful night, and now she would enter it again for the first time in two decades. Hastily she composed a reply to the king, and then she turned her thoughts to exactly what she would say when she met him.

She had told Richard how much Henry had changed, but she wondered if his character and person had altered as much as everyone said. Would he remember her as she had been, and think only of how she had aged? She laughed at her own vanity, but it was true what the Scriptures said, that if a man and a maiden had shared the bond of coupling (married or not), in some way their souls were joined. She loved her husband still, yet nonetheless she cared what King Henry thought of her.

The appointed time arrived, and her son Christopher drove Agnes to the great hunting lodge. It was with a trembling hand that she pulled back the giant rustic door to enter, opening as she did a chapter long closed. But nothing inside the unadorned, even ascetic, room seemed to have changed.

She, however, had changed, and she glanced at herself in the looking-glass that hung in the hallway. She saw a light in a room leading off the corridor, and she paused for a moment, taking a long deep breath, then pushed the door open.

The room was dimly lit, but instantly she saw the enormous silhouette of the portly man the king had become. She made a very low curtsy and said, 'Your Majesty, your obedient servant.'

The king spoke softly but firmly. 'For heaven's sake, get up, my lady. There is no need for such formalities between the two of us. Come closer, that I may see what the years have wrought.'

Agnes stood up and walked very slowly and deliberately toward the light and the king. She had indeed heard stories, and just now she had glimpsed the outline of his form, but she was stunned and shocked at the sight before her: a man of exceeding girth with a sallow complexion and great dark circles under his eyes.

But in spite of what she beheld, she smiled at him.

'Agnes, you are still among the most beautiful women in my kingdom,' he said in his deep, rich baritone. He sighed. 'I fear that Fortune has not been so kind to me.'

She waited in silence, and he waved a hand dismissively. 'But that is of no importance now. We must be quick about this business before anyone knows of our meeting.'

Agnes then told the king of how Richard had learned the secret of his birth, and at first Henry appeared outraged. His face turned red, and he grabbed at his hilt as though preparing to draw a sword. 'Perhaps I have not dealt unkindly enough with the recent Dean of Oxford,' he said darkly.

'Your Majesty, I beg you,' she said, bowing her head, 'not to bring retribution on that man.'

The king thought for a moment, then said in a more gentle voice, 'He is the brother of your late husband, and I suppose that any harm to him would be harm to you - pity the poor man who brought a tear to such a fair eye.' Again he sighed. 'Ah, well! In a way I am relieved and glad that my son knows. Mayhap the time will come when he can indeed prove his Tudor lineage and put himself in the service of those whom I cannot be seen to help myself. I shall see him ere long - from what I hear tell, he is a great deal like I was when young and not burdened by a crown.' He gazed into the twilight of the room for a moment. 'I must say that I am happy for him. He will not have to know all that a king must bear!'

With that the meeting ended, and Agnes made her way down the corridor and out the door without anyone ever knowing she had been there. The rest of the evening passed pleasantly, and she visited with her neighbours, all the while watching the king from the corner of her eye. He seemed in wonderful spirits, more so than he had been for a very long time. More than once, she found him gazing at her, not as he had done long, long before - with lust - but only with the kindly look of a man tempered by frustration and age. She no longer feared, but rather pitied, her king.

Many months passed after that night, and then one day almost two years after his uncle's visit, Richard received a letter bearing the royal seal. His presence, the letter said, was required before the king at Richmond Palace, and he should proceed in all haste, wearing his priestly robes as a precaution against suspicions. No one would know the reason for the summons other than Richard and the king's two daughters, Mary and Elizabeth, and the fact of their expected presence told Richard what he had guessed: the king was dying, and wanted to draw his offspring around him in his final hours.

Richmond Palace, built by Henry VII, had long been a favourite of his son Henry VIII. Perhaps at another time the huge towering structure might have seemed more inviting to a visitor arriving there with a special dispensation from the king, but in the darkness of the night when Richard's coach drew up before it, it appeared dour and dreary. There was a chill in the air, and a palpable sense of sadness and gloom hung about the walls, as though the palace itself knew that its greatest occupant would soon breathe his last.

When Richard reached the great front door, he was immediately escorted to the royal bedchamber. There he found a knot of courtiers gathered around the titanic mass of the king's body, which had been propped up into a half-sitting position. In spite of the logs burning in the fireplace, the air carried an unnatural chill as though from a spiritual and not a physical source, and for a moment Richard feared that he'd been too late. But suddenly the king's voice roared out: 'Everyone out of my chambers!'

Richard turned to go as well, but the bedridden monarch growled, 'You stay, clerk.'

When the others departed, it was as though the shadow of death over the room lengthened, and with it came a smell. This was not the noisome stench of bodies that men who had been in battle never forgot, but an odour that came through the spirit and not the nose. As a leper announcing his presence with loud clapping, so death sent before him this vile and indescribable scent, like a brew concocted in Hecate's kitchen.

With the smell came sight as well, and Richard now saw the full condition of his king. The man's legs, lying above the bedclothes, were covered with weeping sores, and his skin was sallow and chalky. His eyes were half-closed, and his mouth had flaky scabs surrounding it that must have made it difficult to eat or speak. A shiver ran down the length of the young man's body, and he had an urge, not to draw back from the dying monarch in revulsion, but to fall down and wail in despair at the grim final act of the man's life being played out in this bleak theatre.

Richard approached his father's side and knelt before his father and king. Once they were alone, however, His Majesty's tone softened and he smiled, not as a royal person to a subject, but as - 'My son,' he said, beckoning Richard to sit beside him, 'at last we meet without the veil of pretence. Let me look at you.'

'Yes, sire.'

The king's face wrinkled. 'Not sire, lad, father. Take my hand that we may at least once behave as father and son.'

So Richard did, and in his mind he heard the words of the Scripture: 'For ye have not received the spirit of bondage again to fear, but ye have received the Spirit of adoption, whereby we cry Abba, Father.'

Henry beamed with a glow that belied the lateness of the hour in his life; his tender side, so seldom seen in recent years, was now laid bare. 'Ah, a fine young man you are: your mother's good looks and grace, your father's strength and mind.' He spoke as though they had been intimates for years, and Richard must have shown the shock of this on his face, for the king smiled and said, 'You wonder at my words, for you have known me only as your king, but I have watched you through the years and seen how you have grown. I can now confess to you and you alone, I would you had borne the name of Tudor and been there to wear the crown.'

Richard, not knowing what to say, bowed his head slightly.

'But Fate would have it otherwise, I am afraid,' the king continued. 'My time is short, and I must make the most of it. This I will say, my son: make your way and improve your lot within the Court when such can be arranged. You have the soul of the poet, and great talents can best be appreciated and cultivated at Court.' He held up a finger. 'But beware of fools who will tell you lies to gain their way, and be not deceived by fair words - value only fine deeds!' He studied Richard's face for a moment, then concluded: 'You are wise enough to know what I mean, and can perhaps someday give good counsel to a crowned head when such counsel is needed.'

Richard opened his mouth to speak, though he knew not what he would say. Crowned heads! I would you had borne the name of Tudor! Even after the months he'd had in which to reconcile himself to the secrets of his identity, he found himself overwhelmed in the presence of the greatest monarch in the world - his father!

But fortunately he didn't have to say anything, because Henry talked enough for both. 'Would that a son were not such a rare thing,' he continued. 'Would that they grew on trees! For all my labours, I have only Prince Edward to take my place, and he is far too young to understand the things I intend to tell him before I go. Mayhap some of it will record itself on his heart, and he may use it when he assumes the throne - if he does. I fear the lad has not his father's robust physique, but is frail...'

His voice trailed off, and he thought for a moment while Richard sat beside him in silence. 'I know not what shall transpire after I am rid of this earth and this ancient and dying body, but I have called you here so that you may meet your sisters and that they may know of you. Thus they can help you improve your poor estate - and you in turn may one day help them. Now, go to that door over there, rap three times, and return to me.'

Richard did as he was instructed, and immediately two young women entered the room - or rather, a young woman and an old maid. Richard had of course seen the princesses on those rare occasions when they attended the Chapel Royal, but he had never glimpsed them up close, and now he looked at them as though for the first time.

Mary Tudor, thirty-one years old and still unmarried, looked every year her age if not older. Short and flabby, she had already lost many of her teeth (a common enough problem among the populace, but not the royalty), and she looked more like a housewife or a nun than a princess. Her aspect was gloomy, and not, it appeared, only because of her father's illness: the lines on her face gave witness to a person both sullen and distrustful, one for whom happiness was not a habit.

Through the kindness of Henry's sixth and last wife, Catherine Parr, Mary had redeemed her status of legitimacy (which had been taken away upon the king's divorce of her mother and marriage to Anne Boleyn) and returned to the Court; Anne's daughter Elizabeth, on the other hand, who had also lost her legal status as a daughter when King Henry put aside her mother, had been branded a bastard afresh and exiled yet again from Court. But the young woman appeared as brave and confident as if she were the mistress of the house welcoming a visitor.

Fifteen years old and full-grown, Elizabeth was slim, which made her seem taller and caused even her fingers to appear beautifully tapered like those of a figure in a Byzantine painting. She was also very pretty, with a fair complexion and hair of a golden red; though clad in rather plain attire, her manner gave her a glow befitting a true princess.

This young woman had a certain dignity and poise that Richard instantly sensed would never fail her in the worst of circumstances. In her demeanour she was well-mannered, but she spoke to her father with a firm and not a simpering voice, standing erect and not lowering her head or her eyes after the manner of most women, even royal ones. This solidity made her a more and not a less inviting soul, and the impression Richard instantly received was one of warmth. Clearly she suffered few misgivings about herself and her place among others, and what doubts she might have she kept locked away.

In short and succinct words, the king told his daughters who Richard was, and if the news surprised them, their faces did not show it. No doubt they were accustomed to such unusual revelations from their father. Then he proceeded to instruct them as to what they must do to help him gain entry at Court. The princesses vowed that their half-brother's identity would never be revealed, and that they would do as the king bade them; with that, they left the room.

In a last heroic effort, Henry raised himself a bit on one elbow that he might better look his son eye-to-eye. 'One final charge I give you, Richard, regarding the legacy you carry within you. Would that we might have known one another better, but it was not possible without you carrying the stigma of a bastard, thereby bringing shame to one we both know deserves it not. Instead you have a good, unblemished name, and a mother who is as fine a lady as ever lived. Be grateful and unshamed. Mayhap it is your good fortune to be so placed: the royal name can be a heavy thing for a man to carry at times, and you will never be so encumbered.'

He leaned closer, straining to speak. 'And though you do not bear the name Tudor, still you carry the legacy within you, and all its attributes. Use your many and varied talents wisely, and follow that which you know to be right...' He fell back on the pillows. 'Now you must go and I must ready myself for that which awaits. Death stands in the shadows and beckons me.'

6

Richard walked slowly from the room where he and his father had met as common blood for the first and last time. The words spoken there would burn themselves into the very core of his soul for the rest of his life. He felt proud to have known the king in that man's final hour, and he vowed that he would serve this other family of his in any way fate might have in store for him.

But his thoughts were as much on his half-sister Elizabeth as on the man who had sired them both. When first she entered the room, she had smiled at him, and he'd known in that moment that they were friends though no words were spoken. No doubt he and she would indeed see days when they would help one another without anyone knowing their true relationship, and he knew as though it were fact that she too felt these same things even now.

And so Richard departed the palace at Richmond, again a simple priest from Oxford, and inside him he felt equal parts sorrow and joy: sorrow that his father would die without the two of them ever truly knowing one another, and joy at the prospects for the future in service of his sisters.

The next morning it was announced that Henry VIII had died and was to be buried at Windsor, and Richard received the news as a common citizen of the realm. Though he had served in the Boys' Choir of the Chapel Royal, he remained unknown to the people of the Court, and he could not have attended the funeral without stirring up comment - a disservice not only to the memory of King Henry, but also to Mary and Elizabeth. Therefore he waited instead among the crowd at the Windsor gates, kneeling when the great and solemn procession passed by, and saying a silent prayer for his king and father.

Having jostled his way to the front to the see the king's body, Richard witnessed firsthand a horrible sight that would stay burned on his memory for as long as he lived. As the black-draped carriage moved slowly down the road before the silent onlookers, from inside the coffin came a hideous groaning sound, and an instant later a stream of fluid began to issue forth, over the sides of the carriage and onto the street.

A scream went up from the crowd at the sight, and two footmen rushed forward to investigate. Timidly they raised the covering off the coffin, and - though no one could see, this was the rumour - found that His Majesty's body had burst open from its own great weight. The liquid issuing forth, a purplish colour, was his blood mixed with the other fluids of his body, and one last time Richard smelled that hideous scent of death, the noisome stench in the spirit now mixed with the very real odour of rotting flesh.

'It is like our Saviour,' whispered a weeping priest nearby. 'When his sides were pierced by the soldiers, he gave up both blood and water.'

But another, a scornful wag, made a look of disgust and said, 'Forsooth, father clerk! Hast not heard the ancient prophecy?' Others strained to listen, and the insolent youth said, 'In earlier days, the king was given a curse that dogs would devour his body at Windsor.' And even as he said these words, a pack of stray curs rushed forth to the side of the carriage to lap up the blood before a troop of guards chased them off.

'Not like our Saviour,' another man said in a low voice, 'but like Queen Jezebel, cursed by Jehu. God save us all!'

It took Richard many days to put this melancholy memory to the back of his mind, but by the time he returned again in his tiny room at Oxford, he had found some peace and rest in his soul. Upon his arrival in that familiar place, he built a small fire in the fireplace and sat down to ponder the many thoughts and sensations parading through his mind. One thing he knew for a fact: he could never be the same Richard Edwardes known to his colleagues and students, and now he no longer doubted that his fortunes would lie outside the grand stone structures of the ancient university.

He would instead do as his father had bade him do, and would thereby be freed to write poetry and plays and live among (but not as) royalty. It would be as though he were acting a part in a great play of grand design, and only he would know the irony of it all: that as his sire had told him, he carried the great legacy within him.

In the midst of these thoughts, an inspiration seized him, and he set about to record in verse the deathbed message of his father to him. As he gathered paper, quill, and ink and began to write, he felt inside himself a rising sense of excitement: he had begun his true career as poet, and now would unleash the desires long held back by what he'd supposed to be his destiny. That being so, his poem would not be for his eyes alone, and therefore the task required more than a modicum of talent. He knew that his stanzas must be written in terms intelligible to all readers, but such that those few who knew his secret would fully understand its portent.

When he had finished writing, he read his words, and he knew that someday he would share then with Elizabeth his sister:

Fair Words Make Fools Feign

In youthful years when first my young desires began
To prick me forth to serve in Court, a slender tall young man,
My Father's blessing then I asked upon my knee,
Who blessing me with trembling hand, these words did say to me:
'My son, God guide thy way, and shield thee from mischance,
And make thy just desserts in Court, thy poor estate to advance.
Yet when thou art become one of the Courtly train,
Think on this proverb old, that fair words make fools feign.

This counsel gravely given, most strange appears to me,
Till tract of time, with open eyes, had made me plainly see,
What subtle slights are wrought, by painted tales devise,
When hollow hearts with friendly shoes the simple do entice,
To think all gold that shines to feed their fond desire,
Whose shivering cold is warmed with smoke, instead of flaming fire.
Since talk of fickle trust doth breed a hope most vain,
This proverb true by proof I find, that fair words make fools feign.

Fair speech always doeth well, where deeds ensue fair words,
Fair speech again, always doeth evil, that bushes give for birds.
Who hopes to have fair words, to try his lucky lot,
If I may counsel, let him strike it while the iron is hot.
But them that feed on clods, instead of pleasant grapes,
Full loathe I am, yet must I tell them in words plain,
This proverb old proves true in them,
That fair words make fools feign.

Bemoan the time that words so slowly turn to deeds,
Bemoan the time ye fair sweet flowers are grown to rotten weeds.
But thrice bemoan the time that truth is fled,
Wherein I see how simple hearts with words are vainly fed.
Trust no fair words, therefore, where no deeds do ensue;
Trust words as skillful falconers do trust hawks that never flew;
Trust deeds, let words be words, which never wrought me gain.
Let my experience make you wise, and let words make fools feign.

Days, weeks, months, years - in fact, the entire six-year reign of the sickly boy king, Edward VI - would pass before Richard once again saw his sisters, but he did not spend that time in idleness. His new understanding of himself manifested at first in a restlessness with his surroundings. The excitement he used to receive from teaching and studying strangely departed him, and he found that his life at Oxford as scholar and priest no longer satisfied him as it had before.

Inside him, a voice continually reminded him that his destiny lay not in the world of these ivied walls, and the urge to create began to torment him ever more. He wrote more and finer poetry with a greater zeal, but even this failed to satiate the longings rising inside. Nonetheless, his hard work bore fruit, and at least within the halls of the university he soon found great recognition as a poet.

And still his yearnings, unanswered and not even fully identified, plagued him, beckoning him to the larger world outside and echoing the words of the king: 'Make your way at Court.'

How he would accomplish this charge, he did not know. His situation recalled to him the story of Joseph the son of Jacob, who while in prison helped the pharaoh's cupbearer make his return to favour with the king, but was then forgotten by the man for a very long time. Yet Joseph had sought God's will even when events did not go as he'd hoped or expected, and for Richard too this commitment to his Lord took precedence over both his desires to create and his promises to his father and sisters.

Leaving home at such an early age, he'd long viewed himself as a child of God more than of any parent. Though the reformation of the Church of England had changed some details in the outer manifestation of his vows, he remained an ordained priest, and no other bonds could pull him from those. Sometimes he still dared dream of his childhood love, Margaret Babb, wishing that he could be her husband one day, but like a king, he felt the call of duty more strongly than that of his own desires.

Yet service to the Almighty could mean many things, one of which was to make use of the talents he'd been given as an inheritance. Likewise his commitment to serve broadened from a dedication to the church alone to a much larger responsibility toward his Tudor family and thus to all Englishmen. Priest, poet, and brother, they all meant the same thing: acting unselfishly and in love for his fellow man.

Freed by this new understanding of how his role would play itself out, he began to realise that the time had come to leave the comfort of his life at Oxford. Once he made this decision, it seemed that events followed. In 1552 he was asked to take the position of rector for the fine parish of St. Helen's in Worcester, a small village deep in that English countryside from which Richard had long drawn great strength for his soul. Though not precisely what he saw as his ultimate goal, the move seemed a step forward, and he accepted.

The rectorship marked a sharp change from the regimen of cold detachment to which he'd become accustomed at the university. For the first time in many years, he began to deal directly with people daily, and for the first time ever, he found himself in the role of counsellor, listening to the needs of his parishioners and helping them to seek God's wisdom.

As he began to move about in his new ministry, he felt himself relax in his relationships. A new warmth and friendliness came from him naturally and effortlessly, as though the suppression of all this in his life as a scholar had been the pretense and this the reality of Richard Edwardes.

Each week his sermons gained more and more compassion and personal feeling, and his flock responded to the love they felt from the pulpit. Up to now he had cared for people (other than his family, of course) in the abstract, and not as individual human beings, and he matured in the warmth of his contact with these country folk.

As he grew in strength and love, he experienced that serendipitous truth he had long before learned from the Scriptures: 'But seek ye first the kingdom of God, and his righteousness; and all these things shall be added unto you.' Now that he had submitted to a higher purpose, his personal and creative writings began to take on more meaning for him, and the fullness of what he'd come to experience showed itself not only in the quality but the volume of his work. At times, his words and thoughts almost seemed to leap off the page.

As he had placed his writing in the service of God, so for a time he put aside his dream of making his way at Court. Now and then, of course, his thoughts returned to London, and he still believed that his destiny lay there. But in general he found his time so full and demanding that it allowed little opportunity to dream of the possibilities that he knew existed someday for him. Still, every once in awhile he considered that his newfound appreciation and understanding of people would stand him in good stead whenever his sisters called for him, and he always listened with great interest for any scrap of news that came from the capital.

King Edward VI had assumed the throne at the age of nine, but the true power lay in the hands of the 'protector,' his uncle Edward Seymour, Duke of Somerset. Somerset knew nothing of Richard's relation to the Crown, and if he had, might have used that knowledge to his own advantage. Meanwhile the princesses could do nothing to help Richard, for they lived apart from the Court in virtual exile.

Then on July 6, 1553, King Edward, suffering from unknown internal problems and agonising sores on his legs, died at the tender age of sixteen. All that his father had feared regarding his succession now came to pass.

When the king died, Princess Mary, next in line for the throne, was at Framingham Castle in Norfolk, and Elizabeth at Hatfield House, the closest thing to a home she'd ever known. In this interval of mourning John Dudley, Duke of Northumberland, seized the moment to proclaim Lady Jane Grey the new Queen of England, and so she would reign - for a few tempestuous days. The people, however, Catholics and Protestants alike, rallied behind Mary as the true heir to the throne, and Northumberland's rebellion was quickly put down. Both he and Lady Jane were executed, and Mary Tudor became the rightful queen of the realm.

The news and the rejoicing travelled quickly throughout the land, and within a few days, the Rector of St. Helen's in Worcester knew of it as well. Finally, after six years of waiting during which he'd all but put aside his dreams, the moment had arrived when the promises made beside the deathbed of King Henry could be made good. What would his future be now? He did not know, but with a rising sense of joy - as well as melancholy that he might soon bid farewell to his parishioners - he prepared to visit the palace and his sister.

7

For his second meeting with Mary - now Queen Mary - this time at Whitehall Palace, Richard again wore his priestly garments. He thought about his choice before he made it: not only had he presented himself thus the first time they met years before, the vestments made a convenient cover for the true purpose of his visit. Beyond all that, he had heard that his new queen was a devout Catholic, and his appearance in his office as priest could only please her.

Had he gone to her with the assumption that he had on deposit in the bank of her heart even a penny's worth of warmth from their first encounter and her father's revelations regarding his relation to her, Richard would have been disappointed. But even from his limited experience with royalty, he knew better than to assume anything of them, and this protected him from offense.

Indeed, when finally he entered the hall where she held court and was presented to her, the unsmiling queen gazed upon her visitor for a long time in silence as though she'd never seen him before. He imagined that under her imperious veneer, she felt as awkward as he, but he knew the right to speak first belonged to her, so he waited in silence while she looked him up and down.

At last she spoke. 'The queen is pleased that the good clerk could visit.'

Richard bowed again, as he had when he first entered the room. 'It is a great privilege to be allowed an audience, Your Majesty.' 'Leave us,' the queen ordered her courtiers and servants. Still with the magisterial look of one unassailable in her power, she watched them scurry out, and when the last one had departed, she turned again to Richard. 'And now that we are alone, we can discuss your business without employing artifice - for I am sure I know why you have come.'

She paused for a moment, and when she spoke again it was with a slightly more relaxed manner. 'I have given the matter great thought, and I have determined that the best position for you will be in the Chapel Royal. No one will question your background and pedigree there, and because you are a priest, you can be employed on that basis, as well in your capacity as poet and writer. I trust that these arrangements are satisfactory?'

Had they not been, of course, Richard wouldn't have dared to say so, but in the present circumstance he found himself overjoyed. 'Indeed, Your Majesty,' he said, 'such a position would give your servant an opportunity to be of any assistance that he may be to the queen, in any capacity that she may ask.' He had to tread lightly: the fact that he considered the two of them to have a special relationship did not at all mean that she felt the same, and it would be disastrous to speak of their previous meeting - and the injunctions of her father - if she did not mention these first.

She did not, but neither was her tone unkind. 'I trust you will make all the appropriate arrangements for your change in station?'

'Yes, Your Majesty...'

'What else is it you wish to say?'

'If your servant may be so bold,' he said, 'perhaps my first few weeks might be spent in a dual role as rector of St. Helen's and member of the Chapel Royal. This, I believe, would give the Court time to get used to my presence, and thus permit less curiosity.'

She listened judiciously to these words, then said, 'Do as you wish.' She continued to stare at him for a moment, and he wondered if he were supposed to make an exit, but she had not dismissed him, and as with the matter of mentioning their late father, he dared not act first. Then she spoke again: 'What is it, truthfully, that you wish to obtain at Court, Master Edwardes?'

This time he was able to answer in confident words. 'I have no great ambitions or desire for wealth or power,' he said. 'I wish only to be of service to my queen in any way that I can. Whatever your needs or desires may be, you have but to ask, Your Majesty, and your servant will do as you wish.' With daring familiarity, he went on. 'It is said that the queen loves flowers and gardening, as do I, and even if she should require one handy with spade and dirt, she will find me an eager worker.'

For the first time, the queen smiled. 'Your queen is satisfied we shall get on well.' But this was as warm as she would become at this meeting. 'Now, there are many matters requiring my attention, so I trust that you will be able to see your way out.'

He made a very deep bow, then turned and walked from the room. Over the years since their last meeting, he'd thought of her more often as his sister than as royalty, and though from this second encounter he judged that he should reverse that order in his mind, he could not help but feel compassion for Mary. They were both older - he was twenty-eight now, no longer a 'young man' but simply a man; and yet she seemed to have aged two years to his every one. Clearly the experiences of her life had left many scars, and he felt drawn to do whatever he could to earn her friendship.

It would take a long while for that to happen if it ever did, for there were many things about his sister that he would only learn after years at Court. In the meantime, he found himself to his great pleasure living the very life his father the king had wished for him, and he found that he played his part well.

'His part' was just how he thought of it. In previous times, circumstances had never called on him to exercise courtly skills and diplomacy, nor to entertain and amuse, but he soon found that those very talents flowed in his veins along with his royal blood. It was as an actor that he lived at Court, in this case playing a part written for real life and not the stage.

His role, requiring both charm and tact, was that of courtier and gentleman of the Chapel Royal, and Richard found that he played it without apparent effort. He moved with grace and precision, and managed always to have the proper and flattering words for each and every one in the Court - especially the ladies. In a very short time he began to seem like someone who had done this all his life, and his performance made many of the other courtiers appear as novices.

Richard soon became extremely popular with the ladies of the court and was warmly received by most of the lords and courtiers, but there were those who, because of their lesser ease and talents, became jealous of the poet. Lord Hunsdon, the unacknowledged brother of the queen, in particular was less than cordial.

One day when Richard was entertaining a group of ladies with a story, Hunsdon happened to stroll by just as the listeners burst forth with laughter and squeals of delight. At the sight of his scowling face, everyone in the room became quiet. He turned to Richard and, speaking in a tone both impeccably polite but unquestionably icy, said, 'I had not known that the good clerk was also a play-actor; methinks you might just as well have had another calling.'

With that he left the room, and Richard - without a trace of shame or anger on his face - continued his tale. His expression did not lie: he admired Hunsdon as a gentleman, and on any occasion when he might have chosen to take offense at the latter's frequently derisive comments, he said to himself, *At least I had the good fortune of being recognised by our father the king.*

One day when he felt sure enough of himself to do so, he asked the queen if he might recite for her and her ladies-in-waiting a poem he'd written in their honour. The queen agreed to it, and so in clear, distinct, and dramatic tones he began his tribute:

My fancy fanned on me somewhat of ye to see;
good ladies all, accept my will, this thing I only pray
Hawarde is not haughty, but of such smiling cheer
that would allure each gentle heart, her love to hold full dear
Dacars is not dangerous, her talk is nothing coy
her noble stature may compare with Hector's wife of Troy
Baynam is as beautiful as nature can devise:
steadfastness possess her heart, and chastity her eyes
Arundell is well spoken of in these her tender years;
in heart, in voice, in talk, in deed, her future self appears
Dormor is a darling, and of such lively hue
that who so feeds his eyes on her may soon her beauty rue
Mancell is a merry one, and is right worth love
whom nature wrought so freshly, her cunning for to prove
Coke is comely, and hereto in books sets all her care
in learning with the Roman dames of right she may compare
Bridges is a blessed wight, and prayeth with heart and voice
which from her cradle hath been taught in virtue to rejoice
These eight now serve one noble Queen, but if power were in me,
For beauty's praise and virtue's sake, each one a Queen should be

Not surprisingly, these verses greatly pleased the ladies, each of whom blushed in turn when her praises were spoken. But Richard was most anxious to see the response of his queen. She clapped and said in a voice that sounded almost cheerful, 'Well done, Master Edwardes! We will hope for more of your talents.' As she spoke, she looked at him in a way he hadn't seen from her before, as though she wondered what other talents this unacknowledged brother of hers might possess.

He saw the same expression in his queen's eyes on the occasion of her birthday celebration, when he composed and recited a poem for her which he'd secretly feared might seem a bit too flattering, given her demonstrated lack of personal charm and warmth. But by now he'd come to recognise her starvation for love, and he hoped that the admiration expressed in his verses would cheer her. Clearly it did, and she praised him before the rest of the Court.

He didn't realise just how often Mary had thought of him, and what a hard battle he'd had to fight just to win the few smiles he'd received from her. Of course his role as priest had certainly not hurt his standing in her eyes, and it was particularly good that he still served as rector of a country chapel, a position he would not resign until 1555. Though most churches in and around London had converted to the new English faith during the reign of her father, those further distant from the capital had remained loyal to Rome, and many more had returned to Catholicism upon her accession to power.

Mary never questioned Richard about his personal religious views, and he was glad because he believed that such matters should be kept personal and private. Perhaps she kept silent on this matter before she feared he might say something that would make her think less of him.

And so she had remained opaque, but over time he began to build her trust as he proved his unswerving loyalty. Though he gained great acclaim and might have used this to his advantage, he always deflected the glory from himself toward her, and slowly Mary realised that this brother of hers had no intention of threatening her authority. He had made vows, and he remained true to his word - a rare quality, and one more appreciated by royalty than anyone else. Moreover, Mary found herself captivated with his charm and creativity as well as his wit, which brought laughter into a life that had never known much of joy, and she accepted his literary offerings with delight.

So she softened toward him, and even came to rely on his counsel in small things. But she never broached any area of great significance to her, such as her personal decision to marry Philip of Spain, because for her there was no other side to the question.

Still, he could be her eyes and ears if not her conscience: though he too was unfamiliar with the Court, he could move freely and inconspicuously as she could not, and tell her anything she asked to know. She knew she needed help, for she rightly recognised the instability of her rule even if she misunderstood the reasons for this. Perhaps Master Richard Edwardes, son of her father, could act as liaison with the one from whom she perceived the greatest threat of all: her sister Elizabeth.

8

Richard could not have known how much his sister the queen needed a friend - perhaps even she didn't know - nor could he have guessed what a small and frightened woman lurked beneath her foreboding and magisterial persona. The life of Queen Mary, now thirty-eight and on the eve of a marriage to which the groom had agreed for purely political and not personal reasons, had never been happy, and the weight of the crown only further bowed her head.

She wore drab clothing that neither fit properly nor complimented the lumpy lines of her frame. Perhaps with her missing teeth and sallow skin she did not think that jewels would help, or that their beauty would only make her appear even less attractive. Whatever the reasons, she wore only golden bells for adornment, a queer decoration, and did little else to make herself look like anything more than an aging housewife.

Her father, no doubt recognising that her looks would not improve with age, had tried several times to make an advantageous marriage for her when she was still a young girl, but to no avail. Then he'd divorced her mother, and this had placed on young Mary the unpleasant title of bastard. She had lived in virtual exile thereafter, even being denied the chance to pay last respects to her mother when Catherine died in 1536.

As a child she'd received musical training and had proven herself precocious, but this was small consolation to an unattractive girl, and with the onslaught of the years even those qualities seemed to have faded. By the time she ascended the throne Mary exhibited little that would suggest either intelligence or culture; instead she had a sullen, moody way about her that made her dreary company.

Of course no one but an equal would have dared to even insinuate this about their monarch, but Mary knew herself to be unpopular, and for considerably more important reasons than her dearth of good humour. Her sense of inferiority as a woman was matched only by her apprehension at her inabilities in political matters, and these two shortcomings - fatal flaws for a queen - found their fullest expression in her engagement to Prince Philip of Spain.

For her part, Mary looked forward to joining her fortunes with those of Philip, son of her first cousin, the enormously powerful Holy Roman Emperor Charles V. Whereas common folk talked of the financial aspect of marriage in terms of oxen or small plots of land, and the nobility spoke of castles and servants, royalty married into whole countries. Philip controlled not only Spain, but Naples, Sicily, the Low Countries, and colonies in the Americas, and later on would rule over Portugal and his namesake islands the Philippines as well. Mary had only England to offer, and there could be no question that the match would be to her advantage.

But it was not lines on maps that made her giddy down in her fragile royal heart; it was Philip himself. Eleven years younger than she, he brought youthful vigour into her life, and she - half Spanish herself - felt pulled by the tide of his Latin sensuality. She had lived so many years alone, and now she'd truly found love!

That was how she thought of it, anyway; Philip's appraisal was less sanguine. He'd sent ahead an ambassador to survey the English queen for him, and the man's report had been less than enticing. She lacked most of her teeth, the diplomat had observed, and looked a good deal older even than her years; though not fat, she was flabby, and she dressed badly.

Yet whatever his feelings, Philip was a realist (his father advised the marriage for strategic purposes), and a true prince. In public he treated her with all the respect and seeming devotion that befitted a Queen of England, and as was the English custom, he kissed her on the mouth when greeting her.

If Philip was only a grudging party to the match, an even more significant partner in her political life - the English people - had considerably less joy at the prospect of the marriage. For one thing, the groom-to-be was a staunch Catholic like the queen herself, and in the years that had passed since King Henry began the reformation of the English church, the popular tides had shifted away from the old faith in favour of the new. Besides that, his very power threatened to swallow up the kingdom, and they distrusted Spanish ambitions both in Europe and in the newly opened world of the Americas.

Mary, of course, knew of her people's misgivings regarding her proposed marriage, but she would not relent. She had long before decided that if ever she had a husband, he must be a Catholic, and she cared nothing for nationality when love and God were at stake.

Still, she recognised the insecurity of her position at the very palace she supposedly ruled, and the fact that the circumstances of her early years had permitted her little opportunity to visit at Court only added to her worries. With time, she came to focus all her anxiety on her sister.

When the news had reached Hatfield House that Edward VI had died and Mary would become queen, Elizabeth had gone straight to London and joined her sister's court. Mary might have chosen to take on maternal feelings toward her little sister, being indeed old enough to be the mother of the twenty-year-old. But Mary, thirty-seven and looking every year her age, found the presence of her much prettier, more intelligent, and more charming relation much too close for comfort. For one thing, her fiancé had shown just a little too much interest in the younger woman.

It was true that Philip had clearly taken to Elizabeth, and that the feeling was mutual. But Elizabeth's sentiments were only the most charitable and proper. She evaluated him not as a possible suitor but as a future brother-in-law, and she reckoned Mary to be fortunate for making the match. Indeed, she rejoiced in her heart for her sister, and hoped the Spanish prince might improve Mary's troubled spirits.

Still, Mary chose to be jealous, not only as a woman but as a monarch. Though the interest of her husband-to-be in her sister must have hurt her the most, it only added to her growing unpleasant realisation that many of her people would be happy to see Elizabeth and not her on the throne. So she set about to make life uncomfortable for the princess, humiliating her in front of others and treating her as one of lower rank than she actually held. As she demeaned her sister, she raised other women in her place.

Finally one evening following a dinner at which Mary had seated Elizabeth in a place much lower in rank than protocol would have required, Elizabeth approached her sister and quietly asked, 'May I have a word with Your Majesty in private?'

Mary looked at her with scorn for a long, tense moment before finally saying, 'If you will be brief.'

With this, the queen led the princess to a small parlour near at hand, and when they had shut the door behind them, she turned to her and said with evident disgust, 'What is this for which you take the queen's time, dear sister?'

Elizabeth stood up straighter, her long slender hands at her bodice, and said, 'Dear sister' - the words sounded sincere from her mouth, unlike

Mary's - 'why do you put others in my place at dinners? In so doing, the disservice is more to you than me.'

Mary glowered at her contemptuously and snapped, 'It surprises me that one who was declared a bastard by my father would expect any place at all at the queen's table. 'Tis more than you deserve with all your posturing, your airs with your learning, your throwing yourself like a strumpet at Prince Philip.'

She paused for a moment and walked toward the window, then turned with a face flushed by anger. 'How dare you carry on as you do in my, your queen's, palace! The time has come when you should retire to one of your own residences, where you can practice your airs to the walls or the servants.'

And then as though they had reached an agreement, she announced, 'Very well, I shall inform the Court that you are not feeling well, and are returning to the country for a time. Take care that you show my story to be true, or I'll find far less favourable quarters for you!'

Elizabeth stood in stunned disbelief for a moment, then said in a soft and composed voice, 'Yes, Your Majesty is quite right. I had hoped that I might prove some help to my sovereign, but I can see now that I was wrong. It would indeed be best if I were to go away; therefore I will do as you bid me do.'

Showing none of the indignation and hurt that must surely have burned in her bosom, she bowed, turned, and left the room with dignity and calm - but without being excused by the queen. She returned to the others who had dined with them, and told them she was not feeling well. That night she began preparations to take up residence at Ashridge in Hertfordshire.

All this Mary had done, in spite of the protests both of Richard and of Philip. On the day of Elizabeth's departure, the prince could no longer contain his disgust with Mary's treatment of her sister, and there ensued a row of royal proportions.

'I ask you how any person,' he demanded in his heavily accented but impeccable English, 'let alone a queen, one who is supposed to be both wise and fair, can treat her own sister as badly as you have Elizabeth? Have you so succumbed to the blindness of jealousy that you cannot see she wants only to be your friend and do your bidding?' With a gesture of disdain, he issued forth a special expression of contemptuous doubt: 'Forsooth! You do yourself and your kingdom no service with such behaviour!'

Despite her mousey appearance, Mary had strong passions for her God and her man, but at this moment her malice toward her sister took precedence over both. 'You ask me how I can do this,' she retorted, 'and I ask how you, a Christian of the holy Catholic church, can call this daughter of a - of a common whore - my sister? Does your faith mean so little?' Spite made Mary's never too lovely face even more unattractive. 'She must have you beguiled with her womanly charms!'

Mary's outburst stunned the prince, who stared back at her in speechless anger. Then he turned and stormed out of the room.

When he was gone, Mary seethed in private, taking comfort in her abject heart from the searing warmth of hatred. 'Elizabeth!' she said aloud with distaste, rolling out the syllables - Elizabeth, issue of that awful Anne Boleyn, who had stolen her father and caused her mother such disgrace. Mary smiled a bitter smile. She was glad to see her sister go, but Elizabeth would not so easily escape her wrath.

In the midst of these quarrels, it would have been difficult for Richard to have remained unaware of the turmoil, but he considered it wise not to attempt intercession with the queen on her sister's behalf. His position was difficult at best: Mary had often demonstrated her unwillingness to brook protest on any matter where her opinion was firm, and more importantly, he had given his word of loyalty to their father. Clearly this meant that the greater fidelity belonged to the one sitting on the throne.

But this did not prevent him from going to Elizabeth in secret to comfort her in any way he could. The princess understood why he had come, and before Richard could speak said simply, 'Only God can help my sister. I surely cannot. Trouble yourself not with these things; I know and understand your heart, and the vows you made to the king.'

Richard stood there without speaking for a moment, then said, 'Then might we pray together for understanding and guidance before I go?'

Saying nothing, Elizabeth knelt, and he bowed down beside her. A few minutes later, without speaking another word directly to her, Richard let himself out the door.

Still he wished for words that would change the queen's heart even as he knew the impossibility of this. On those occasions when she did ask him for his wisdom, it was almost always with questions that required only the answer of 'yes' or 'no'. Mary was all heat, and no light; here where the illumination of understanding was required, he could do nothing.

Soon after Elizabeth left for Hertfordshire, a rebellion broke out against the intended marriage and alliance with Spain, and for a few troubled days, everything that Mary had feared seemed to have come upon her. But after Parliament rallied and sent troops to quell the revolt, the queen began hearing rumours that her sister had known of the conspiracy against the crown and perhaps even been involved in it. This was just the sort of thing she wanted to believe, and when she'd quite convinced herself that these preposterous claims were true, she ordered that Elizabeth should return to London immediately to be interrogated.

Elizabeth, plagued with a kidney ailment, sent back word that she was too ill to travel, and pleaded with Mary to let her remain in the countryside for a time. Both Philip and Richard beseeched the queen on behalf of her sister, saying that she had no interest in taking the throne that rightfully belonged to Mary, but this only intensified her anger.

She sent her personal physicians to examine Elizabeth, and they reported back that though she was not completely well, she could no doubt make the trip to London. Mary then dispatched three of her counsel - Lord William Howard, Sir Edward Hastings, and Sir Thomas Cornwallis - to bring Elizabeth to London. Perhaps if she'd known of these men's sympathies for Elizabeth, she might have chosen otherwise, but then it was becoming increasingly hard to find anyone who opposed her younger sister - ironically, for the very reason that Mary had so clearly determined to destroy her. The three made the trip to Ashridge as slowly as they dared, hoping that by the time they returned, Her Majesty's anger would have cooled.

They found Elizabeth looking quite sick, her normally rosy face ashen in complexion - a condition no doubt abetted by her current worries. On the trip back to the capital with her three escorts, she ordered the curtains of her horsedrawn litter pulled back, an indignant gesture to illustrate to the people of England the truth of her claim of illness.

When they arrived at Whitehall Palace, two of the queen's councillors, one of whom was Thomas Radcliffe, Earl of Sussex, met them with orders from Queen Mary that Elizabeth be taken to the Tower of London.

The Tower! Even the name had a ghastly ring to it. Common criminals died in common prisons, but the Tower was a special place of misery for high-born offenders, and it offered forms of suffering that a lover of cruelty would have called exquisite. But the worst pain of all lay in the anticipation of the tortures and punishments that dwelled within its foreboding gates, and at the very sound of it, Elizabeth was seized with fear.

Yet even then she kept enough of her wits to conceive a plan that might still purchase her freedom. She asked Lord Sussex if, before departing for the Tower, she might be given pen and paper in order to write a plea to the queen. Sussex, yet another sympathiser who did not at all relish his mission, decided that there could be little harm in allowing her request, so he ordered the writing materials brought to her.

Elizabeth sat down and composed a lengthy missive in which she attempted to convince her sister of her innocence and her good will, but that was not her true purpose in writing the letter. She spent considerable effort over her words, and erased them many times. When she had finished and could think of no other way to use up additional time, she took as long as she possibly could in drawing lines across the bottom of the page, ostensibly so that no one could make additions without it being obvious that they had done so.

By that time, her party had missed the tide for the boat trip from Whitehall to the Tower, and would have to wait for morning. Elizabeth's plan had worked, and though it had bought her only twenty-four hours, perhaps in that short period Mary's anger would cool.

But no further word came from the queen, and on the next day the dreaded journey from Whitehall Palace began. That day - Palm Sunday, March 17, 1554 - dawned cold and dreary, with a drizzling rain only adding to her sorrow as she descended into the boat and made her way toward the ominous Tower of London. On the occasion commemorated in that holy day, the Saviour had entered Jerusalem to the shouts of the throng gathered there, who spread palm branches in his way and praised him as their king; but less than a week later, many of those same well-wishers would call for his blood on the cross. Elizabeth could not help but think of this as she sat in the boat and it began its slow passage down the river.

Another thought occurred to her, one with even more chilling portent: by arriving at the Tower via the waterway instead of by land, she would have to enter through the gate opening onto the Thames, the 'Traitor's Gate!' No one who passed into the Tower by that entrance ever left it alive. As recently as the unfortunate events involving Lady Jane Grey, three highborn persons - Lord Northumberland, Lord Guildford Dudley, and Dudley's wife Jane herself - had entered here, and within a few hours had faced the executioner.

If ever in her life Elizabeth had known terror, this was the time, and as the icy rain trickled incessantly onto her craft, she trembled in fear.

The barge drifted past the points along the Thames she knew so well - Savoy Stairs, Somerset Water Gate, St. Paul's Wharf, Old Swan Stairs - and finally under London Bridge. Then through the misty rain Elizabeth could make out the black iron grating of Traitor's Gate. For a moment, she sat as if frozen with her ladies-in-waiting and two male escorts, then as befitted one of royal blood, she struggled to regain her composure. Speaking with difficulty, for the dryness in her throat made it almost impossible to enunciate without revealing her fear, she asked if she might be allowed to enter by another way.

But Sussex, clearly pained by what he had to say yet nonetheless compelled to follow the orders of his monarch, answered that the queen had given explicit directions. He must follow them to the last word, he said (perhaps thinking that he'd already erred by permitting the letter which had cost them a day), or be in danger of his own imprisonment in the Tower - with all that meant.

The barge suddenly thumped to a halt and Elizabeth's heart sank within her. One of her male attendants gallantly proffered his cloak to protect the princess from the rain as she stepped from beneath the canopy and onto the land, but in indignation she rejected this well-meant offer. She would need no pretense of chivalry, not at such a dreadful moment as this.

When she stepped ashore, Princess Elizabeth turned and spoke to those assembled there. 'Oh Lord!' she said in a firm and loud voice, 'I had never thought to enter here as a prisoner, and I pray you all bear me witness that I come in as no traitor, but as true a woman to the queen's Majesty as any now living.'

Many of the guards, moved by this impassioned utterance, stepped forward and knelt before her. 'God preserve Your Grace!' one shouted, and the others joined in. 'God preserve Your Grace!'

With these words still hovering in the misty air, Elizabeth turned toward a large stone by the water side, walked to it, and sat down. One of her attendants, glancing up at the sky from whence the chilly drizzle still poured, beseeched her to enter the Tower and get out of the rain.

' 'Tis better to sit in this ungodly place,' she replied majestically, 'whatever the weather, than to go where it is planned that I be seated! Would the people of England have me walk cheerfully to the chopping block when I am without fault? Is there none who cares what becomes of a princess royal? Has England, which I love with all the passion in this frail heart, sunk so low as this?'

One of the guards, who a moment before had stood by in impassive silence, burst into tears. Elizabeth rose suddenly in a fury and said, 'Would you cower and weep tears for me when it is your strength to defend me that is needed? What has become of the valour of brave hearts who would defend their princess?'

But the princess could not sit forever in the gray mists by the banks of the Thames; night would come, and with it no reprieve from her sister the queen. Finally she allowed herself to enter and face what lay within the Tower.

There she found her prison, an apartment with a large vaulted chamber, an enormous fireplace, and three very narrow windows that let in a little light through the thick walls of sullen gray stone. To a common thief, it would have been a palace, but then common thieves never saw the inside of the Tower, and it was hardly proper lodging for one of royal blood.

Yet she had no choice of where to lay her head, and thus the Tower became her home. As days ebbed into weeks and weeks into a month, Elizabeth went time and again to sit before her inquisitors, and on each visit gave the same answers to the same questions. Her hope began to fade, and many times she would gladly have confessed to anything in order to end this slow torture of humiliation with certain death to follow, but something kept her going. Inside her she carried not only the knowledge of her innocence, but the conviction of her destiny - and the memory of one who had died in order that she might one day hope to reign.

She'd been only three years old at the time of Anne Boleyn's beheading, and she could not remember her mother at all, but now more and more she understood what that woman had suffered by going to her death in this very place. Anne had fought to preserve the birthright of her baby daughter, and even though it appeared now that her mother's efforts had been for naught, Elizabeth resolved to live as long as God and the queen permitted.

In spite of her abiding sense of dread, Elizabeth discovered the saving grace of that tendency - common to all human beings - to make a routine out of any ongoing experience, no matter how dreadful. The place called 'The Tower' actually consisted of many buildings enclosed by an ancient wall that had once marked the boundaries for the City of London, and it housed not only the prisoners but the guards and their families. She was permitted to walk around outside twice a day, and Sir John Brydges, Lieutenant of the Tower, invited her to take her meals in his timber-framed quarters within the Tower complex. There was also a small lad, son of one of the guards, who daily brought her flowers and often spoke with her as she walked.

All these things made for a cheering respite from the gloomy sameness of her captivity, and she was even allowed a visitor: her brother Richard. He came as often as he could, posing as a priest there to hear her confession, though in fact his visits had other purposes as well.

Richard confirmed his initial impressions of the princess, made many years before, that she would be a friend and a true sister, but this was a time to give and not to seek aid. Therefore he did what he could to reassure her that she would be released, reminding her that he was not her only ally at Court, and that whenever he dared to speak well of her to the queen, he did.

Often he entertained her with his writing, reciting new pieces of poetry as he wrote them and telling her of his plays. Other times they discussed the works of other authors, or passages from the Scriptures. But always they would pray together for the needs uppermost in Elizabeth's mind for that particular day.

Her brother's visits meant more to her than the princess could or would express. As time passed and he brought her more and more comfort, the bond between the two became stronger and stronger. Though he would have seen her free, Richard had done the next best thing: made her captivity bearable.

But then just as Elizabeth was becoming used to her present circumstances - as used as anyone could become - her sister tightened its terms. Soon the privileges of walking and taking her meals with Sir John were taken away as well, and the little son of the guard came to her one day and told her he'd been forbidden to speak to her. Now her confinement became even more rigid with each passing day, and once again she grew to despair of any hope for freedom.

As Richard saw these new restrictions unfolding, he simply intensified his visits by staying longer. Now he began bringing her small gifts such as pastries or bouquets of flowers, and these did much to soothe her soul in this darkest hour.

Though if the queen had inquired about these visits, he could simply have claimed to act in his capacity as a man of the cloth, still Elizabeth recognised how daring it was for him to come to her as he did. From this she drew strength, and with each passing day she cherished him and their blossoming friendship more and more.

9

It was clear that the queen intended to see Elizabeth beheaded, and nothing Richard could say on her behalf seemed to sway Mary from her resolve. He felt himself torn nearly to the breaking point, for he had a commitment first to serve Queen Mary, and regardless of the greater affection he felt toward Elizabeth, he had to stand by the words he'd spoken to their father.

At his last visit to Elizabeth on the evening of May 18, 1554, Richard reached for her hand, a gesture he had never before dared make, and said, 'Dear princess, let us kneel and ask Almighty God for strength, understanding, and deliverance.'

The princess did not pull away, as he'd feared she might, but rather gently knelt as he bade her do, and as they had many times before, together they went before the throne of a monarch greater and more powerful than the Queen of England. As Richard left her cell that night, he again assured her that God would see her free of this place, that she had not come this far only to suffer such a cruel fate as her sister intended.

The next day, Elizabeth looked out the small window of her barren cell and spied a company of armoured men with several liveries in the courtyard. With an icy sensation in her heart, she leaned back against the wall, certain that Richard's prayers had failed.

When she could speak, she walked to the door of her cell and demanded to know from the guard who those men outside were, and why they'd come. If she was to die, she wanted to know - and to prepare herself. With a cautious smile, his eyes betraying his gladness at bringing the good news, the man informed her that they had come to escort her to a more comfortable place of confinement, the manor of Woodstock near Oxford.

But Elizabeth was not to be so easily comforted. Perhaps this was only to put her at ease before her execution.

She was partially right. The group did escort her to Woodstock, but when they got there several days later, she was immediately made to understand that little had changed: she was still to be watched every minute of every hour.

And yet she had some consolation that at least she had left the Tower alive, as few people had ever done before. Perhaps God had heard Richard's prayers after all.

At Woodstock, Elizabeth was not permitted to speak or even write to anyone, and the sickness of hope deferred now took its toll on her physical body. Out of exhaustion and despair, she fell ill, and when physicians came and bled her, she slipped into unconsciousness.

For Elizabeth, oblivion was bliss. When she awoke, after she knew not how long, she found herself alone, and managed to rise from her bed with great effort. She limped to the window, and there on the leaded pane she scratched these words with the diamond in her ring: 'Much suspected, by me - Nothing proved can be - Quoth Elizabeth, Prisoner.'

As the days passed by slowly at Woodstock, Elizabeth received a piece of news from outside. Philip, who had departed England soon after she'd left for Hertfordshire and wed Mary by proxy a few days before she entered the Tower, had on July 20 joined his new wife in London. She took this as a good sign, and it was.

Summer became autumn, then winter and spring. Finally in April 1555, with the persuasion of Philip and Richard, Mary freed her sister and absolved her of the charges against her. Elizabeth was brought back to Hampton Court, where Philip and Mary were in residence, and for the first time in a year, she lived once again as a princess and not a prisoner. She even dined in the great hall with the royal couple, and though thenceforth her relations with Mary would seldom rise above the temperature of ice water, she resumed her friendship with Philip.

Perhaps feeling guilty now, Mary declared Elizabeth her rightful successor, thus saving England from the dynastic squabbles to which it had been so prone in recent years. Elizabeth understandably found it difficult to muster within herself great reserves of amity toward this half-sister who'd nearly sent her to her death. The thirteen months from March 1554 to April 1555, during which Elizabeth at twenty-two should have enjoyed all the delights to which young women at that age are given, had been the worst year of her life.

Now she felt within herself not hatred but weariness, not only with her sister but with the whole dreary life at Hampton Court in which the latter had enveloped all those around her. From time to time Richard came to her in his role as her personal minister, and they were allowed to visit at great length, but neither he nor anyone else could shield her from the pall of misery that seemed to follow her sister wherever she went.

Finally Elizabeth asked permission to retire from Court for awhile in order that she might again visit her palace at Hatfield, the only home she'd ever known. Mary consented, and Elizabeth readied her things for the journey. In final preparation, she sent a note to Richard entreating him to meet her at the church of St. Botolph's Without Aldgate.

Aldgate was one of six entrances to the city built by the Romans 1500 years before, and the church just inside it had stood there as long as any record had existed. The east gate to the city was not on the normal route of departure, and would therefore less likely draw any attention; besides, it was quite normal for pilgrims on their way into or out of London to stop at the sanctuary for prayers. Therefore no one would take notice of it if the princess did so as well.

When the procession reached the steps of St. Botolph's, Elizabeth informed her ladies-in-waiting and guards that she wished to enter alone. One of the men insisted on seeing her as far as the vestibule of the church, where he would remain until she left the sanctuary, and she consented. As she walked into the cool twilight within, she immediately saw Richard at the front kneeling in prayer, and stepping quickly and silently, she knelt beside him.

Richard had sensed her presence before she appeared, and he remained silent for a moment with his head bowed. Then he opened his eyes and gazed upon his sister - his friend - and as they sat back on the pew behind them and looked at one another, words seemed almost unnecessary. But Richard did speak, and he did so first, for with Elizabeth he felt as natural and comfortable as with his mother - so different from Mary, and not simply because the latter was queen.

'I was just thanking the Lord,' he said now, 'that you had been spared, my lady, and I prayed that somehow from your ordeal would come something good. I am quite sure that such may present little possibility in your mind at this time, but I at least hold the hope that my prayer will come to be.'

'Something of value has already come from it, Richard.' Elizabeth's gaze, kind and appreciative, was intent, but what captured his attention was the manner in which she'd addressed him - never before had she called him by his given name. 'I have discovered the worth of your friendship, and the comfort of having a member of my family who truly cared and unselfishly sought the best for me, even at risk to himself.'

'My lady - '

'Shhh!' She held up a long and graceful finger. 'I may not always be able to speak as I do now for fear that idle heads and tongues will make more of it than either of us would wish. But I know, and you will know, that there is a bond between us that nothing can alter. Perhaps in time there will be other occasions when we can speak thus, but it will serve neither of us to forget the roles we must play.'

She paused and shut her eyes as though in prayer while he waited in silence. ' 'Tis a sad circumstance,' she said, and she turned and looked at him. 'And yet it is a great comfort to me: though in words I may not often confess these feelings, your princess shall not forget her brother - nay, her prince. Indeed, I find myself regarding you as something akin both to the father I could never know and the brother for whom I have always wished.'

Richard wanted to speak, but at first his voice failed him. He slipped off the pew and knelt before her. 'My lady,' he managed to say, 'I shall be your faithful servant and friend for as long as my life shall last.'

She smiled down at him serenely for a moment, then she assumed the posture of one making ready to leave. 'And now,' said the princess, 'with our mutual understanding spoken only between us and Almighty God, I must be on my way. Perhaps at Hatfield I may find some peace away from Court. Things are better now between my sister and I, but I never know when all may suddenly change yet again, and I want to be well away from her for a time. She is ill, and I know not how grave it may be - therefore you must keep me informed.'

Richard rose along with her. 'I will be your eyes and ears, my dear lady,' he said, 'and will keep you daily in my prayers. May the Good Lord go with you, bless you, and keep you.' Then, as though in an afterthought, he pressed a small piece of paper into her hand. 'I have written some lines I pray will please you.'

Elizabeth smiled as she took it from him, then turned and with her characteristic short, quick steps silently left the sanctuary. Richard knelt back down, and he tarried there for a moment, praying for her safety. When he was sure the caravan was out of sight, he left the church and made his way back to the stifling world of Whitehall Palace.

IO

Richard would not see Elizabeth again for some time - and under quite different circumstances than before. By now Queen Mary had concerns other than her sister's loyalty. As women before her had done and would continue to do down through the ages, she'd married a man not unlike her father, but she chose to ignore the well-substantiated rumours of his infidelity. She knew that, like the man he so resembled in temperament, only one thing could hold his affection - especially given the fact that she lacked many of the womanly attributes so abundantly possessed by the wives of Henry VIII - and that was an heir.

Due in part to the lifelong ill health that often prevented her normal menstrual cycles, and abetted no doubt by her fierce love for Philip and her desire to keep him, on two occasions she became convinced that she was with child. But she was not, and in the summer of 1555 Philip, weary of both her and her country, announced that he had to return for a time to Spain and matters of state there. Mary recognised this for the polite good-bye that it was, and though he came back a few other times it was never for long; in July 1557, now as King of Spain, he left for the last time.

After her womb failed her, Mary became strangely docile for a time, during which she made her peace with Elizabeth. It was a period of eery calm, just before she turned on her religious foes and unleashed a lifetime's worth of bitterness against them - thus earning for herself the name of 'Bloody Mary' by which history would know her. In the course of this, many were burned at the stake. She also, at Philip's bidding, entered a disastrous war with Henry II of France which resulted in terrible losses for England and which Philip ended by making a separate (and advantageous) peace with Henry.

Her sense of reality began to desert her. In the early months of 1558, long after such would likely have been possible due to her relations with Philip, she became convinced yet again that she was with child, and she sent for him. But he already had plans to court her sister after she died, and he sent her a polite and condescending note of congratulations at her pregnancy.

She became so fearful she resorted to wearing armour even when she slept, and when sleep did not come she wandered the halls of the palace like a phantom. All had forsaken her: her dead mother, her indifferent father and husband - even the Church, whose Pope declared her papal legate Cardinal Pole a heretic.

All, that is, except for Richard Edwardes, the brother of whom the world knew nothing. When all others had failed her, he had stood by waiting to help in whatever way he could - and this was not an easy thing. Mary had proven a great challenge for Richard, who found her views of life utterly alien to his own, and he was constantly on his guard not to say or do anything that would ill affect his, or Elizabeth's, status.

But through it all, he managed with skill to walk the tight rope of her temperament. When permitted, without anyone's knowledge of his true identity, he appeared and comforted her as her brother and priest. Mary found it as difficult to express herself to Richard as to anyone, but in little ways that did not require words, she did her best to let him know that she appreciated his loyalty, love, and concern. Perhaps his was the only true friendship she'd known since that of her mother.

A plague of ague was afoot in the land, and it struck the queen, along with dropsy and what her doctors diagnosed as 'a superfluity of black bile.' Now her body began to die even as her spirit had already done, and then in the early hours of November 17, 1558, the stormy life of Queen Mary ended.

Only a shroud could conclude her tragedy and misery, yet because of her station, her name lived on - with ignominy. In truth she had killed far fewer 'heretics' than her more zealous counterparts on the Continent, but then the English had always prided themselves on possessing greater civility than their cousins in France or Germany. Forgotten were her many good deeds, for instance her visitations (under disguise) to the homes of the poor, where she learned of their needs and sought to help them.

But perhaps the greatest irony in the unfortunate legacy of Queen Mary lay in the famous rhyme known to all English-speaking schoolchildren from her time onward:

Mary, Mary, quite contrary, how does your garden grow?
With golden bells and cockle shells,
and pretty little maids all in a row.

It came from a verse meant to please her, a corruption of lines in her praise - written by her friend and brother, Richard Edwardes.

Richard was not there when the queen died, but he was woken up and told the news. His first thought was of Elizabeth: with her position guaranteed by her mother's sacrifice long before and her sister's sending of the crown jewels just eleven days previously, she would be the next Queen of England. He dressed quickly and after questioning a courtier, learned that Sir Nicholas Throckmorton was to bear the message to Hatfield House. With no time to lose, he found Throckmorton and offered himself as a travelling companion. Throckmorton, who knew and liked Richard, considered it an asset to have a priest along at this momentous occasion, and he readily accepted.

Hatfield was an easy day's journey from London, but they wanted at all costs to be first to bring the new queen the tidings, so the two messengers set out immediately. It was mid-afternoon on the seventeenth of November when Throckmorton and Richard Edwardes reached the long drive leading to Hatfield House.

The palace, a gigantic structure of russet brick nestled in a secluded stretch of country under a cluster of ancient English oaks, spread out before them as though welcoming the news they bore. Built in 1497 by Cardinal Morton, Bishop of Ely, it had been confiscated by Henry VIII upon the reformation of the church and used as a home for all three of his legitimate children. The king's younger daughter had spent her early years there with her baby brother Edward, the two waifs ill-clothed and often unsupervised, but she'd retained happy memories of the place into adulthood.

On that afternoon Elizabeth, drawn out of doors by an unseasonably crisp and clear but cold autumn day, had nestled into a comfortable spot under an oak tree with a book. She made a point of reading in different languages that she might enhance her linguistic skills, and it was no mere trifle that consumed her attention now: in her slender, delicate hands she held a copy of the New Testament in Greek. So intent was she on the text that at first she didn't hear the approaching messengers.

They stood in respectful silence for a moment until the princess realised she was not alone, whereupon she wheeled about and demanded, 'What mischief brings you to disturb Henry's daughter when she is studying?' She put up her hand to shield her eyes from the sun, and for the first time she recognised her visitors. Instead of acknowledging them, however, she stood up in a single regal movement, as though she knew what news they brought.

'Your Highness,' Sir Nicholas said ceremoniously, 'it is with both sadness and joy that we come! Your sister, Queen Mary, has died, putting an end to her suffering and pain.' He paused that his queen might fully grasp the import of his words. 'It is my duty to tell you that Your Majesty is now the Queen of England!'

Elizabeth received the news at first without any detectable emotion. For a moment her eyes flickered toward Richard's, then she sank to her knees and said, 'This is the Lord's doing. It is marvellous to our eyes!'

Both Richard and Throckmorton rapidly followed their sovereign's lead, and Richard spoke a brief prayer of thanksgiving. He asked God to grant his new queen the wisdom, the courage, and the understanding that she would need in the tasks that now lay before her, and to stand by her in the face of the heavy responsibilities that she now bore. Finally, he prayed that she might for the rest of her days know the happiness that her sister had not.

When he had finished, Elizabeth stood up and with true royal tones spoke the second utterance of a reign that was to span forty-five years. 'Do not condemn your knees to this cold sod, gentlemen.' She smiled. ' 'Tis poor homage to the queen to have her subjects suffer and limp. Sir Nicholas, please go in and order tea for us while I have a brief word with this clerk.'

After Throckmorton had bowed and departed to do his queen's bidding, Elizabeth turned to her brother. 'Richard,' she said, in a tone quite different from that with which she'd spoken a moment before, 'I know not how I shall be able to do all that is required of me, and I must confess that I meet this news with near as much fear as I had on the way to the Tower.'

For a moment Elizabeth, for all her strength and reserve only a young woman of twenty-five, had made herself vulnerable to Richard, and he chose his words with care. 'Your Majesty - what a joy it is to call you by that title! - if my humble view counts for anything, your abilities are more than sufficient for the task. Forget not that you are of the Tudor line, with your father's blood flowing through you.' He stopped there, but he could see from her face that she wanted him to go on, so he continued. 'Only brief words will I give, Your Majesty, for you know already what it is you must do, and I am pledged to serve you in any endeavour you choose to undertake.'

She sat down and listened as he began to speak words he'd considered long before this day. 'Your father said once to your servant that he should trust in deeds and not words, and though this is so, in the minds of men appearances speak for truths of the inner person. Therefore think upon your new duties as but a role within a play, which you must perform with all the skill of a great actress.

'When you walk, walk not quickly and glidingly, as is your custom, but rather with long, slow, and deliberate steps, head held high to show you as no mere mortal. It should seem always that any path you trod is familiar to you, as though you had taken those very steps before. As to your dress, Your Majesty, clad yourself not plainly in sombre colours, without curls and jewels - as you might prefer for your own comfort - but rather in elegant garb, richly adorned with jewels and crown as befits the queen. Likewise lower your voice a bit so it is not that of a gentle maid, but rather that of a queen, who is above all maids, and rivals the male his assurance of superiority.

'You are no longer Elizabeth Tudor, but rather Queen Elizabeth, sovereign and protector, shepherd and friend to all your subjects. Your people must know that their queen is wiser, more deliberate, and stronger than any king.' He paused to study her face, for she was watching him intently. For a moment he had become someone different, speaking not merely from his position as servant and priest, but from all that he had considered in his many hours alone. He made a slight bow. 'Therefore I bid my sister Elizabeth adieu and greet my queen, Elizabeth, as my sovereign. And, now, Your Majesty, if your humble servant may be so bold, a portion of your realm awaits within to greet their queen and rejoice in her presence.'

Elizabeth, Queen of England, smiled at her brother before she rose and entered the great hall of Hatfield House. There the staff down to the lowliest servant had assembled, and they instantly dropped to their knees, raising their voices with a shout: 'God save the queen - God save Queen Elizabeth!'

From that moment forward, though her heart might have trembled and on occasion she might have found herself unsure, an inner voice would always repeat the words Richard had spoken to her. At those rare moments when no one's eyes were on her, she might forget herself and walk in her usual quick steps, but then she would quickly recall her brother's advice and return to the mannerisms required of the English Queen. The world over which she reigned would indeed believe their queen to be something more than a woman, someone wiser than a prophet, and her every word and deed would seem to arise from prior knowledge and from greater wisdom than any subject had ever known.

Elizabeth had little chance in the years that followed to tell Richard how important his words to her had been, but he knew. His reward came from serving her, and in so doing he played somewhat the role of prince - though the world knew him only as a priest and poet. He would stand behind her, far in the shadows, advising her in creating an image that would inspire her people and hold their allegiance.

As the time approached for the coronation, Richard reminded her that her subjects wanted their monarch to symbolise an opulence that they might never personally achieve, but which they wanted for their country. Pageantry and apparel would be integral to it, and the coronation should exceed any spectacle England had ever seen. There should be guards resplendently attired, and everyone who participated should look polished and elegant beyond anything known before.

What might have seemed a preoccupation with ornament had practical and very serious reasons behind it. Mary's misguided adventure in France had cost the country more than lives and land: England teetered dangerously close to bankruptcy, prices had risen to new heights, and the royal treasury was all but bare. To counter these dispiriting realities, Richard encouraged the new queen to appear as often as possible in all her splendour in order to assure her subjects that times were far from being as bleak as they seemed.

Ten days after her accession, Elizabeth took possession of the Tower where once she had prepared to die. Dressed in a deep royal purple which complemented the fairness of her face, she rode as far as Cripplegate in her coach, accompanied by a phalanx of palace guards, and from there proceeded to the Tower on horseback. This was a symbolic act, honoured by time as part of the pageantry that attended the assumption of the throne, and the sight of the glorious new queen in her magnificent dress upon a fine steed struck admiration in all who watched.

Almost weekly processions were staged, with ornate costumes and ever-increasing numbers of guards in elegant uniforms to present Elizabeth as a goddess figure. Once she appeared on a litter with an elaborately embroidered canopy overhead, carried by Knights of the Garter. At other processions she would move amidst hundreds, with a luxurious robe of velvet trailing behind as she walked with her increasingly natural measured step. No length was spared in creating the illusion of the virgin goddess who now oversaw the well-being of all Englishmen.

For her upcoming coronation, new uniforms of brilliant red, gold, and silver were ordered for the palace guards. All ladies of the court were given yards of velvet for dresses and robes, and lesser quantities of gold cloth. To Richard the Court allotted several yards of crimson for a new outfit as befitted a poet in service of the greatest monarch on earth. Meanwhile the date of the coronation, carefully selected by the most respected astrologer of the time, was set for Sunday January 15, 1559.

On the Saturday prior to her crowning, Elizabeth set out on yet another procession from the Tower to Whitehall Palace. This time she wore a gown of gold with an ermine cloak and was seated on a cushioned litter draped with velvet and borne by four knights. Her entourage was halted many times along the way as children recited poems and gave her gifts of flowers. One child even presented her with his own Bible, his dearest possession willingly and cheerfully offered up to his queen.

The people took this symbolism to heart, and it was a good thing in such trying financial times. The uniforms and the splendour, the pageantry and spectacle, pointed toward a new England stronger and more prosperous than anyone had thought possible, a new era in which past injustices would be righted. Clearly the best days of the realm lay in the future and not the past.

On the day of the coronation, Westminster Abbey teemed with throngs anxiously awaiting the arrival of the queen whose crowning would usher in this new golden era. And then she appeared, proceeding slowly and majestically toward her anointing with a long red velvet train, borne by ladies in waiting, trailing behind her. Few alive remembered the coronation of her father, but many present had witnessed those of Edward and Mary, and even now the memory of those two began to fade in the face of Elizabeth's much greater splendour.

A hush fell over the great hall as the Bishop of Carlisle placed the heavy Crown of St. Edward upon her head, and immediately thereafter came a blaring of trumpets and a booming of cannon. The assembled choirs sang at the top of their voices and the music from the great pipe organ swelled to such heights that one envoy said it sounded as though the end of the world were at hand. But this was the end of the nothing; it was only the beginning.

II

Thus began the age of Elizabeth, first queen to lend her name to an entire era. It would be an age when the English, often humiliated and outdone by their stronger rivals on the Continent, would rise to new triumphs, greater prosperity, and intensified national pride. In these years, it would become a commonplace among Europeans to say of their cousins on the isle of Britain, 'If they see a foreigner very well-made or particularly handsome, they say, ' 'Tis a pity he is not an Englishman.'

At the centre of this glory sat Elizabeth, but unbeknownst to her people, underneath the glamorous trappings of power she was a shy and very conservative woman. She despised the lavish dinners of state and unbridled indulgence in rich foods and wine which had been the hallmark of King Henry's reign; frugal by nature and temperate in all things, Elizabeth did not care for rich red meats and heavy drink, preferring fowl and fish, fresh fruits and vegetables, and at most a very light and delicate wine.

Often at dinners and feasts she would eat sparingly if at all, sometimes only moving the portions of food around on her plate as though attempting to inspire her appetite with a more creative design. The very act of dining in public had little appeal to her, and if she could, she would excuse herself early and retreat to her own private chambers for a simpler meal.

As queen, Elizabeth found herself increasingly jealous of her moments alone. She had spent her early years outside the company of other children, a fact which added to her abiding sense of self-reliance, and had become quite content with her own thoughts. And yet as Richard had told her, she had a role to play, and at times the private person of Elizabeth Tudor conflicted with the public persona of Elizabeth the queen.

A great banquet at Westminster Hall, attended by 800 guests, followed the coronation. Elizabeth appeared once again in purple velvet, and was seated beneath the enormous window to inaugurate the feast that Sunday afternoon at three o'clock. The banquet lasted until one o'clock the next morning, and she left exhausted from the demands of the day, so tired that another festivity planned for Monday had to be delayed forty-eight hours for the newly crowned queen to catch her breath.

Her instinctive desire for privacy, however, came only from her particular experiences and not from any aristocratic snobbery. Elizabeth's popularity when she ascended the throne far exceeded any in remembered history, and she was truly a woman of the people even as she ruled over them. She enjoyed referring to herself as 'merely English,' meaning that for the first time in years, England had a monarch with no marital or kinship ties to Spain, France, or any of the other threatening great powers on the Continent.

In spite of her desire to be alone, Elizabeth showed no fear of crowds, and would take time to speak to her subjects in the middle of a grand procession. She did many things, some great and some small, to illustrate to her people the fact that she had their interests at heart. When she and Richard met at St. Botolph's, she had noticed that the ropes for ringing the beautiful bells were in a state of disrepair, so she made a gift of very fine silk rope to replace the tattered ones.

The significance of such seemingly minor acts was not lost on the English people, who likewise saw the queen's concern for them demonstrated in larger ways, such as her reevaluation of the currency. She had appointed William Cecil, a dear life-long friend, to a seat on her Council, and Richard too became a friend and confidant of Cecil's. When Richard heard from his brother William, now a wine merchant, apprising him of the problems merchants were having in the international market because England's coins had twice been debased in the reigns of Henry VIII and Edward VI, he brought this to the attention of Lord Cecil.

The coins were of gold, and monarchs in the past had been wont to artificially inflate their treasuries by recalling the coins of the realm and either having small portions of gold shaved off each piece, or melting down the coins and adding base metals to their content. Now this irresponsible policy had begun to take its toll for England's businessmen, and when Richard informed Lord Cecil of this, Cecil in turn presented the problem to the Queen's Council.

Elizabeth listened quite attentively, and with the help of her advisors, she determined that the coins should be reminted with their value restored. To do this, the Court enlisted the help of all London's goldsmiths, and though the task of recalling and redeeming the currency was an enormous one, it was soon done to the satisfaction of both the merchants and the government. In time England's businessmen began to fare far better in the markets, and prosperity returned to the land.

Elizabeth was applauded for her wisdom, her reevaluation being declared the work of genius and one of the greatest achievements in many, many years. And though she took credit in the public eye, at Court she did not fail to praise those who had given her wise counsel. On the occasion of the reminting, she had celebrated by handing out new coins to those around her, and when she next saw Richard (in the presence of several others), she said, 'Perhaps, Master Edwardes, you believed your queen unaware of your wise advice to Lord Cecil, but you are mistaken. Your queen is not only quite aware, but truly grateful.'

Richard had smiled and bowed, as befitted a humble advisor in the queen's Court. Some time before, Elizabeth had informed him that she intended to transfer him temporarily from the Chapel Royal to the position of her personal chaplain. In that closer capacity, he could advise her more easily, and she could consult with him at any time she wished without the uninvited attentions of anyone.

She valued his advice, not only because of their secret tie of kinship and his demonstrated wisdom in the past, but also because he'd served in the Court of Queen Mary and could make beneficial suggestions to the inexperienced queen. Therefore whatever Richard's personal life might have been, he was constantly on call as chaplain - and as the beloved brother of the queen, the only friend she'd ever known with whom she could exercise complete honesty.

The days and weeks now seemed to vanish in quick succession as Elizabeth became more and more confident in her new and very demanding role. As he'd been in a smaller way for Queen Mary in the last days of her reign, Richard was there in the background to advise her, and Elizabeth drew strength from his guidance. Soon he would work himself out of a job, though, for she was rapidly becoming so accustomed to her rulership that she needed his help less and less. She began to work instinctively, as though she'd come into this world with all the traits and talents of a king intact.

Yet even as confidence grew within her, the matter of her sex meant that she had to prove herself every day to the people of England. At one procession before her crowning, a woman standing by was heard to say, 'Oh Lord, the queen is a woman!' This comment, which greatly amused Elizabeth, nonetheless indicated an enduring problem. All monarchs had to establish their legitimacy, but Elizabeth had to prove herself in ways seldom expected of kings, and her predecessor had done little to alleviate the popular apprehension at the idea of a female ruler.

Her role required political acrobatics, for though as a woman she had to tread softly, the security of her reign required that she demonstrate her ability to rule as well as or better than any man. As Richard had advised that she do, she began to mould her mannerisms to counteract the image of a frail woman: no longer could she be the soft-spoken, well-mannered young lady she might have remained if left to her own. She had to be strong and forceful and beat men at their own games, to do her destined job and perform it better than any king had ever done.

Whereas Mary had always longed for a suitor and found few men willing to ask for her hand, Elizabeth had exactly the opposite problem. Just as he'd done with Mary, their father had used the possibility of marriage to his second daughter as a diplomatic trump card, and while she was still an infant he'd presented her 'in the altogether' (that is, naked) to a group of foreign emissaries.

This rather barbaric ceremony was the result of an equally barbaric rumour: not only was it said that Henry could not sire male heirs because of his syphilis, but also that his daughter had been deformed by her father's disease. The dignitaries had seen to their satisfaction that she had not, and the response to the prospect of marrying a king to Elizabeth was more favourable than at the earlier attempt to auction off Mary. But when Elizabeth was declared a bastard, Henry turned his attention to matters other than his daughter's prospects.

Perhaps it was then that Elizabeth first decided to remain a virgin. Or it might have happened much earlier, when as a little girl she'd learned of the fate her mother had suffered for her own marriage; or later, when she very nearly went to the same end for the jealousy of her sister. Then again, throughout her life she'd had the opportunity to observe a number of unhappy marriages - her father's and her sister's most of all - and it could have been this that galvanised her resolve.

She knew only that she wanted to be alone; having survived those lonely early years of her life, she had grown up with inner strengths that seemed to preclude the need for a great love. Besides that, with her great beauty and power, she could never be certain that any man's love was truly for her and not for the wealth and advantage she had to offer.

Aside from the personal reasons, she had political ones as well. A king could marry, and unless he were an exceptionally weak man, no one would accuse him of being overshadowed by his wife. The same, however, could not be said of a queen, and not trusting the feminine traits she knew she carried within her, she feared placing the welfare of her nation at the mercy of her allegiance to any man. A woman, whether she be the daughter of a peat-digger in the furthest corner of the realm or the offspring of a king, was expected to marry upward socially; by definition she would have had to marry the monarch of another country, and that would have negated her crucial distinction as being 'merely English'.

Thus she became the Virgin Queen, and if Mary's eagerness for a man made her all the less attractive, the opposite could be said of Elizabeth. Thenceforth she never hesitated to use her unwed status - and the possibility that she might change her mind - as a tool of diplomacy, ever turning the advantage for herself and her country.

Mary would have done somersaults in her grave if she could have seen her sister's first suitor now that she'd become queen: Philip of Spain, now King Philip II. In spite of the fact that Elizabeth's fortunes had changed, the cocky monarch could not imagine she would reject his offer: not only did he rule the world's greater power, but he guessed she still had plenty of lingering affection for him.

And Elizabeth did dally with the king, as she would do many another suitor. She kept him guessing for as long as she dared, for she needed Spanish support at the tripartite peace talks with France currently taking place at Cateau-Cambresis. But when she could no longer stall the eager Spaniard, she summoned his ambassador, Count Feria, and informed him that she could not accept His Majesty's most flattering proposal because she as a Protestant would be considered a heretic by his people.

The count left her presence spluttering and fuming, fearful of the reaction his sovereign would have to the news and its bearer; but to his amazement he found Philip actually relieved. The latter immediately proceeded to marry the daughter of the French king, and upon hearing of this, Elizabeth feigned the wounds of a woman scorned even though she and Philip both knew who'd done the scorning. By now she'd had what she wanted, having won diplomatically in the peace talks.

The queen was not long without a suitor, for Philip's uncle, the Hapsburg Emperor Ferdinand I, Suzerain of the Holy Roman Empire, soon decided that his younger son Archduke Charles would make the perfect husband for the English queen. In May 1559, Emperor Ferdinand's ambassador, Baron Caspar Breuner, arrived in London to relay his proposal to Elizabeth. Once again she played her cards wisely, saying that while she had not to date felt any compulsion for marriage, she was but human and therefore subject to changes of the heart. The baron, considering his mission hopeful, reported back to his emperor that after seeing both Elizabeth and her great material possessions, the English queen was well worth the trouble.

But this was not to be. Elizabeth had discovered the powers inherent in her status as the Virgin Queen, and she would always keep her men guessing.

12

Virgin she might be, but this did not mean Elizabeth eschewed male company - or that she didn't enjoy the thrill of having many men pursue her. In fact she tended to prefer the company of men to that of women, and she kept the finest among them around her.

She let it be no secret that she liked to surround herself with good-looking, preferably young, people. In part this arose from a trait in her that a later age might have called perfectionism, in some cases fastidiousness. Though far from squeamish, she had rules regarding matters of good taste that far exceeded what was ordinarily expected in an era when bathing was still considered a somewhat exotic practice.

Thus she insisted that her apparel be so stored that it never picked up odours of any kind, and in part disdained large banquets out of disgust with the crude table manners of many of her guests. When one aspiring courtier appeared before her, a fellow not bad-looking save for the fact that he was missing a tooth, Elizabeth saw to it that he was barred from Court. On another occasion, a man with extremely bad breath so offended her that she remarked on it to another person, not thinking he would hear. But he did, and excused himself, never to return.

Such things as good teeth and clean breath were a minimum, but the queen required far more. She expected her gentlemen of the Court to be handsome, intelligent, and talented both in arts and sports. The queen herself loved to dance, and considered it a mark of breeding in a courtier to be both an incomparable dancer and a witty and charming partner. When she showed favour toward Sir Christopher Hatton for his fine dancing, and one of Sir Christopher's rivals claimed he knew a man who could dance better, she retorted, 'I will not see your man. It is his trade.'

A successful courtier should be able to converse knowledgeably in more than one language on the subjects of art and poetry, and likewise be an accomplished horseman and tennis player. Indeed, when she was offered the hand of Archduke Charles, she discreetly inquired into his ability to 'ride superbly and dance well,' for she did not wish to be married to a man 'who sits all day among the cinders.'

As for the queen of the arts, music, the Tudors had always been enthusiastic patrons. Henry VIII had been a composer in his own right, and even the dour Mary had played competently in her youth. But under Elizabeth, not only poetry, dance, and theatre, but the art of which Cecilia was the patron saint flourished as never before.

The average Englishman could sight-read music and play at least one instrument well, and lutes and citterns could commonly be found in barbershops for the amusement of waiting customers. At a time when few could read the poetry of Richard Edwardes or travel to London to see the latest play, virtually all could sing or play the newest music by Thomas Tallis or William Byrd, or could make up their own ballads for a local hero.

The queen had at least sixty musicians in her service, including the singers of the Chapel Royal and the instrumentalists of the Queen's Musick. All of these - not least among them Richard himself - enjoyed the privileges of possible advancement associated with attending her at Court, and Elizabeth was willing to go to great lengths to employ the greatest musicians in the realm. Thus she hired William Byrd, the foremost composer of his day and a Catholic, as an organist of the Chapel Royal - a heresy to some.

Courtly entertainment likewise included masques, plays, jousting, barriers (a sport in which two men on foot fought with a fence between them), tennis, and horse racing. Nor did the queen shrink from the more visceral forms of amusement that had heretofore been the province only of men: her favourite sport was bearing, an extremely violent pastime in which dogs were pitted against bears, the result being much ugliness and bloodshed.

Yet she hated true wars, and this informed her choice of so many warlike entertainments. Having seen Mary's dreadful blunder in France, she detested the thought of sending handsome young men off into battle to be killed and maimed. Better to keep these young gallants at Court, their attentions taken by artificial battles and their careers forever under her guidance.

Indeed, none of her courtly diversions were for show alone. The Court fulfilled several important functions: not only was it the physical residence for the queen and her government, but it had to be a place glittering enough and entertaining enough to draw the high-born, high-spirited young men who might otherwise have found more dangerous outlets for their energies

- such as intriguing against the crown. And so even at times of financial crisis, she spared no expense in making hers an exciting court in which to serve.

This spoke much for the importance which she placed on keeping her noble young men occupied, given her natural tendency to pinch pennies. Another reason why she despised warfare was the waste and the drain on the treasury that ensued, and this queen was frugal to a fault. (In spite of this, no doubt heeding her brother's advice to carry herself always in regal splendour, she managed to build a tremendous wardrobe and collection of jewels - most of it gifts from her Court.)

She thrived on flattery, and insisted on being the central figure in her male courtiers' lives - whether they were married or not - as Richard himself would soon see. Above and beyond all else, Elizabeth's men had to be utterly devoted to her. Once she had a bad toothache, the result of overindulgence in her one culinary weakness, sweets, but she quite naturally shrank back from the agony of having her tooth removed. (The word dentist would not even enter the language for two more centuries.) In order to convince her that she could endure it, one of her courtiers allowed a perfectly good tooth to be pulled from his mouth.

Elizabeth could not abide secrecy in any area, unless the secret were a pleasant surprise for her. She had to approve all romances and marriages among her courtiers, and those who failed to comply were quickly banished - at the very least. If a gentleman and lady of the Court fell in love, even if she did not consider it a good match, she would give her consent and blessings so long as they were open with her and did not carry on behind her back.

No doubt her early experience of living in the midst of intrigue and conspiracy, not to mention her later tribulations at the hands of her sister, had instilled in her a need for complete loyalty and honesty. Whatever the reason, in the Court of Queen Elizabeth there were definite rules to achieve success and even to survive, and so long as her men observed those rules, they were handsomely rewarded. If they forgot themselves, however, their lives at Court could be quite brief.

This system of friendly competition between the men around her worked more often than not. Lord Hunsdon, who had long before appointed himself Richard's rival, thrived on competing with the latter in courtly graces, and Richard often let himself be bested for the sake of maintaining harmony. Thus there was an order among the courtiers - with one striking exception.

Upon her accession to the throne, she'd had to appoint many people, and in general Elizabeth had exercised great wisdom, for instance in balancing Catholics and Protestants among her Councillors. Sir Nicholas Throckmorton, whom she named as Chief Butler and Chamberlain of the Exchequer, had advised that she strive 'to succeed happily through a discreet beginning,' with 'a good eye that there be no innovations, no tumults or breach of orders.' It was advice well-given, for she could not yet afford to rest in the security of her claim to the throne.

Nonetheless she dispensed with most of the ladies who came to her from Mary's court, preferring to have around her those who would make no comparisons - even though she warranted she would triumph over Mary in any such contest. Katherine Ashley, Elizabeth's former governess and dear friend, became her First Lady of the Bedchamber, and John Ashley was appointed Keeper of the Queen's Jewels. But her appointment of Robert Dudley as Master of the Horse brought sharp criticism and ugly rumours.

Dudley, who in the future would become the Earl of Leicester and owner of Kenilworth Palace, had been Elizabeth's friend since childhood, and at one point they'd shared the degradation of confinement in the Tower of London. (It was his father, uncle, and aunt who fomented - and died for - the Jane Grey conspiracy.) The queen made no secret of her fondness for him, and he was ever mindful to lavish gifts of all sorts upon his queen, sparing no expense to please her. Elizabeth rewarded this devotion time and again with special favours that brought him income or prestige. Thus at her coronation, she placed him in the position of highest honour and recognition after herself, walking immediately behind her.

It was no wonder that the Virgin Queen should find this man appealing. At slightly under six feet in height, he was considered tall and strikingly handsome, his swarthy features having earned him the somewhat scornful nickname of 'Gypsy'. Nor did he lack the many talents required of Elizabeth's courtiers: he was one of England's most accomplished horsemen, an expert jouster, a keen fisherman, and an archer and tennis player of distinction. He excelled in intellectual pursuits as well, speaking fluent French and Italian and possessing a considerable knowledge of the classics. Most of all, though, he had the ability to make Elizabeth laugh, and he kept her entertained with his wit.

In spite - or no doubt because - of his many assets, Dudley had plenty of enemies among the other men around the queen, who outside her presence derided the ambitious Gypsy. Not only had his father, the traitorous Northumberland, been executed during the reign of Queen Mary, his grandfather, Edmund Dudley, had died on the orders of Henry VIII for offenses committed during the reign of Henry VII. His numerous detractors liked to throw about the accusation that Dudley was descended from a 'tribe of traitors'; even Elizabeth, when out of sorts with him once, had taunted him - in the way she could only have done toward a man who held a genuine attraction for her - by saying that the Dudleys had been 'traitors three descents.'

He could hardly help his ancestry, but some of the accusations levelled against Dudley were more well-deserved. There could be no question of his ambition, and his pursuit of Elizabeth's hand in the early years of her reign appeared to come as much from a desire to improve his station as from his equally strong admiration for her. He used every device and ploy in that pursuit: never one to hold back out of shame, wherever possible he undermined her multitudinous suitors.

He had served as King's Master of the Buckhounds during the reign of Edward VI, a position of great symbolic importance, as was his appointment as Master of the Horse under the Elizabeth. In the latter capacity he had the responsibility of running the royal stables of 275 horses, supervising the stud farms, and procuring and training horses to be used by Elizabeth and her Court. Thus he had assured lodgings at the palace, and this habitation at such close quarters with the queen resulted in rumours even after he married Amy Robsart, daughter of the Lord of the Manor of Sidersten in Norfolk.

For a time the marriage seemed almost idyllic, and Robert moved out of the city with his new bride. But his father-in-law, of all people, soon lured him back to London, where he once again became an integral part of the Court. Thenceforth his relations with Amy were not those of a normal and happily married couple, if nothing else because his visits to her (she had not been invited to the Court) were infrequent.

Rumours grew of a torrid affair between the Virgin Queen and her Gypsy lover, and worse things were said than that. People began to speculate that Dudley planned either to divorce his wife, or - it was whispered in the most scandalous tones - do away with her so that he could be free to marry Elizabeth whenever she relented.

Regardless of whatever suspicions Dudley could be said to have justly aroused, those close to the queen could attest to her virtue, simply because Elizabeth remained surrounded at all times by her ladies of the Court. Nevertheless, Kate Ashley threw herself at Elizabeth's feet in despair and implored her to take care lest her goings-on with Dudley irreparably sully her reputation. The queen assured her that in no way would she marry in haste to squelch the rumours; less pacifying was her regal statement that her life was hers to lead as she saw fit, and that if she wished to live immorally, there was no one who could forbid her doing just that.

Whatever anger she might have felt at Kate's inference, Elizabeth, out of long-time affection and respect for her First Lady of the Bedchamber, kept it restrained. Others were not so fortunate: when a Brentwood woman, Anne Down, spread tales that Elizabeth had a child by Dudley, the queen did not take this preposterous invention lightly, but imprisoned the woman for slander.

In the midst of all this, something happened which seemed to confirm every suspicion about Dudley if not Elizabeth. One day Amy Dudley gave her servants leave to attend the fair at Abingdon, and upon their return, they found their mistress lying under the staircase, dead of a broken neck.

The news of her death quickly reached the queen and Dudley, who were together at Windsor, and both of them acted immediately to allay any suspicions. Dudley demanded a thorough investigation of the circumstances surrounding his wife's death, and Elizabeth sent him away from the Court until a proper verdict could be reached. Despite the fact that the tribunal appointed to the case ruled the death an accident, this was not sufficient to calm the rumours now spreading rampant throughout England.

Dudley, though no doubt free of guilt in the demise of his wife, did indeed still have designs for the queen's hand. In spite of his ambitions, he knew when events demanded patience, and he waited until the gossip died down before he began once again in all earnestness to pursue the affections of Elizabeth.

She of course was pleased, and encouraged him to a point. Had she ever been willing to marry any man, it might well have been Lord Robert, regardless of what anyone thought - and yet she'd decided that she would remain the Virgin Queen for the rest of her life.

Dudley took this merely as coyness on her part, and the more she evaded him, the harder he pressed. Finally when his proclamations of love became more than she desired to hear, she announced to him, 'There is room for only one master of the royal household, and the queen is that master. There will be no changes, and there will be no marriage.'

Naturally this both crushed Dudley's heart and embarrassed him as a man. Yet he had good sense as well, and finally recognising that his pursuit was in vain, he resolved to be the queen's friend. He remained that until his death in 1588.

In the course of pursuing Elizabeth, Dudley got to know the man whose relation to her he would never know. Richard was only six years older than he, and the two had much in common, so they became fast friends and greatly enjoyed one another's conversation. Richard, of course, knew the truth beneath the rumours about Elizabeth and Dudley, and he trusted the latter implicitly, welcoming the advice and friendship he offered the queen. Thus whenever no answer seemed appropriate to a situation, he would suggest that Elizabeth consult with Dudley for his opinion.

One day when Elizabeth and Richard found that they could converse openly, she confessed to her brother, 'Oh, Richard, you know me well enough to guess my true sentiments toward Robert.' Richard wasn't about to offer an unwarranted opinion, so he only listened as she continued: 'I love him, I truly love him!' She sighed. 'And therefore I've found it difficult to put an end to his pursuit, but I could no longer tolerate the brazenness of his offers of marriage.' She looked at Richard. 'You know full well, dear brother, how such a union would affect my position, both with my people and with other nations!'

Knowing that no platitude would suffice in such a matter of the heart, Richard listened instead of speaking.

'It is for the queen,' she continued, her tone becoming ever more reflective, 'as though she were already married to the throne and the people were all her children. Marriage and the luxury of having mate and lover would take away from, not add to, my stature. In being subject to my husband, there is risk to judgment, and peril that he might come to think himself greater than his sovereign. He would want to give me counsel, as befits a man with his wife, and in either case I should be the lesser: were his judgments wise, then all would say, " 'tis his wisdom, and not hers, that steers the country toward greatness"; if not, then I should have betrayed my nation for the desires of my own heart.'

She looked away. 'And this is not to mention the abiding doubts I would always have regarding the chains that bind him to me. How would the queen ever be sure whether it was for love of her or love of her power and wealth that a suitor declared his love?' Turning back to Richard, she said, 'In sum, the risks are great, and the numbers of those who would suffer for a mistake far outweigh the burden of the queen's heart. Duty transcends all else.'

Richard thought about this for a moment, then said, 'Yes, dear lady, you have acted wisely in this situation, even if to do so was not easy for you.'

' 'Tis a pity always to act as queen and never as a woman,' she said with emotion in her voice.

'But you have done well by your people,' Richard replied, 'and have remained ever the queen England needs in this hour.' He looked down at his hands. 'And yet believe me, as a priest I know what it means to foreswear marriage in favour of higher vows.'

13

A time would come when, in another moment of unguarded conversation, Richard made a suggestion to Elizabeth regarding his appointment. Perhaps, he said, he should soon separate himself from the innermost part of the royal household before anyone came to regard him as something more than her private chaplain. Knowing the wisdom with which he spoke, the queen agreed, and soon returned him to the Chapel Royal.

In spite of this apparent demotion, Richard's fame for his poetry and plays had begun to spread even wider, so it became only natural that he should return quite frequently to Court, this time in the capacity of poet and dramatist. In fact his lodgings placed him even closer to Court than before, when he had boarded at a house not far from St. Paul's; now, upon orders from Elizabeth, he was given an apartment within the palace at Whitehall.

Thus he had the opportunity to remain the secret eyes and ears of his sovereign without being too closely identified with her and her household, and this suited Richard. Though he missed his earlier proximity to his sister, he found himself relieved not to be placed under the scrutiny accorded anyone who came near the queen. Instead he could return to his writings and his creations, that other and of late often neglected half of his destiny, and he knew that these would in time bring Elizabeth great pleasure.

Soon after his change in position, he presented the first fruits of his new solitude, a play with poetry and music of his own composition, and he begged the queen's indulgence to present it for her entertainment. Elizabeth, well aware of her brother's talents and his need for an outlet to bring forth the genius that ran in his Tudor veins - and flattered by his sincere and uncalculated desire to amuse her - readily consented.

On the occasion of that maiden performance, Richard himself mounted the stage first to dedicate the work to 'the fairest queen who e'er has reigned.'

And then, with all the charm and courtly manners that now came to him as easily as his own breath, he spoke the lines of a poem dedicated to Her Majesty:

> The strongest guard that Kings can have
> Are constant friends, their state to save;
> True friends are constant, both in word and deed,
> True friends are present, and help as each need;
> True friends talk truly, they gloss for no gain,
> When treasure consumeth, true friends will remain,
> True friends for their true Prince, refuseth not their death.
> The Lord grant her such friends, most noble Queen Elizabeth.
>
> Long may she govern in honour and wealth,
> Void of all sickness, in most perfect health;
> Which health to prolong, as true friends require,
> God grant she may have her own heart's desire;
> Which friends will defend with most steadfast faith,
> The Lord grant her such friends, most noble Queen Elizabeth.

The queen, by now much accustomed to such praise, was nonetheless touched because she knew the unalloyed affection from which his lines sprang.

The play itself was of a classical theme, but it marked a departure for Richard, for it included ballads which were sung by the actors in addition to ordinary lines of speech. Elizabeth was delighted with this development in his talents, and she showed as much to all around her by her rapt attention and her occasional exclamations of pleasure.

When the drama had finished, she led the house in standing to applaud, and after the cheering had subsided proclaimed, ' 'Tis tribute to the queen, indeed, that such talent and time should be given to the end that she be entertained. Thank you, Master Edwardes! We are pleased and commend you for your skill. Never has king or queen been better pleased or more greatly entertained! With great credit to her poet, your queen does indeed have such true friends as you spoke of in your poem.' The audience, as entertained as their queen, needed no cue from her to stand as well and shout, 'Hear, hear, Master Edwardes!'

Soon word began to spread throughout the kingdom that England had in her midst one of the greatest poets and playwrights ever known, and Richard found among his countrymen increased acknowledgement and acceptance for the talents he'd always had within him. This to him was a prize of far greater worth than any sceptre a monarch ever held - he, Richard Edwardes, was making a name for himself by his talents and not his bloodline. He would always know that praise came to him purely for what he did, and not for who he was, and happily he took his place among the budding poets of what would become England's golden age.

And yet he lacked for one thing, a missing part of his life he'd never dared hoped for until the continuing reformation of the Church made its fulfilment appear possible for the first time.

During his short reign, Edward VI had decreed that priests need no longer remain celibate, but when Mary assumed power, she had rescinded that new law along with all others that loosened her country's ties with Rome. Under Elizabeth, however, this matter once again became a topic for discussion, and she chose to reinstate her late brother's decree. And now Richard ventured to think once again of fulfilling a desire as dear to his heart as his poetry and his service to the queen.

One evening following the presentation of a short play by him, he managed to steal a few moments alone with the queen. Catching her in a lighter mood (brought on no doubt by the amusement she'd just witnessed), he began to approach the subject: 'My queen, do you recall the discussion we had not long ago on the subject of marriage?'

For a moment she glanced at him sharply, for the subject of her own virginity was a closed topic. 'Of course I do.'

'As your servant said then,' he continued, hurrying to allay her apprehensions, ' 'Tis fortunate for all Englishmen that so wise a queen as you sits on the throne and bears her countrymen's best interests always. And yet I ask you now if one not so bound by duty to the people - one whom the queen's own law has freed to marry - might now choose to do so without causing her offense?'

Elizabeth walked to the window so that he could not see the expression on her face, but when she turned back it was with a look of lightly sarcastic amusement. 'Would my poet be thinking to better his poor estate by wooing one of the wealthy and beautiful maidens the queen has chosen for her court?'

Richard inclined his head. 'It is not my poor estate that I was considering, Your Majesty, but rather the possibility I might advance the legacy of the Tudors, even if under a different name.'

Preposterous as these words might have sounded coming from any other mouth, Elizabeth recognised the sincerity in Richard. Now she demurred: 'Perhaps I spoke too quickly, without attention to the seriousness of your query, and both for that and for questioning your innermost thoughts, I ask that I may be forgiven.'

Richard, waiting tensely for the meat of her reply, barely noticed that he'd been given that most unusual of commodities, a royal apology.

'Your queen,' she went on, 'has no quarrel with members of Court marrying, so long as they do not hide it from her notice for fear of her disapproval. I will never countenance skulking. But in all sincerity, if you wish to marry - and choose one whom I feel is worthy - 'tis my blessing you shall have indeed, dear Richard.'

Richard detected a trace of tears on the royal visage, and wondered for an instant if this came from joy at his prospects or sorrow for her own. Then he said, 'In truth, dear queen, I would think it awkward should I wish to wed someone at Court, feeling as I do that such would take away from my queen. In fact there is a young lady in Somerset named Margaret Babb whom I have known since childhood. She is fair and temperate and has long been a very dear friend. I know not if she will accept a proposal, for I have only my talents and love to offer her, but if it would please Your Majesty I will put the question to her, and if accepted, will request that she come to visit you so that you may know the truth of my sentiments.'

Elizabeth smiled and said, 'Let it be so then. Take your leave to visit your home and find out if the maiden will have you, but this much I must confess: if she does not find you prize enough, I should have to question how bright she may be.'

Richard bowed. 'As always, my queen is far kinder than deserved. It shall be done, and for this thy humble and ever-grateful servant gives thee thanks.'

Elizabeth grinned broadly, and Richard thought a little slyly. 'As will ever be true, the poet with his silver words could melt the coldest heart that e'er was. You have learned too well at Court, sir, but knowing as I do the sincerity of your heart, your queen could scarcely question or deny whatever your heart desires.' She waved a hand in mock annoyance. 'Begone with you, now! Make haste and bring her here that the queen may pass her judgement. For truth I am curious to see the damsel who could steal your heart.'

In a sweeping gesture that would have pleased any queen, Richard bowed low and left with an excited heart to make ready for the journey home. To hasten him on his way, he arranged for a small ship to sail to

Somerset, thus reducing the time for the trip, which would have taken two weeks by land, to a matter of two days.

Agnes Edwardes was overjoyed to receive her son, and it was with even greater pleasure that she learned of his mission. Margaret Babb, the daughter of a neighbouring family some years younger than Richard, was a beautiful young woman with hair like spun gold, large sparkling green eyes, and a perfectly oval face that had earned her the informal title Agnes herself once had held, prettiest maid in the shire. Delicate and almost fragile in demeanour, her presence nonetheless radiated with a joy of life that infected all around her.

Richard's only apprehension concerning the proposal he brought her was the fact that so many other men with much more to offer would gladly have taken her to wed. The day after his return to Somerset, he made his way to the Babbs' home, where he had often visited before as priest and friend - almost as one of the family. The Babbs received him thus now, never guessing what romantic purpose he carried with him, and Margaret was as friendly as ever.

He took a few days to determine that, strange as it might have seemed, she remained unbetrothed, then one afternoon he suggested that he and she go for a walk. The two of them had always been friends, and as they strolled across the meadows they talked and laughed. Naturally it fascinated her to learn all about life at Court, and this gave him an opening: he mentioned that the queen had decreed that the clergy might marry, then paused to let his meaning sink in.

Margaret became strangely quiet, appearing puzzled, and for a moment Richard feared that he'd touched on a subject she didn't wish to discuss. But he had not come this far to be turned back even before making his request, and so he proceeded: 'Margaret, you have always been my friend, and indeed I know of no one I care for or respect more than I do you.'

They had stopped walking, and they stood facing one another in the middle of an open field. The sun was at his back, and she shaded her eyes to look at him so that he could not see if his words pleased, amused, or even offended her.

'Perhaps,' he continued, 'these words I speak may seem to you rash, but believe me when I say that they have been long considered, and my silence until now has been a matter of duty to God. I had always wished, were it possible, to make you my wife.' Was that a smile he saw on her dear face? 'And now that such is possible, I would like to ask your father for your hand in marriage. I have no idea if you might have me, dear lady, but it has always been my fondest hope that you would.'

He saw tears like jewels at the ends of her long lashes, and her face was flushed with excitement. She started to speak, but words would not come for a moment, and she caught herself with a laugh, then said, 'Richard, even before I was old enough to think of marriage at all, I loved you, and I love you still with all that is in a heart which, like your own, had never dared dream or even hope. Yes, dear Richard, it would make me the happiest of all women to be your wife.'

Richard stepped toward her, and for the first time in long years of friendship their lips met. As he held her in his arms, a surge of love sweeping over him even as her trembling shoulders told him it had her, Richard thought that he'd long written about love without ever knowing it. And now love was his!

'You have made me the happiest man in all Christendom,' he said finally. 'I feel as though my heart might burst with joy. Let us go now to your father at once, and pray he will give us his blessings.'

And so hand in hand they ran down the hill back toward the house, wondering that they had been so foolish to walk so far away. When they rushed in, panting from their run, Margaret's mother looked up at her daughter's face, more radiant than she'd ever seen it, and knew in an instant what news they brought.

No words needed utterance, and yet the women had to withdraw for the practice already old when Jacob asked his uncle Laban for the hand of Rebecca. When Richard posed the question to Robert Babb, the latter gave his response without hesitation: 'Son,' he said, laying a friendly hand on Richard's shoulder, 'I have long known what was in my daughter's heart, and no doubt you have as well. She is pretty enough, and there isn't a young man who has seen her who would not have courted her on the least bit of encouragement, and yet she loved you and only you. She never spoke of such to me, but I knew all the same, and my only grief has been that marriage was not possible for the man she loved. And now the Good Lord has removed all obstacles...'

He stopped, feeling himself becoming emotional, then resumed in a more manful tone. 'Of course, I am delighted to give you my daughter's hand. Any man in my place who did not consent to such prospects would be a fool, and I do not think myself a fool.'

Richard, overwhelmed with joy, said, 'Thank you, sir. You have made me a very, very happy man.' Then he remembered his promise to Elizabeth, forgotten in the midst of her enthusiasm. 'But if I may, I have one more request of you.' Robert Babb looked at him, wondering what more he could possibly ask besides the hand of his fair Margaret. 'Our queen has her rules about the marriage of courtiers, and requires that she give her consent. 'Tis only a formality, for I know she will love Margaret as much as we do, but it is a formality I would do well to respect. Therefore I must ask if you and Mrs. Babb and Margaret would return with me to London, so that I might present you before the queen?'

At this the old man's eyes twinkled, and he flung open the parlour door with great gusto to announce to his wife, 'Mrs. Babb, we are going to Londontown to see the queen!'

Within two days the happy group was on its way, travelling by sea to hasten their progress. The Babbs had never sailed before, and their every experience was a new thrill. When finally they reached London with its palaces and churches and many people, they all agreed it was far grander than they had ever imagined - though Mrs. Babb said she feared she'd get a stiff neck from looking up at all the tall spires.

Elizabeth soon granted the group an audience, and Richard was touched to see the excitement with which Margaret's parents greeted this prospect. Margaret herself was anxious, but Richard coached all three carefully as to what they should do and say before the monarch. When the dread moment arrived, he could tell that the queen had anticipated their nervousness, and she made herself more gracious than he'd ever seen her.

'Your Majesty,' he announced when he entered the throne room with the three visitors from the country, 'allow your servant to present Mr. and Mrs. Babb and their daughter Margaret. They are dear friends of long standing, and it is with utmost honour that I present them to you.'

Elizabeth rose and said to the parents, 'Has this young man always used so many words, or are these only for special occasions to impress his queen?'

This put them at ease, and Elizabeth chatted with them for a few minutes before turning to Richard. 'If you are to be married to this pretty lady, Master Richard, 'tis best you make haste before she changes her mind. You're not the only man she could attract, I will allow. Be gone and be happy! Your queen has less pleasant tasks that she must be about.' But before she let them go, she turned to Margaret and said, 'Richard Edwardes is a very fortunate man, but in all fairness I must add that he has a kind heart and deserves you fully. Not only he, but you as well, have chosen wisely, and you will be very happy.'

14

Though Richard had assured them the marriage could take place at the Chapel Royal, Margaret and her parents were of one accord that the two should be wed in the Church of St. Mary the Virgin in North Petherton, where both Margaret and Richard had been christened. Therefore without delay they made the necessary arrangements, and were soon on their way back to Somerset.

On the day of the wedding - April 22, 1560 - North Petherton was in the full glory of spring, adorned with all the gorgeous flowers of the season. Richard's mother, who like the Babbs had never dared hope for this day, appeared as joyful as the bride herself, and her tears fell without shame as the couple exchanged their vows before the very altar where she and Will Edwardes had stood not so very long before. And then with the speaking of the words 'I do,' Richard and Margaret were joined as one before God. The whole congregation seemed to sense the rightness of this union, and everyone left the chapel that day rejoicing for the happy couple.

Because Richard could not remain long from his post, they decided to honeymoon in London, so they soon made their leave and returned to the city. There they found that Elizabeth had granted them an apartment at Whitehall larger than the one Richard had occupied as a bachelor, and had seen to it that it was brightly furnished, with bouquets of flowers to await its new occupants.

Days and weeks now melted away in quick happy succession, and the two fell completely under the spell of their own childlike love for one another. All else now seemed only background scenery in an enchanted world where love ruled supreme. Whenever it was appropriate, Margaret visited Richard at Court, where the splendour of it all made her feel as though she had wakened in the middle of a fairy tale.

Within a month of their return, Richard received word that he had been appointed Deputy Master of the Children of the Chapel Royal. The health of the aging Master, Richard Bower, who had taught Richard himself when he was but a boy in the Choir, was beginning to fail, making the job of the Deputy Master twice as challenging. Master Bower had become quite set in his opinions as to how the children should be tutored, and it required great tact and patience not to upset him, but Richard - remembering his own lonely days in the Choir - recognised that the boys needed encouragement as well as upbraiding, fatherly affection as well as paternal discipline.

Soon he found himself getting on well both with his pupils and with Master Bower, but the job took Richard away from Margaret many days and evenings of the week. Nor was it to be the only intrusion on the wonderfully carefree, ecstatic state of love they vainly hoped might be theirs forever. Soon Margaret learned that she was with child.

Richard was ecstatic, knowing that she would have a son even though Margaret protested that it just might be a little girl. In any case, there was a rule at Court, strictly observed, that ladies in waiting were not to present themselves in the delicate state of pregnancy, and moreover that in the echoing halls of the palace would be heard only the cries of royal babies and no others. (And that had not been heard in more than twenty years.) Therefore Margaret would have to go back to North Petherton, and so it was with a deep loneliness that Richard brought her back to her parents' home.

There she would stay until the time of the child's birth, when Richard would bring her back to London. Though they might not retain their apartment at Whitehall, they could obtain lodging elsewhere, and 'It matters more to me,' he told her on their parting, 'that my wife and child be by my side, and the three of us live in a garret, than that I should dwell alone in a palace.'

Now as he rode back toward the capital, his heart not nearly as light as it had been when he'd gone this same way just months before with his new bride, Richard could not help but think how unjust it all seemed. Once he'd been quite content in his solitude, but it was hard to go back to it now that he'd known the joy of married life, and he could hardly bear to part from Margaret. Yet this was the price one paid for service to the queen. The queen - suddenly it occurred to him that he'd glimpsed how she must have felt, condemned to eternal virginity. From that moment he carried himself with a little more ease, knowing he did not bear such a burden all alone.

And yet in all his travels to the capital from childhood onward, this was the first time when the sight of her glittering towers did not put him in mind of the New Jerusalem described by St. John in his *Revelation.* Instead the great structures of London appeared so much cold stone, holding within them so many cold hearts. Likewise he found his time back at the palace taken up with tedium, and though he performed all his duties well, he did so without the customary delight that had made work seem little different from play.

As time passed, he began to have mutinous thoughts. Perhaps he should indeed give up his life here at Court, his poetry, his plays, his queen, his hopes for the future - and return to Somerset to be with the woman he loved. It recalled to him the saying of Agur in the *Book of Proverbs*, that there were four things he did not understand: the majesty of an eagle in the sky, the sinuosity of a snake on a rock, the sureness of a ship on stormed-tossed seas, and the passion of a man for a maiden.

Only one thing held Richard back in these desperate days, and that was his promise to his father and king. Such words were not lightly spoken, and as King Henry himself had said to him on his dying bed, words without deeds lack worth of any kind. And so, encouraging himself with the knowledge that he would bring his family back to London when the child was born and Margaret could travel again, Richard set about once again to act his part at Court.

But his queen, and she alone, could see through the mask he put over his emotions as he trod the living stage, and when she had an opportunity to do so in private, she remarked on this to him. 'You may think your queen does not know or understand your sentiments,' she said, 'but you are quite mistaken. To know joy, one must also pay a price - your queen has reckoned such things for herself as well. I would spare you if I could, but I cannot, for destiny makes the rules by which we are harnessed, and we merely step into them.' She gazed at Richard, her usually foreboding gaze for once softened in the tenderest of affection.

'You may not think so, but I understand your condition, and am saddened myself. But 'tis only for a short time, and you and she shall be together again. Then it will seem all the more worth waiting for.'

Richard knew she was right, and he bowed his head. 'I pray that I have not served thee less well for it, Your Majesty. My first allegiance has always been and always will be to my queen.'

Her reply was quick and unwavering. 'Fear not! You serve me well indeed, and it is only because I have a window to your heart that I know your misgivings. It is like that with us, you know! We are of the same blood, and there is a bond that no one else shall ever know, save us.' She beckoned Richard to come closer, and he knelt before her in silence. 'Now take yourself to Somerset.'

He looked up at her, wondering if he'd heard correctly. 'Yes,' she said with a smile, 'there is a woman there I expect longs for you as you do for her. 'Tis near time she should deliver, and you must be there to see your child - the legacy of the king!' She sighed. 'Would that your queen might be so blest, but as you have seen through a glass darkly, I see in full - that the weight of duty does extract all too dear a price. Though I have the body of a woman whose duty it might have been to bear children, I have the stomach rather to be a king, and that is what I must be...'

Leaving off these thoughts, she waved him away. 'Begone with you! I'll have no more love-sick poets in my presence for a while. The kingdom and your queen will still be here when you have regained your heart and can return.'

As he made ready to journey once again to Somerset, Richard's step was lighter than it had been at any time since he'd last bade Margaret farewell. From time to time he paused to thank God for giving him a sovereign with such a heart of compassion. Soon he was on his way, and by the time he reached his family's home in North Petherton the world of Court seemed dim and far away.

Agnes had seen the coach coming, and was waiting at the door to welcome him. As he threw his arms around her, he asked about Margaret, and his mother told him that she had been resting for awhile but was now sitting up in the parlour waiting for him. Richard walked toward the parlour with his heart racing at the expectation of seeing his bride again and holding her in his arms.

Margaret stood up and started toward the door. The moment he saw her, Richard thought she seemed pale, as though she'd been ill. But this was the first time he'd ever looked so closely at a pregnant woman, and perhaps it was only her condition that made her so. Certainly she was as beautiful as he remembered her, and her ample swelling signified life and good health.

His bride stood trembling before him, and he moved her quickly toward the nearest chair, but she resisted. 'I do hope,' she said, looking into his eyes, 'that with the great size motherhood has added, your wife does not now seem ugly to you.'

From her expression, he couldn't tell if she meant it sincerely or in weak jest, but Richard hastened to dissuade all her fears. Taking her in his arms, he kissed her passionately and then, after telling her how much he loved and had missed her, knelt down before her and said, 'You are more beautiful than ever, dear one. Indeed, motherhood becomes you most handsomely that methinks we shall have a dozen children.'

She smiled. 'Perhaps not quite so quickly as all that.' She made a circle with her arms around her enormous belly. 'At the moment the weight of motherhood is quite tiring, though I am told that all this quickly fades from one's memory.'

When they went to bed that night, little did they suspect how soon Margaret would be delivered of her child. Perhaps it was the excitement of her husband's return, but for whatever reason she awakened Richard at about the time the giant clock in the hall struck two.

'It is time, Richard,' she whispered, moaning from the pain. 'Pray call both our mothers.'

Richard lit a candle, and in his face she could see his shock. 'Dear, are you...?' She held up a hand. 'Now is the time,' she gasped, 'for the ladies to do that which needs to be done. You must keep Father occupied while we do.'

Richard kissed her gently and slipped his clothes on, almost at a run, and he rushed first to rouse Agnes and then Mrs. Babb in her house. By the time he returned with Robert Babb, the two ladies had taken charge, and they quickly turned the men away with instructions to keep plenty of hot water boiling on the stove and make ready a supply of linens.

Richard and Robert, knowing full well that they were being given harmless tasks to keep them out of the way, moved to the kitchen. There they tried to busy themselves for a time, but eventually both fell into a pose of meditative expectancy. Hours passed in this same dull but anxious state until the sound of birds and the light of the sun outside shook the two as from a delirium.

But the waiting continued, punctuated only by occasional assurances from one of the mothers, speaking noncommittally and looking back toward the bedroom as though afraid she'd already stayed away too long. The clock continued its relentless revolutions of the hours, until noon passed and then evening slipped into the blackness of night.

Through all those agonising hours, both men had remained determined not to let the other know of his growing concern. But as time and fatigue wore away their resolve, their fears began to show. Robert had gone through this before, not only when his wife gave birth to Margaret but with their other children as well, and yet even he began to wonder aloud what was happening. Richard, for his part, began to pace the floor, and the anxiety he'd held back all day seemed to settle on him with the darkness. For a while they tried to talk, then they again fell into their own troubled thoughts, which with the passage of hours dwindled into a restless half-sleep.

Suddenly the silence of the night was pierced with the cry of a newborn child, and both men jumped to their feet in shock. A moment later Agnes, looking like she'd just come off a battlefield, appeared at the kitchen door. In spite of her obvious exhaustion, she managed to smile. 'You have a fine son, Richard, as fine as ever I have seen. Margaret wants to see you.'

She knew her son would be quick to rush to the side of his wife, and with what strength remained from her ordeal, she hurried behind him up the stairs to stop him just as he reached the bedroom door. 'You must not stay long,' she cautioned. 'She has had a very hard time of it, and she needs her rest.'

Showing by a nod of the head that he heeded his mother's words, Richard stepped noiselessly to the side of the bed and knelt beside Margaret. She looked like a child herself lying there, delicate and beautiful, though the rosiness was gone from her cheeks and her eyes had dark circles. She held their son in the crook of her arm as she looked into Richard's eyes, beaming back at her with pride and wonder.

'Give your son to my mother now,' she murmured softly. Richard took the tiny bundle from her arms and handed the precious burden to his mother-in-law. Mrs. Babb took the baby and hastily left the room so that Margaret and Richard might have a moment alone. When Richard returned to the bedside, he saw a strange expression on his wife's face, a look he'd never seen before and could not attribute merely to fatigue. Margaret was frightened.

Clutching the bedclothes to her breast as though she dared not let go, she whispered in a plaintive voice, 'Richard... hold me in your arms.'

He pulled her close to him, and he could feel her body, abnormally warm and wet with perspiration, trembling. He planted tender kisses on her forehead and cheeks, and though he wanted to say something - anything to comfort her - he could find no words.

'Richard,' she gasped, 'I love you so... I am so happy I could give you the son you wanted...' Suddenly the trembling ceased.

Richard pulled back and looked into her face, but her eyes were half-closed. 'Margaret,' he said, shaking her. 'Margaret!' And then he realised that she had slipped away from him.

The silence of the room became deafening. 'Margaret!' he yelled, clutching her lifeless body to him, and for the first time since childhood he burst into tears. Now all the dammed torrents of emotion burst their restraints, and he was sobbing, covering her matted hair with his tears. He held her for a very long time, and long after the others entered the room, he became aware that Agnes and Mrs Babbs were kneeling beside him, weeping too.

And so that day - November 9, 1561 - the date when his son was born and fulfilled the Tudor legacy, a date that should have been the happiest in Richard's life, became his saddest. As for the days that followed, he passed through them as one walking in a mist, awaking each morning to the terrible truth and living out the long hours as in a nightmare.

Richard shared little of his innermost thoughts with his mother, but in the way all mothers who love their sons do, she ached as he ached. Yet she knew the stuff of which he was made, and recognised that for those in whose veins Tudor blood flowed, victory would always come sooner or later. Somehow he would emerge a better man.

In those dark days, Agnes was there for him in ways he couldn't have known at the time. Had it been up to him, the child (named William after his father and brother) might have died, but Agnes took him to a village woman to nurse, and Agnes alone had the presence of mind to pen a note and send it to the queen.

Most Gracious Queen:

Richard has a fine son whom he has named for his father, William. Margaret fought bravely and fiercely to bring him life, and she paid for his with her own. Richard is devastated. Whatever can we do?

Your Devoted Servant,

Agnes Edwardes, Richard's Mother

Within less time than anyone might have expected, the queen's messenger brought a letter bearing the royal seal. Richard, by now awakening from his daze, opened it with trembling hands. It read:

Richard,

Although I can never know your grief as you, my thoughts and prayers are with you daily. How proud you must be of your son! The palace is not so cold nor your Queen's heart so hard that the presence of an infant shall upset either. Your apartment at Whitehall awaits you and your son, and has been furnished with the things for a baby.

You will, of course, need someone to care for the child. Bring your mother, if she will consent. The Queen would like very much to know the courageous and brave lady of such great beauty of whom my father spoke. It is time these palace walls saw something of new life!

Your faithful friend,

Elizabeth R.

Richard read these words with tears in his eyes. Perhaps the queen knew better than he - perhaps he could indeed begin again, serving his queen still while loving and raising the son that his beloved had fought so valiantly to give him. He knew, of course, that nothing would ever be the same for him, but there was a new life now, one that shared in the Tudor legacy and would pass that legacy on. He had loved and been loved as he'd never dreamed could happen, and that love would linger with him even now, reaching out to him across the wide chasm of death.

He knew that he had to move on to fulfil his destiny. It was a choice made purely from his will and not his feelings, yet he believed that in time he would again regain the joy he'd once known.

15

At long last, Agnes got to see the splendours of London, the grand and mysterious things she'd only imagined before, sitting in her simple house in Somersetshire and reading her son's enthusiastic letters. Once the three of them were settled at the palace, Richard wrote a brief note to the queen.

Her Majesty, Queen Elizabeth

Your humble and obedient servant requests permission to present his son and mother to Her Majesty. As ever, your wisdom and compassion fall upon this your poet.

Richard Edwardes

The appointed day arrived, and for the first time two of the great ladies of Richard's life met. From the moment they first laid eyes on one another, Richard saw that just as he'd expected, they understood one another at a glance. Agnes was everything that Elizabeth had ever heard or believed she would be, and Agnes in turn could see the stamp of the Tudors - the strength and poise of King Henry - on his daughter the queen.

Elizabeth had little experience with babies, but when she saw Richard's son that first time she was moved, and commented that there could be no mistaking the infant's bloodline. Richard and Agnes, knowing the import of what she said beyond the mere words she could speak in the presence of other courtiers, were pleased beyond what they could have said even in private. Richard sensed a bond, not only between Elizabeth and himself, but also including his mother, and he knew it would always be there whether anyone spoke of it or not.

Everyone treated Agnes with warmth and kindness, welcoming her with open arms to the family of Whitehall, and she quickly became accustomed to her new home. The palace was a great sprawling city within itself, with huge kitchens and bakeries in the floors beneath the living quarters, and all the trades and shops needed for a self-contained town tucked here and there within the palace walls. It had its own pier on the Thames, the lifeline of London from whose banks the construction of the city seldom strayed far, and across the river one could see the open fields to St. Paul's and the towers of St. James. One need not even go outside Whitehall to attend services, the Chapel Royal being just a few steps beyond Richard's door.

Little William thrived and grew before their eyes, and Agnes often remarked how very much her new grandson resembled his father at the same age. She felt happier than she had been in a very long time, and with her home in Somerset placed in the hands of her son Christopher, who always saw to his responsibilities with painstaking care, she concentrated her attentions on the duties at hand. Richard and William needed her in a way that she had not been needed for a very long time, and in caring for the simple needs of the baby while giving her son companionship, she felt a renewed sense of purpose.

It gladdened Richard to see his mother so happy, and in turning his attention to her needs (not to mention those of the queen), he soon laid his own sorrow to rest in the innermost chambers of his heart.

The year 1561 was to bring many changes in the life of the poet. Richard Bower died, and as expected, Richard was appointed his successor. He welcomed the demands the new position placed on him, and moved quickly to fully implement the changes he'd begun as Deputy Master. Among those was a relaxation in the rigours of the curriculum, which as a student he'd felt failed to recognise the youthfulness of the boys under instruction. They were, after all, boys still, and should have an opportunity to act their age at times. Therefore he allowed daily for physical exercise and games.

In so modifying the strictures of their daily life, he instantly won the boys' love and respect, and in turn behaviour problems - which had begun to get out of hand under old Master Bower - ceased almost completely. Each of the children, most of whom had left their homes at an early age as he had, came to regard Richard not merely as a teacher and disciplinarian, but also as a father.

Along with his new post, Richard began to have thoughts of a new play, with his students serving as actors. The boys were excited at the prospect, and so Richard went to the queen with his idea.

Elizabeth approved the notion wholeheartedly, but just as he was about to leave her presence, he brought up another subject of great (though secret) importance to him.

On one visit to Court some months after returning to London, he'd noticed a new face among the queen's ladies in waiting. She looked about sixteen, and extraordinarily beautiful, with deep black hair and a gentle face. Her green eyes and long, full dark lashes seemed to draw in anyone who looked at her, and as he noticed her moving about, he thought to himself that she had the manners of one much more mature. Though a newcomer, she appeared as though she'd always been present at Court, and her grace reminded him of another young girl he'd once known - Elizabeth.

So now, trying to sound nonchalant, he observed, 'I see the queen has a new and lovely flower in her garden. The lady in question seems quite young, yet not ill at ease at all to have so recently come into the Court. Is her family here in London?'

Elizabeth smiled, and when she answered she complemented his offhand manner in kind, acting as though Richard's interest in the girl were of the most mundane sort. 'The queen is pleased,' she said, 'to see that her poet has not lost his eye for a pretty young maid. Yes, her name is Hellene, and her family are the Griffiths of South Wales.' Always with an eye toward the treasury, Elizabeth did not fail to add, 'It appears they are the richest family in the kingdom.

'And yes, she is very young, but do not be fooled by age: she speaks and reads Latin, Greek, and French, and moreover has wisdom of surpassing degree. She is a delight to the queen, as we can talk of things about which most of the pretty faces at Court know nothing - in fact, we talk on much the same level as you and I.'

Richard soon heard through Court gossip that Hellene was the second child in a family of twelve, her father having been married twice and fathering six children by each wife. Coming from such a large family, the young woman had gained the special advantage of learning how to get along with others of necessarily differing temperaments, and her position as oldest girl had early laid on her the responsibility of helping with the younger children - thus her maturity.

Her father, in hopes that she might someday grace the Court, had seen to it that she was well-educated and trained in all matters a lady of quality should know. She became accomplished in music, and was said to do some of the very finest needlework the ladies of the Court had ever seen. Her talents, as well as her beauty, had not gone unnoticed either by admirers or foes: already there were those among the Court who, seeing Elizabeth's quite obvious favour for her, had begun to react to her in a somewhat jealous manner.

Richard, having experienced the same in the Court of Queen Mary (and even now on occasion from Lord Hunsdon), could sympathise. As for his interest in the girl, he told himself that as the queen's eyes and ears, he needed to stay informed about all matters at Court. And indeed, he still carried much sorrow in his heart for Margaret, and though he didn't let this show in his outward demeanour, those who knew him well could see it.

One evening not long after Richard's inquiry, the queen and her new favourite lady-in-waiting were conversing over a number of topics: upcoming events at the court, a new book Hellene was reading, and sundry small talk. Hellene rose from where she sat and walked over to a bookcase to explore the shelves for new treasures. Seeming preoccupied with the volumes, she said casually, 'I hope Your Majesty will forgive my noticing, but this Richard Edwardes seems to stand quite apart from most at Court. He has a certain grace or quiet calm, something that is different. Perhaps it is only because he is so tall, but one might think him a duke or someone of that stature.'

Elizabeth did not respond immediately, and Hellene turned quickly to face the queen. 'I hope that I have not said something I should not have,' she said hastily, then added, 'but he is quite a remarkable man.'

Letting her face betray nothing, the queen replied, 'He is indeed, but imposing in manner as he may be, he is no duke; he is only the son of a yeoman in Somerset. And yet he is quite talented and wise, and the Court is fortunate to have one such as he.'

Feeling reassured that she had not stepped out of place, Hellene let herself go back to looking through the books before she said again, 'He certainly must be a joy indeed to the queen, for he is so handsome and such a gifted poet.' She chose her next words very carefully. 'Though I am sure most would not notice, for it arises not from any words spoken and deeds done, I sense a special bond between Your Highness and the poet. It appears he is a special friend and someone you rely upon very much.'

People seldom surprised Elizabeth, but she had to ponder her lady-in-waiting's words for a moment before she replied. 'Yes, my dear Hellene, he is indeed a special member of my Court family, and he can always be counted on when others may not be. You are perceptive to notice such, but lest you think otherwise, he is of no romantic interest of the queen. He is only a man who has served as my personal minister, and has come to be a special friend.'

Hellene turned from the bookcase, her face red. 'Your Majesty, I did not mean to imply...'

Elizabeth held up a hand. 'You need not worry that you have offended the queen, my child.' She beckoned Hellene to come sit at her knee, and when she did, the queen gently stroked the girl's head. 'I recognise that you perceive things of which others are blind, and this is one of your charms for the queen. And now let me presume upon you.'

Hellene turned around and looked up at her, and the queen went on. 'It is pleasant that you think well of my poet and friend, but do not let your observations and feelings carry you beyond what is appropriate. Remember that this man is old enough to be your father, whereas you are young, beautiful, and more wise than your years would warrant. There will be many an eligible and handsome young courtier, and from their ranks you may ultimately choose one to marry. In the meantime, however, you can learn much from a friend such as Richard Edwardes. There is no finer gentleman in the land than he.'

Hellene's expression was earnest. 'I fear that I have offended thee in some way, and do beg Your Majesty to forgive the prattlings of a young maiden. Sometimes I proceed too far with my observations, and do not heed the chance that others may interpret my words differently than I meant them.'

The queen looked down upon her with a kind smile. 'I assure you that no offense was taken, dear child, and if such ever happens - as unlikely as that may be - you would know the difference quite well. Your queen is not hesitant to let those who displease her know that they have done so.'

But Hellene knew that, even if she hadn't invoked the queen's displeasure, something she said had hit far closer to the truth than Her Majesty thought proper. She concluded that henceforth she should keep such observations - and questions about the poet Richard Edwardes - to herself.

That, however, did not prevent her from approaching the handsome priest with sincere questions about poetry, philosophy, and theological matters, which she put to him frequently in the weeks that followed. Not once did they speak other than as student and schoolmaster, yet a friendship began to flower nonetheless.

Richard found himself again and again marvelling that inside of Hellene's beautiful young head could be stored so much wisdom and learning. She absorbed knowledge quickly, and thought through complex questions with the skill of a true scholar; thus despite her years, he began to look upon her almost as his equal in maturity. Nor could he help but take note of the fact that as their friendship grew, she became even more beautiful to him.

Elizabeth, like the wise virginal goddess Athena whom she so resembled in her ways, seemed to see and know all that went on at Court, and she soon became aware of Richard's frequent visits to Hellene. Not that the two tried to conceal this from her - they were not so foolish as that! But she forgave Hellene for her apparent disregard of the injunctions she'd offered.

Still, Elizabeth had to wonder how two such attractive people could remain mere friends, without either seeming to regard the other in anything but the most appropriate manner. But then they were both extraordinarily intelligent and perceptive people, and she took comfort in their honesty and openness with her. She found herself pleased with the events unfolding before her eyes, despite the difference in years between the two. In her private thoughts, she reckoned that she would have no reservations if their friendship took a more serious turn, but then she rebuked herself for seeing more there than truly existed.

One evening after Richard had read bits and pieces of a new play to Hellene (which he frequently did because he appreciated her ability to understand and make intelligent comments), the two of them fell into a silence, lost in thought.

Then Hellene broke the reverie with one of those forthright comments of hers she'd so aptly characterised before the queen: 'Is it still so very painful to you - your loss, I mean?'

Richard, taken aback only slightly, fixed a steady gaze on her for a moment, then said slowly, 'Yes, I suppose it ever shall be in some ways. One cannot love so well and not feel a loss.'

He paused again as he tried to find the right words for something he had felt deeply for a long time, and yet had never put into words for anyone. 'I have the son she bore me, and he is a great comfort because a part of her is still with me. I don't know if I can ever again feel about anyone as I did her, but perhaps time will provide the answer.' He regarded Hellene tenderly. 'These are thoughts I seldom share, for there are few I judge deserving to know the innermost sentiments of my heart. And yet these thoughts are always with me, waiting only to be unlocked by one of wise and gentle demeanour.'

Hellene looked down at her hands. 'Your honesty means much to me.

You have become a very dear friend, and I do so hope that someday you may love and live again as you did then. I pray that God may help your poor heart heal.'

But she did not stop there. Trembling slightly, she said what was most deeply on her mind: 'Whoever she may be, the woman you choose will be the most fortunate in this world, for you truly are a man of great talent and tender heart.' She looked up at Richard. 'Forgive me if I have been too bold in asking you about these things, but I have wanted to speak with you of this for ever so long. I knew not if I dared speak, whether my thoughts might be regarded as an intrusion, and I do hope that I have caused you no pain.'

'Fear not,' he said gently. 'You too are my dearest friend, and your concern has helped me already. I shall always treasure what you have asked, and what you have said.'

To Hellene it seemed that perhaps they had lingered too long already over this interchange, and she stood up. 'Perhaps I had best retire for the evening.'

Richard reached for her hand and planted a gentle kiss on it, one perhaps more imbued with feeling than propriety would have allowed. Then they went to their separate chambers, but as Richard stood before the door of his own, he knew that something special had begun to happen. Inside himself he felt emotions almost forgotten, and again - this time in a much happier context - he wondered at the four things that had perplexed old wise Agur. The way of a man with a maid...

When he stepped inside the suite of rooms, he found Agnes embroidering before the fire. 'Something special for the queen?' he asked.

She looked up at him as he bent down to kiss her on the forehead. 'What's that I see in your face, my son? Since you are not given to strong drink, I can only guess that something remarkable has happened.'

He laughed, knowing that she would always see through his most impenetrable facades. 'No, mother, it is only that I have just become aware of a wonderful fact that I had not known before. It has been present before me for awhile, and yet I have not had eyes to see it. Perhaps I shall share it with you at another time.' He looked into the fire. 'The Lord does move in most mysterious ways, does He not?'

Agnes smiled knowingly. 'Yes, my son, He does indeed, but I doubt that is the realisation of which you were speaking.' Going back to her work, she said, 'Never mind. I will be here when you wish to tell me about this wondrous realisation of yours. I must admit, however, that you have piqued my curiosity a bit, but that means only that I have a surprise to look forward to, doesn't it? How pleasant it will be to contemplate.'

The days melted away, and the Richard that Elizabeth and his mother had known before began to reappear. Indeed, he seemed to glow with an inner peace he'd lacked before his time of tribulation and sorrow.

Hellene saw it too, and was grateful. Perhaps, she thought, her impertinent question, which permitted him to unburden his sorrow, had served him well. But whatever the cause, she rejoiced in Richard's new-found happiness without wondering too long over the joy this brought out in her.

One night after a banquet at Hampton Court, Richard approached Hellene as though to bid her good night, but instead he said, 'Dear lady, may I speak for a moment with you alone?'

She nodded her assent, and took his arm as they walked together down a quiet hallway.

Stopping out of sight of the others, he looked into her eyes. It was only a moment's glance, but in that instant Hellene saw through the crystal-blue of his gaze into his very heart and soul. She knew what he would say even before he said it: 'My dear Hellene, there is something I would like to...'

She raised a finger gently to his mouth to stop the difficult words. 'Yes, I know what is in your heart, as it is in mine.'

'Would you...'

And again she touched his lips lightly with her delicate hand. 'Of course I would, my love,' she sighed.

He pulled her to him in an embrace, and neither cared who saw them at that moment.

'I never dreamed I would ever love again, Hellene,' he whispered, 'but I love you with all my heart. I know the great difference in our ages...'

Yet again, she stopped him. 'Shhhh! Speak not of things which matter not at all. I, too, love you with all my heart, and were I to die at this moment, I would die the happiest mortal on God's earth.' She held him tightly. 'I once told you that whoever she might be, the one you chose would be the most fortunate of women, never daring then to dream it might be me. But if this is what you would wish, then let us not waste a moment of this life on useless words.'

Richard kissed her again, and then, mindful of the queen's presence in the room adjoining, took Hellene back into the great hall where they had been. When they entered again, the queen's eyes met those of Richard, and she smiled as if she knew already what he would come to tell her on the morrow.

16

Richard's pace quickened when he saw the first lights of Whitehall shining in the moonlit night. It was late, and he didn't know whether he would find his mother awake, but so intoxicated was he with happiness that he could not bear to keep his wondrous news to himself. So he was glad when as he approached his door, he saw a light shining through the crack and knew that she had waited up for his return.

Agnes sat in a comfortable chair, reading her Bible by candlelight, and as Richard walked in he took off his hat and spun it into a nearby chair in a customary display of boyish joy - something she hadn't seen from him in a while.

'Your steps are light, my son,' she remarked. 'You must have had a good evening.'

'Oh, 'tis better than good, my mother dear, far better than good,' he replied, sitting down. Putting his hands behind his head, he leaned back in his chair and stared up at the ceiling with a look of supreme pleasure on his face. 'This is the best of all possible evenings in a world that is beautiful to behold.'

Agnes shut her Bible. 'As serious as all that?' she asked with a quizzical smile. 'Well, then, I suppose you are going to tell me now that which you only mentioned in veiled terms a short time ago. Come closer to the light so I may see your eyes - they always betray you, Richard, and unless I miss my guess, this newfound lightheartedness I read on your face has something to do with a certain young lady from Wales.'

Richard looked startled for a moment, then with a laugh he said, 'Oh, Mother, it is true that you see all and know all, is it not?'

'Only where my children are concerned. Now pray tell me your tale.'

Grinning broadly at this, he took his mother's hand in his. 'Yes, Mother, it is about Hellene that you see me so glad. Tonight we have spoken of our mutual love, and she has consented to be my wife if the queen will approve of our marriage.' He looked down at their two hands. 'I suppose such a union makes no sense in the world, given the vast gulf between our years, but...'

'For heaven's sake, lad, what has age to do with anything?' said Agnes scornfully. 'Why, one would think you close to the grave to hear you talk, and you but six-and-thirty in years! As for your concerns about the queen's approval, put them to rest. Her Highness is no fool, and no doubt has wondered what has taken you so long.'

'Am I so obvious?' he asked earnestly.

Agnes laughed. 'Your queen is your good friend, as am I, and wants only what is best and will bring you happiness. By now I suspect half the world knows what that should be, dear boy.'

'That is so, indeed,' said Richard pensively. 'And yet one other fear does but slightly cloud my joy in this hour...'

'I know the battle that has raged within you,' said Agnes, putting her other hand on Richard's shoulder. 'You love Margaret still, and feel even guilty for loving another. Let it go, son, let it go! You will always love her as long as you live, but she is with the angels, and no doubt would want you and your son to be happy.'

'You have seen part of it,' said Richard cautiously, 'but there is also this fear that my new wife may sense a spectre hanging over our marriage, a ghost of Margaret.'

Again Agnes reassured him. 'Give the girl credit for the very wisdom which, as much as her beauty, draws you to her! By my reckoning, she is plenty strong enough that she will not feel a threat from the memories of another. Indeed, from what I can guess of her, she would know that in some ways your past sadness would only make your life with her all the more rich and full.'

'She is wise, is she not?' said Richard, his sudden tension softening with his mother's comforting words.

'She is a lovely girl in all ways, Richard, and you are indeed fortunate to find a flower so rare.' She cupped her hand under Richard's chin so he would look at her. 'But then, being your mother, I happen to believe her quite fortunate as well.'

'I know not how you manage always to say the things I need most to hear, Mother,' said Richard, 'but you do.'

'You forget that you are of my body, and a bond runs between us. It is not unlike the family tie between you and your queen, making it so that at times the two of you act in a harmony for which words are unnecessary. Truly such a kinship is a strange and wonderful treasure, and now once again you have seen this special love flower between yourself and Hellene. You and she can be as one, and in that being share to a degree in the Divine Love that surrounds us all if we have but eyes to see and hearts to feel.' She glanced at her son. 'Now what is that look I see on your face?'

'I was just thinking,' he said, 'that your words outdo those of a poet, and I could not improve by line or word on what you've said.'

Time in the next few weeks sped up for Richard and Hellene as they busied themselves with plans and dreams. They agreed that the wedding should take place in the Chapel Royal so that the queen might attend, and the bride and groom sent word to Hellene's family in Wales and Richard's brothers in Somerset.

Soon the hour came when Richard found himself standing in front of the altar waiting as Hellene's father walked toward him with the most beautiful bride anyone had ever seen. The Chapel was lit by long tapers along the aisle, and in the light of them Hellene glowed even more brightly, her satin dress shimmering as in a vision.

And so began another passage in the life of a lad from a modest background in Somerset, who through fortune and destiny had grown tall, famous, and wise. Not once did he compare his love for Hellene to that which he'd shared with Margaret, for though there could be no distinction between these two loves in the degree of their intensity, their qualities made them as different as youth and maturity - though in fact not two years separated the one from the other. With Margaret he'd had all the fresh excitement of a first love, whereas he felt as though he'd always known Hellene, but would continue to discover new mysteries in her even as their two lives moved inexorably toward eternity.

Following the wedding, a reception was held in a spacious room at Whitehall Palace. The queen attended, wearing one of the most spectacularly resplendent gowns she possessed, and in her usually sober countenance she could barely contain her joy at the marriage of her dearly loved brother.

When she determined that sufficient celebration had taken place and the couple should be on their way, Elizabeth signaled a guard, who in loud and resonant tones proclaimed, 'Her Majesty, Queen Elizabeth, wishes your attention!'

All eyes quickly turned to the queen. ' 'Tis a glorious occasion,' she announced, gazing at the assembled well-wishers, 'when the queen's poet weds so fair a maid.'

The crowd responded with applause, and Hellene could only blush and lower her eyes.

Elizabeth continued. 'Though all are enjoying this lovely celebration, 'tis time that the newlyweds take leave and be on their way. My poet will be pleased to know that the queen's wedding gift is leave from his duties for the Crown and a handsome purse to permit a lengthy honeymoon.' The crowd showed their obvious approval for this with another round of applause. 'The groom's mother assures me,' the queen went on, 'that she can get on quite well with young William, and would be delighted to have time alone with the little chap. Therefore I say to you, the bride and groom, enjoy your holiday well, for you will find more than enough to fill your days on your return. Go with my blessings and good wishes!'

Richard made a deep bow before Elizabeth, and kissed her hand. While the celebrants applauded, he said quietly, 'How may I ever thank thee enough, Your Majesty?'

Elizabeth smiled majestically. 'You may regard the payment too dear from such a demanding queen, sir, but fear not - I shall not make the task too great.'

Soon afterward, the couple departed to begin their holiday away from London. They had talked many times of visiting Somersetshire and going on from there to the home of Hellene's parents just north of the small hamlet of Llandaff, but they'd never dreamed such would be possible. Now that the queen's beneficence had made this hope a reality, they set off in haste as though to prevent her changing her mind.

Hellene being an excellent equestrian, they decided to proceed on horseback with an extra packhorse to carry provisions. Thus they would make better time, and more importantly they could be alone. Their first major stop was in Salisbury, and as they approached the town, they could see from a goodly distance the magnificent spire of its cathedral. Though both of them had gone there before, it was as though they saw it all for the first time, for now they gazed on this sight from the unity of their love.

They visited the cathedral late in the afternoon and soon thereafter found suitable lodgings at a very old inn nearby. When the proprietor learned of their recent marriage and that Richard was a member of the Chapel Royal, he immediately insisted that they should have the largest room - the one King Henry had always used when lodging at Salisbury.

It was a lovely suite indeed, but the young couple were so totally enraptured with one another that it could have been a stable. The kindly and solicitous proprietor provided them with a special banquet, fit for royalty, and yet the two had thoughts only of what awaited them later that night.

It seemed an eternity until they were alone in their chambers, and as he watched Hellene slip into the huge canopied bed, Richard caught his breath at her great beauty. 'Never has any man been as fortunate as I!' he said when he could speak.

Her large green eyes glowed up at him with the light of a love from within. 'If that is your perception, I am grateful for it, but 'tis I who has been blessed, my love!'

They kissed passionately and without restraint, and then Richard blew out the candle.

Their breakfast the next morning, an event to which they found themselves more attentive than at the meal the night before, was only slightly less elaborate than the supper they'd enjoyed, and Richard paid the proprietor well before he and Hellene set off once again.

At each stop, it seemed as though their hosts knew of their coming in advance, and they were wined and dined as though they were a king and queen. Every innkeeper had a special room for them, and Richard returned their kindness not only in coin, but with stories that excited these news-hungry country folk. Night after night, Hellene listened without growing weary to his tales of the queen, her Court, and London itself. On one occasion, she persuaded him to recite some of his poetry, which his listeners received with hearty approval.

Another memorable stop, not long before they reached Richard's home, was at Wells in Somersetshire, an ancient village that had taken its name from the artesian wells that supplied its citizens with crystal-clear cool water. At the edge of the town, they took lodgings at a small but inviting-looking inn, and after they had eaten a delightful dinner, they decided to see the town's cathedral.

Unlike Salisbury, this one lay hidden behind a screen of trees, walls, and buildings, and they did not find it easily. Finally they asked directions in a bake shop, and were told to go down a large street with arches overhead, at the end of which they would see the cathedral. And just as they'd been told, there they saw the magnificent structure atop a knoll. It was a breathtaking sight, with its stone lacework and statues, and to Richard the evening light made it appear as though it were made of alabaster.

It being too late to go inside, they returned to their inn and set out for the cathedral after breakfast the next morning. This time, in the fresh dewy light, the building appeared even more beautiful, and Richard was reminded again of the New Jerusalem. No sooner had they entered the doors than a little old man, a retired choirmaster, greeted them. When they told him who they were, he offered to give them a tour.

Their guide informed them that most of the cathedral had been built during the time of their most illustrious Bishop, Jocelyn de Welles. Descended from a Norman knight of the same name, Jocelyn and his brother Hugh, Bishop of Lincolnshire, had been present at the signing of the Magna Carta. In fact Hugh de Welles had with his own hand made the copies of the great document, the foundation stone of English government, that were given the barons at the time of the signing.

After giving the couple a complete tour of the cathedral and the bishop's palace, their guide took them to the small line of quaint stone cottages - which looked more like an illustration from a storybook than something from real life - where retirees and rectors lived. Suddenly aware of the time, Richard realised they'd been on tour for almost three hours, and he invited the guide to join them at the inn for lunch. The latter accepted with delight, and they were able to continue their visit over generous servings of shepherds' pie and bread fresh from the oven, spread generously with butter.

The next day they arrived at the Edwardes home in North Petherton. Richard's brother Christopher, who had not been able to attend the wedding because of responsibilities at home, was there to greet them on the doorstep. 'My dear brother!' he said with a smile when Richard introduced him to Hellene. 'You did not tell me you were marrying an angel! You are a most fortunate man indeed - perhaps even more fortunate than deserved!'

Hellene's wit was a match for his own: 'My husband neglected to tell me he had an Irish brother,' she said, and in response to Christopher's quizzical look added, 'for surely you have kissed the Blarney Stone.'

All three shared a laugh over this, and immediately Christopher and Hellene got on as though they'd been brother and sister all their lives. They ended up staying an extra day at North Petherton, and it was an enchanted time for everyone. Christopher, eager for news of their mother in London as well as their brother William the vintner, kept Richard talking till the late hours, and the latter joked that he would be glad to move on for the rest it would afford him.

And so they bade the Edwardes home good-bye and continued on to Llandaff in Wales. It would have been quicker and more direct to go by boat, but they already had their horses, and therefore they proceeded by land. At mid-afternoon, they stopped by a gentle Somerset stream for a rest, and the area being secluded and the afternoon warm, Richard suggested they go in for a swim.

Hellene was still a bit modest about disrobing in front of her new husband, but Richard had no such qualms, and he quickly stripped and plunged into the water. Seeing him splashing about and clearly enjoying himself, she relented, and went behind a tree to remove her clothes. A moment later she slipped into the stream beside him.

It was a lovely afternoon, and the water refreshing and stimulating. Here among the trees with no company but their horses, they reminded Richard of another couple placed alone in a Garden planted with all of God's goodness around them. As they were wading out onto the bank, he suddenly grabbed Hellene's hand and pulled her toward him. Their wet bodies came together as they sank into the rich green grass and flowers that bordered the stream.

They passed the next few days of travel in pleasurable companionship, and soon their horses had carried them to the gates of the palatial manor of the Griffiths of South Wales near Llandaff. Hellene's parents were delighted to see them again, and to have them at last in their home. The mother and father quite obviously adored their daughter, and within a matter of minutes, Richard was getting along with them as though he'd been part of the family forever.

On the second day at Griffith Manor, the newlyweds took a ride into Llandaff to visit the cathedral there. The terrain was rugged, and the church nestled amidst hills and trees as though for protection. Upon leaving the cathedral, they decided to ride down Cardiff Road to the south toward the village, and along the way they passed an ancient Norman fort. Richard asked Hellene about the building's history.

'It is strange you should ask,' she replied. 'It is called Edwards Hall, named after King Edward, who is said once to have stayed there. It last belonged to the Earl of Warwick, who acquired it through marriage to Lady Isabel le Despenser, and now it belongs to the crown. I've never been inside, but have heard that though it looks rather stern from without, it is quite warm within.'

'Hm,' Richard said, looking up at the imposing structure as their horses passed by it. 'There is something about that place,' he said. 'Somehow I feel drawn to it.'

The days that followed were filled with lavish meals, long walks through the countryside, and many a night of wonderful talk and laughter with Hellene's parents. But soon Richard became anxious about the amount of time they'd already spent away from London. They'd been gone two weeks, and though he could have spent two more months - indeed, two years - this way, he didn't want to tax his queen's generosity. So within a few days, they set off on their return trip, laden with gifts and good wishes from the Griffiths.

As they rode away from the manor, sad to leave but glad to move forward into their new life together, Hellene turned one last time to wave back at her parents. Richard, seeing the slightest look of girlhood longing in his new bride's eyes, told her he hoped the family would soon come to visit them in London.

One night in Oxford, with their honeymoon soon drawing to a close, they lay together in bed, and their mood was as filled with melancholy as it was expectation. 'I know not what to feel,' Hellene whispered to him. 'Soon we return to Court, and there I shall have to share you with all others. Perhaps it is selfish of me, but I wish I could have you only to myself.' She raised herself from his side to look at him. 'Oh, Richard, I do love you so, and you have made me happier than I imagined a woman could feel.'

Richard smiled. 'In these last few days,' he said, 'I have shared more happiness with you than in all the rest of my life. It's as though you've opened up the other half of my being, Hellene, a part of me for which I yearned all these years without knowing quite what I missed.'

One final stop remained for them on their way back to Whitehall, St. Dunstan's, an old church in the elegant Stepney district of London. It was not on their way, but Richard had heard this place had a stone rood or cross that dated back to the time of the Saxons, and more importantly, a Glastonbury thorn that grew out of a cutting taken from the original shrub.

The church, separated on a large parcel of land all its own, seemed to exist in a timeless world set apart from the city beyond. They soon met the vicar there, a man clearly proud to serve in a parish where prayers had been heard for nearly three-quarters of a millennium, and inquired about the rood. The man took them to see it in the cemetery beside the church, and as he gazed upon the stone cross, Richard marvelled at how new it still appeared after having weathered almost seven hundred years of snow and rain.

The vicar offered to give them a tour of the church, and as Richard and Hellene followed him through its vast and solemn interior, they sensed that they had entered an especially sacred place. It was as though, Richard thought, the love the parishioners shared in their worship of God reached out in its warmth to envelop all who entered its chambers.

They were about to leave when Richard remembered he wanted to see the Glastonbury Thorn. The vicar, impressed at his visitors' knowledge of the shrub, walked with them to the side of the church, where a small garden flourished. But of course the shrub itself would not be in bloom, for it was neither Christmas nor Easter nor the occasion of a visit by royalty.

'And here,' said the vicar proudly, 'is the bush of which you have inquired.' He glanced at it, then looked again. 'Why, that's strange,' he said, and the three of them gazed at the flowers that had somehow bloomed. 'I cannot understand this at all. Well, whatever the cause, you have had the rare privilege of seeing the shrub in flower.' He appeared pensive and more than a little troubled. 'Very odd,' he said under his breath as he walked away without even bidding the couple farewell. 'Can't understand it at all.' He scratched his head and disappeared into the church.

Hellene and Richard looked at each other in consternation. Staring down at the blossoms, Richard felt a little disconcerted, and he could sense his wife's eyes on him. He glanced up at her, and she smiled upon him in a strange and knowing way.

But she couldn't possibly have guessed the secret of his birth, and he had pledged to go to his grave with this one fact about himself locked away even from the woman he loved.

17

Agnes and little William were delighted to have them home, and the child accepted his beautiful new mother immediately and completely. Hellene could see much of William's father in the boy, and that made her love him as much as if he'd come from her own womb.

Soon the four of them settled into a comfortable, happy family life within the walls of Whitehall Palace. Everything was so much in harmony - between husband and wife, daughter-in-law and mother-in-law, stepmother and stepson - that it seemed as though it had always been this way, and memories of any time before this great period of joy seemed to recede into the shadows of forgetfulness.

At least once a month, normally on a Sunday, the four of them would go to the house of Richard's brother William for dinner. William, second of Agnes's sons and Richard's best man at his wedding, had moved to London even before Richard, and had prospered in the wine trade. Once he'd established himself in his profession, he'd gone back to Somerset to take a wife - Elizabeth Babb, younger sister of the late Margaret.

Elizabeth Edwardes, as she was now called, resembled her much-loved sister in temperament if not appearance. Whereas Margaret had been golden-haired, Elizabeth was a brunette, but inwardly she possessed Margaret's sweetness and quiet strength. She had borne William eight children - the seven boys Robert (named for his maternal grandfather), Joshua, William, Thomas, Leonard, John, and Jacob, and the sole girl and youngest child, Martha.

Though not rich, William and his family were quite well-off, and lived comfortably in a house with seven bedrooms outside London. Because the queen had to put money into other things, the Chapel Royal often lacked for funds, and Richard's brother made generous donations. But his most valued assistance was in guiding Richard to make investments in property that in turn would bring in extra income. Many times the properties acquired were in need of repairs and refurbishing, and William lent Richard the necessary capital to make these improvements, to be repaid when the properties were leased out.

Elizabeth Edwardes was a wonderful cook, and enjoyed entertaining her husband's family when they came to visit. She and Hellene and Agnes got along quite well, and while the women busied themselves in the kitchen cleaning up after dinner, Richard would gather the children around him and tell them stories. They loved to hear tales of King Arthur, especially the ones about Merlin; but whatever the story, they sat transfixed, hanging on to every word Richard spoke.

His sister-in-law, observing the way in which he managed to keep so many youngsters utterly enraptured (and thus silent, a rare thing in such a household), observed to him one day, 'Brother Richard, you have a wonderful way with children. Your boys in the Choir must consider themselves most fortunate to have one such as you for their master. It is certainly easy to see that you enjoy what you do, and I imagine you find your work most satisfying.'

'True, 'tis very satisfying,' Richard replied. 'But strange as it may sound, I believe that I learn as much from the boys as they do from me.'

'Methinks you a bit too modest,' said Elizabeth with a teasing smile. 'Oh, it must be most exciting to live in a palace and see the queen almost every day! I find it hard to imagine just how grand it all must be.'

Richard exchanged a knowing smile with Hellene before replying: 'Yes, I suppose that in some ways it is, but sometimes I find it far more pleasant simply to relax with family. Here I can be as I truly am, whereas there I must play a role. And when I am in that role, I have to exercise constant care and be ever on the alert lest someone object to this or that! The glamour one sees from outside is only part of it, I'm afraid.'

And it was true: Richard enjoyed being with family, retreating into his true self as a lad of Somerset and not having to be 'on stage' at Court. Oftentimes he envied William his freedom to live always as he was, never playing a role, and yet he knew that even had he been given the choice, he would not have lived differently than he did.

Back at Court, Richard and Hellene would continue to participate in the drama of great events, and even to play a small part in history. Not long after they moved into their apartment at Whitehall, Hellene began making a large and elaborate lace ruff of gold thread for Her Majesty. Richard, seeing the work in progress, marvelled at his bride's artistry and patience no less than he did her ability to find the time amidst her many other responsibilities to craft such an intricately beautiful thing.

She had learned by way of palace gossip that the queen was soon to have a portrait painted. Many paintings had already been made of Elizabeth, but this one would be different. In the past, artists had fashioned their illustrations of the Virgin Queen from stylised models, and the results usually reflected a far more stern demeanour than the queen's true self, likewise showing a woman less attractive than the true Elizabeth. This time, however, she would pose for the picture in person - at least she would take out the time to model the face and hands.

In time the ruff was completed, and on a special Sunday when the queen attended the Chapel Royal, Hellene presented the gift to her as a token of gratitude for her friendship and special favours to the family. The queen was amazed at the beauty of Hellene's fine handiwork, and promised that it would be worn in the sitting for the portrait. When it was finished, the portrait did indeed show Elizabeth's true beauty, and because in it she seemed to be holding a rainbow in her right hand, thenceforth it would be called the 'Rainbow Portrait.' Elizabeth was very pleased with it, and she told Hellene that it would not have been nearly as fine a depiction had it not been for the gorgeous ruff.

And so a piece of his wife's work would live on long after he and she were dust; likewise Richard's writings now seemed spun from a mystic and immortal substance of which he could only guess the source. He became an inspiration to everyone he knew and met, and his acclaim - not only as a poet and dramatist, but as a man - spread far and wide. In characteristic fashion, his ever-heightening reputation served only to humble him, and as he'd learned to do long before, he deflected glory toward his queen and dear friend.

His life, not only the outward life in the Court but the inner one at home and the still more intimate one of his internal self, took on a new dimension. Words had renewed meanings, colours became brighter, and music seemed richer than ever before. All of his senses were keener, his insights sharper and in clearer focus, and this recalled Solomon's wise saying in Ecclesiastes: 'Cast thy bread upon the waters: for thou shalt find it after many days.' It seemed that the more he loved Hellene and gave of himself, the more his understanding and appreciation of the world around him grew. The more he released his dearest goods - his love and his talents - the more he found his treasury replenished.

All he had searched for and wanted throughout his life was here and now. His writings came more quickly, as though he had only to take time to set on paper the words running through his mind. A new flame burned within his soul, and he felt he'd become a vessel or channel through which truths and knowledge might spread to those around him.

This he thought, but he did not share his musings even with Hellene for fear she would think him mad. And yet he believed that she felt the same things for herself, and when finally he did find the courage to speak his thoughts, it was as though she'd only been waiting for him to say so. Yes, she too sensed that God had begun a special work through their two joined lives. How fortunate they were to share in that Divine love, and how richly blessed!

As with the inner life, so with the outer, and it seemed to Richard that he moved inexorably toward ever greater recognitions and honours. Though he had never studied law, because of his reputation he was asked to become an honourary member of Lincoln's Inn, an organisation for men of the legal profession. This was a great honour, and applicants had to formally prove their credentials both as men and as scholars by answering a series of questions.

When he appeared before the committee which would approve his membership, they asked only one question that troubled him slightly. Having inquired of his background in studies of jurisprudence, one of the men turned to him and asked, 'And your father, sir?'

Richard smiled slightly, then answered, 'He was a gentleman!'

The interrogator looked a bit puzzled for just a moment, then said, 'Oh, but of course - quite so.'

Sitting in that dignified anteroom with portraits of great barristers of the past adorning its walls, Richard had a waggish temptation to add, 'The King of England, you know.' He would have loved to see the reaction on that scrivener's face when he heard that!

18

By the end of their first year together, Hellene had presented Richard with a daughter, whom they named Elizabeth after the queen, but Richard would forever know her by her pet name of 'Lillibet'. The second year brought another daughter, and rather than make it too obvious that he was naming his girls after his sisters, Richard suggested the French version of Mary - Marie. In 1564 would come another little girl, whom they named Gwen for Hellene's mother.

Hellene had practically raised her younger siblings as a girl, and the presence of the child William had given her an opportunity to freshen her skills. Now all her experience stood her in good stead, and she proved herself an excellent mother. She was calm and serene with the children, and they responded to her quiet strength.

There was little of crying or bad manners in the Edwardes household, and other residents at Whitehall were amazed at how beautifully the children behaved. Hellene became quite used to the approving comments of neighbours and strangers, seeing her with her troop of baby girls led by the boy William. Nor did the sweet spirit of these children come from docility or any lack of liveliness; every day, weather permitting, they would leave the palace and romp and play outside the castle walls, thus expending the energy that might otherwise have troubled the other residents of Whitehall. 'Oh, they are perfect cherubim and seraphim!' one neighbouring matron always said, and Hellene would smile, knowing she'd brought the children up well in the belief that quietude and a spirit of fun could exist side by side in one personality.

As the oldest, William fell right into step, and became a great help in taking care of those younger than he. Hellene in turn treated him no differently than she did her own children. She praised him for his help with the younger ones, and he too responded to her gentle style of parenthood.

Richard's duties at Court often kept him away, but he almost always managed to find a few minutes in each day to take the children one by one and spend individual time with them. He hadn't been at all handy with babies and small children at first, having grown up so quickly in the Boys' Choir of the Chapel Royal that he could scarcely remember being a child himself; but soon he won their respect and deep love.

He was determined that his offspring should have the things he lacked, including plenty of time for play and exercise. Ever the consummate teacher, he would invent games to challenge their imagination, and whether in his study at Whitehall or on the green playing fields of the palace, he helped them to see learning as a game itself rather than drudgery. Studies as well as sports became affairs of competition, with the children each vying for their father's praise. He became their best friend, such that Hellene would often joke, when she saw him playing with them, that she had a fifth child to care for. Yet in spite of this chumminess, Richard had no trouble administering discipline when needed - which meant that he seldom had to do so.

Though such opportunities were not frequent, whenever possible the children were allowed at very short intervals to visit the queen. They always behaved with the utmost of politeness, and usually had some new treasure to bestow on their monarch: a poem filled with childish non-sequiturs or an endearingly ill-proportioned portrait. Elizabeth, smiling and clapping for these charming young performers, once observed to Hellene that if all children were so well-mannered, the world would become overpopulated in just a few years. 'But then,' she once added with a far-off look, 'these are special.'

Hellene, of course, didn't dare to ask why these children should be as special to the queen as they were to their mother. Though she'd never spoken of it again since her rather artless observation to Her Majesty some time before, she knew that Elizabeth's relationship with her husband had as its basis something deeper than the merely professional interaction of a monarch with a poet and priest. Of course she knew they weren't, and had never been, lovers, so that left only one other possibility for the intimacy she glimpsed when she saw their eyes meet. But she wouldn't speak of it now, not when there were so many other things to think of.

And so life went on for the happy little family, which with the passage of time became a happy big family. It delighted Agnes Edwardes beyond measure to watch her grandchildren grow up at such close range. When she'd first come to London with Richard, it had been a sacrifice, but by the time he married Hellene, she found herself hoping that her son's new bride would not expect her to return to Somerset now that she was no longer needed.

Indeed she was needed, and much loved, by her daughter-in-law. They laboured together over the many chores of running the household, and often when the children were asleep and Richard away, the two women would talk for long hours of many things. Hellene, who had to be a mother to so many little people, appreciated Agnes's willingness to mother her, and she found her a great help in times of trial.

Such a time, a near-tragedy, came to the family in the fall of 1562. Despite the fact that great epidemics raged not infrequently through the City of London, the children had all been healthy, with nothing other than an occasional cold during the winter. But one day William got caught in a sudden rain shower, and before he could be brought back to the apartment to change his clothes, he had become quite chilled.

Hellene wrapped a blanket around him and told him to sit in front of the fire, and he seemed to have recovered by the time she put him to bed. But by morning he was burning with fever, and complained that his throat hurt. Hellene made him stay in bed, and she and Agnes began a vigil, bringing him freshly made broth at meals and keeping him covered. He slept through most of this time, which stretched into days, but showed no improvement. In fact his fever became worse rather than better.

Richard was worried for his son, but when on the third evening of the boy's illness he received a summons to the queen's apartments to discuss a recent communique concerning Mary Queen of Scots, he had no choice but to do Her Majesty's bidding. Late that night, William awoke suddenly and called in an urgent voice for his mother.

A weary Hellene had gone into the next room to take a short nap, but she awoke instantly and ran to the side of William's bed. 'What is it, William?' she whispered. 'What can Mother help you with?'

'They won't let me have my turn,' he cried.

'Your turn? Your turn at what?'

'The angels are swinging down from heaven, and they won't let me have a turn to swing!'

Hellene stepped back in terror just as Agnes ran into the room. The boy had fallen silent, and she told her mother-in-law what she'd just heard, whereupon Agnes threw on her cape and bonnet and ran for the physician.

Recently they'd heard through palace gossip about a Dr. Burcot, a German, who was familiar with the most recent epidemic, but when Agnes got to his home, she learned that he was away on another call. She waited for what seemed like hours, wishing she could get a message back to Hellene and fearing the worst for her grandson, but finally the doctor returned and they jumped into the carriage to hurry back to Whitehall.

When he got to the apartment, Dr. Burcot quickly examined the boy and took particular note of his throat. By now Richard had been summoned, and he stood by the bed with Hellene and Agnes.

'Yes, it is the same with him as the others,' Burcot observed. 'I have seen this thing before, for there is an epidemic of smallpox in the city. I've already lost ten patients from the illness this week.'

'Oh, dear,' said Hellene, looking as though she might faint.

'But I've saved more than I've lost,' he added. 'There is an ancient Arabic treatment which as far as I know is the only cure, though I must warn that the sickness in the throat can result in a temporary loss of speech.'

'As long as the child is saved,' said Agnes.

'Yes,' the doctor answered, looking down at the patient. 'He is fortunate not to be more ill, and there is a critical point when the right steps will save his life. His fever will go higher still, and he will ramble in his mind and speech, so you must prepare for that. I would suggest that you give him cool liquids to drink to perhaps lessen the fever, and then all that can be done is to wait for it to run its course.'

While Agnes ran to get water, the doctor went on with his instructions to Hellene and Richard. 'When his fever has gone as far as it can, he will suddenly become very cold, and before that happens he must be wrapped warmly in red cloth and placed on a bed before the fireplace. That alone can save his life. If he survives that, he will get well, but I must warn you that you should prepare yourselves for the worst.' With that, the doctor took his bag and started for the door. 'Pray!' he said, turning back one last time. 'When all else fails, pray to God!'

Hellene and Agnes recoiled from these sombre words in horror, but Richard had heard the other half of what the doctor said - the half that held hope. The three of them took turns giving the little patient sips of cool water all through the night while the other two got down on their knees before God, and at a late hour Richard ordered the two exhausted ladies to retire. He pulled William's bed close to the fireplace and stoked up the fire to keep the child warm for the impending crisis.

Thus he sat through the long hours before dawn, his prayerful vigil recalling to him the agonising wait he and Robert Babb had endured on the night the boy came into this world. The room was sweltering hot.

Richard had stripped to his shirt sleeves, and the perspiration ran in long ticklish rivulets down his forehead and face. Every few minutes he would administer more cold water to the child, a sip at a time, and he piled more and more blankets on the little body.

As dawn was just beginning to shade the edges of the sky in purple, Richard got up and walked to the window to stare out at the sleeping landscape. Then he returned to the side of William's bed and gave him a few more sips of water. The slow progress of approaching morning would remove the need for the candle that had now burned down to a stub, and Richard blew it out.

He sat down and put his head back against the chair to rest for a moment. William's breathing had become more rapid and wheezing, but Richard was weary and needed an instant's rest. Before he knew it, he was asleep.

Suddenly he awoke with a start. The room was deathly quiet, and fear stabbed at his heart as he realised he didn't hear any breathing coming from the little patient on the bed. Richard rushed to his side, and in the wan light just before dawn, the child's face looked as white as that of a corpse.

'William!' he cried, grabbing his son's hand, and the lad opened his eyes. 'Oh, thank God!' Richard exclaimed, and when he put his hand on the forehead he discovered that the fever had broken.

Hellene and Agnes, awakened by Richard's cries, rushed into the room. 'Hellene, Mother!' he said breathlessly. 'He is well again - my son is well again!' Tears ran down his cheeks, and he clutched William in his arms.

The morning that followed was filled with the heightened joy that comes on the heels of great relief. William remained tucked in his bed, but now he had a great smile on his face as bright as that of the sun shining in through his window. The whole family sat in the room with him, laughing and talking, and every time someone stopped in to visit, Richard regaled them with praise for the great Dr. Burcot.

But then there arrived a messenger from the queen who had not come to check on the child, but rather to bring troubling news. Her Majesty had taken gravely ill herself, so ill she could not speak. Her physicians were quite sure she would die, and wanted to spread the word to all those close to her.

19

The queen might well have taken ill simply as a result of fatigue, for of late she'd faced concerns of the gravest possible nature for the kingdom and people of England. Two issues had occupied her attention almost daily from the moment the crown was placed on her head, though in fact they might be counted as one. First there was the urging of her advisors to marry and thereby provide an heir to the throne. Given her demonstrated unwillingness to accede to their advice on this, the second question was that of a likely successor in the absence of such an heir. Until now, Elizabeth had not been ill, but no one, not even the queen herself, knew what Providence might have in store for any mortal, and her own family's experience had proven the importance of arranging an orderly transition of power.

Now storm clouds had begun to gather from the north. Though many could have made a case for themselves as successors, in pure point of fact Mary Stuart, often called Mary Queen of Scots, had the best claim. Granddaughter of Henry VIII's elder sister Margaret (which made her Elizabeth's first cousin once removed), she was nine years Elizabeth's junior, but had reigned for much longer. Her father, James V, had died when she was six days old, and she'd been crowned queen. Her mother, Mary of Guise, a Frenchwoman who would rule as regent until the daughter reached the age of majority, had enormous ambitions for Mary, and in order to protect her, had sent her to France to live.

Mary grew into a beautiful young woman much praised by the French courtiers, and would not see Scotland again until 1561, when she travelled there as a nineteen-year-old widow following the death of Francis II. But before that happened, she would face her greatest adversary in the world, her cousin Elizabeth.

Despite the fact that Mary was tall and willowy, with an abundance of feminine charm that many claimed could never be captured in any portrait, in actions if not appearance she resembled her late cousin Mary Tudor. Like the other Mary, she had forfeited her chances at winning the affection of the English people by marrying a foreigner. Even more like the woman given the unfortunate appellation of 'bloody,' she had embraced the Catholic faith at the very time when most of England was moving away from Rome as quickly as it could.

What made Mary Stuart a grave danger to Elizabeth, then, was not her popularity but her propensity for intrigue. Her father-in-law, Henry II of France, had sought to have Elizabeth declared a bastard once and for all and to install Mary on a joint English-Scottish throne in London. In his palace he'd allowed Mary to quarter the arms of England on her escutcheon, the place where a monarch displayed his or her insignia. Even more pointed had been his commissioning a set of engraved plates that proclaimed Mary as the rightful queen of England, tableware from which he impudently served English diplomats whenever the latter dined at the French court.

The situation vis-a-vis France and Scotland did not look good for England. It would be relatively simple for French and Scottish troops, working in concert from Calais and Edinburgh respectively, to strike at England from the north and south. The English, caught in the pincers movement of their two historic enemies, would quickly be overpowered.

But there were good signs as well. Lord William Cecil had closely monitored the international situation, and in so doing had found that the Scottish nobles were becoming restive under the rule of Mary of Guise. He had quietly done whatever he could to inflame their discontent.

A part of his work was already being done for him, unwittingly perhaps and for religious and not political reasons, by the Protestant leader John Knox, who was stirring up his people against the Papist queen. And yet Cecil might have wished for some other ally, for he knew that his own queen detested Knox. In the year of her coronation, he had published his First Blast of the Trumpet Against the Monstrous Regiment of Women, an attack on both Marys and indeed on any other woman who presumed to lead men: 'Woman in her greatest perfection,' he'd written, 'was made to serve and obey man, not to rule and command him.'

Well aware of his sovereign's misgivings regarding the Scottish cleric, Lord Cecil forbade anyone to speak of Knox's involvement; yet he knew that Elizabeth had other reasons for demurring in the fight. To intervene in Scotland would constitute a violation of a kinswoman's divine right of rulership - the very right by which Elizabeth claimed her own legitimacy - and would therefore be a great and unpardonable sin.

After Henry II died in July 1559 of injuries sustained in a jousting tournament, and Mary's husband Francis began his very short reign, it soon became apparent that the Guise family were running France. Mary Stuart, at the goading of her relatives, became bolder, and publicly referred to herself as queen of France, Scotland and England. Lord Cecil learned from an informant that upon leaving a service at chapel, she'd been greeted by a crowd of well-wishers crying 'Make way for the Queen of England' - and she had not urged them to desist.

This intelligence broke down Elizabeth's last shred of resistance to the urging from Cecil and others that she intervene, whereupon she sent £3,000 to the rebellious Scottish nobles. Upon learning of this, Mary of Guise ordered the French ambassador in London to confront the queen with the fact, but in the absence of any proof, Elizabeth daintily parried his accusations. After the angry Frenchman left her presence, Her Majesty found herself hardly able to control her laughter.

Finally, on October 21, 1559, the nobles publicly stated that they no longer recognised Mary of Guise as their regent. Now the stakes began to escalate, and Elizabeth's representatives at the border anxiously watched for further evidence that the cold war with Scotland had heated up into full-fledged conflict. As though in confirmation, the French began to mass their troops along the line separating the kingdom of Mary Stuart from that of Elizabeth.

Initially the Queen's Council had not been informed of the financial aid to the Scottish rebels, but with news of the French build-up, it became necessary by the twelfth of November to apprise them of this. Soon afterwards they agreed to station 4,000 men at Berwick on the borders, with the Duke of Norfolk dispatched as Lieutenant of the North. Likewise the fleet was made ready, and on December 16 the Crown sent an experienced sea captain, William Winter, northward with official instructions to enter the Firth of Forth, seize the French ships, and blockade the area from possible French reinforcements.

Yet these events hardly meant that the queen and her most prominent councillor saw eye-to-eye. Cecil still believed that further steps needed to be taken and, in spite of opposition from many colleagues on the Council, managed to gain enough support to send the queen a message outlining the necessity for further reinforcements. Four days later the missive came back to him with the notation, 'Not allowed by the queen.'

Elizabeth's reluctance came neither from cowardice nor an excess of deference, but rather from her close scrutiny of the treasury, combined with her perception that the military was not prepared for conflict and that the results of a misjudgment would be disastrous. Her caution seemed warranted when soon thereafter the news reached London that Captain Winter had been successful, whereupon Elizabeth reasoned that enough had been done.

This unnerved Cecil, and in desperation he tendered his resignation. He gave it with his deepest assurances that he would serve his queen in any other capacity desired, but that under the prevailing circumstances, he could no longer continue as her adviser.

If he was bluffing, his bluff worked: in spite of her misgivings, Elizabeth relented at the thought of losing her advisor, and agreed to enter into a formal alliance with Scotland - that is, with the nobles and people. With the signing of the Treaty of Berwick, worded in such a way as to acknowledge Mary Stuart as Queen of Scotland - that is, it indicated that the military action was only to protect England against a hostile foreign power, France, and not to aid rebels against Queen Mary - she officially took Scotland into her protection.

But Elizabeth was, uncharacteristically, of two minds about the French, and to the consternation of her Council, she still attempted conciliation with Paris. Clearly the aim of King Francis was only to stall her until additional reinforcements could reach Scotland, but she nonetheless engaged in continued dialogue with his emissaries.

It was against this propensity for inaction in this particular situation that her councillors, led by Cecil, finally persuaded the queen to action. On March 31, 1560, an English army of 8,000 men under the command of Lord Grey crossed the border into Scotland, where they joined forces with the Scots. The enlarged force camped outside Leith, the port adjacent to Edinburgh, where Francis had based his troops. And yet Elizabeth persisted in stalling what by now appeared an inevitable war, refusing to permit her men to attack Edinburgh Castle, in which Mary of Guise had taken refuge.

Then on May 7, the combined English and Scottish troops stormed Leith, but the assault failed, resulting in the loss of 1,500 Englishmen and many more Scots. Upon first hearing of the setback, Elizabeth's reaction had been to fly into a rage, but on further consideration she determined that, having commenced the attack, the troops must now continue. Therefore she wrote to the Scottish nobles, assuring them that fresh troops and supplies would be immediately dispatched.

The latter arrived soon afterward, and the tide began to turn for England. Fortunately for the combined British force, France faced religious problems requiring a military presence at home, and this cut into supplies at Leith; soon a dispatch from the king in Paris gave instructions to his generals to begin peace negotiations. But before talks could begin, the English had another stroke of good fortune when Mary of Guise, the arch-predator, died on June 10. After much haggling, the two sides reached an agreement including Mary's renunciation of the Scottish throne and a complete French withdrawal from Scotland, which they formalised in the Treaty of Edinburgh, signed July 6.

The queen, at first so reluctant for war, now seemed to have joined in the spirit of things a bit too much. Lord Cecil was extremely disturbed when on the day following the signing of the peace, and in spite of England's poor military performance, Elizabeth demanded that the French return Calais (lost by her sister) along with £150,000 for damages. Fortunately for all, the queen's demands arrived too late to prevent the signing.

The French left, but Mary, on advice from her husband, did not ratify the treaty. When Throckmorton remonstrated to Mary's uncle, the Guisan Cardinal of Lorraine, the latter answered flippantly that such should be considered no great matter among friends. Further efforts to obtain ratification met with no better results, and the problem remained unresolved when Francis died in December 1560.

Besides making Mary Stuart a very pretty and potentially dangerous widow at the age of eighteen, this event left France in the hands of Catherine de Medici, who ruled as regent for Francis's brother Charles IX. With the Guise family now eclipsed by the Medicis, prospects for resolution seemed brighter - but the English did not count on the fact that Mary herself would elect to return to her native land. From the English side of the chess board, it appeared that the opponent had brought his queen over to the other side, with an eye on their king - who in this case also happened to be a queen.

Mary Stuart sent an emissary to petition Elizabeth for safe passage through England, and Her Majesty received the diplomat rather curtly, refusing to answer for her cousin's safety should she make an unnecessary English landing on her way back to Scotland.

Perhaps reckoning on her weak bargaining position, Mary determined not to make an issue of her journey, and arrived without incident at Leith on August 19, 1561. To the surprise of everyone, the lovely young queen met with a warm reception; emboldened by this, she turned her considerable charms toward the task of winning over the Scottish people.

Once safely ensconced in Holyrood Palace, she proceeded to conduct herself with great moderation and judiciousness, and openly declared a desire to make peace with England. To that end she sent an emissary, William Maitland, to negotiate with Elizabeth for a modification of the treaty: Mary would make no moves for the English throne, this revision stated, during the lifetime of either Elizabeth or Elizabeth's children if she had any, but upon the death of either, she would then be declared heiress presumptive.

In her discussions with Maitland, Elizabeth expressed her contempt for any other claimants, and admitted that she thought no one more worthy than Mary Stuart. However, the decision was not completely up to her. There was the matter of Henry VIII's will, combined with the desires of the English people, not to mention the fact that she might imperil her own fate once she named her successor. As example of the latter, she cited the way she had been treated by her sister where the succession was concerned.

Relentless and almost brutal in his pursuit of what he perceived to be his queen's interests, Maitland inferred that nothing would prevent Mary from taking what was rightfully hers anyway. Elizabeth, attempting to appease, went so far as to suggest that perhaps a council might review the treaty, then even suggested that the two queens meet in an attempt to resolve the matter.

Upon receiving this news, Mary was jubilant, but her advisors reluctantly pointed out that with all her charm, she was no match for the quick wit and cunning of the English queen. Besides, it appeared that the religious unrest in France might provide a proxy battleground to test Elizabeth's good intentions. The Queen's Council had repeatedly urged that she give aid to the Protestants in France, but she clung to the hope that Catherine de Medici would prevail, and therefore she would want to stay on the good side of the French Catholic monarchy.

Finally, negotiations proceeded to the point where a meeting between Mary and Elizabeth was arranged for some time between August 10 and September 20, 1562. An excited Queen Elizabeth began to lay out plans for great pageantry with which to impress her visitor, and the future looked bright.

But then civil war did break out in France as everyone had feared, and plans for the meeting had to be shelved. England would enter into the conflict on the side of the Protestants, and there would be no hope of rapprochement with Mary Stuart.

It was in the midst of these events that Elizabeth was taken suddenly ill with a fever. Upon hearing the news, Richard's first reaction was to fetch Dr. Burcot once again, but he suddenly realised that this direct approach might only lay his relationship with Elizabeth open for suspicion. Though recognised as a member of the Court and a poet, he had no reason or authority to intrude on the purview of Her Majesty's physicians; to do so, he would need the aid of someone more publicly recognised as enjoying the queen's trust.

He quickly decided on Lord Hunsdon, the queen's first cousin (and half-brother, though no one spoke of such), and after locating Burcot, the two men rode to the earl's house. Hunsdon had never put aside his unexplainable dislike for Richard, yet with the passing of years he'd become less pointed about it; in any case, when he learned the cause of the present visit, his concern for the queen caused him to lay aside any animosity he might have held, and he jumped into the carriage to ride with them to Whitehall.

By the time the three reached the palace, the queen's fever was raging, and she'd fallen completely unconscious. Hunsdon soon convinced the Court physicians to at least attempt to see what could be done for the queen. He had a pallet laid for her in front of the huge fireplace, which was soon glowing brightly with a brisk fire. Then the vigil began.

It soon became abundantly clear how close they had come to being too late, for within two hours the queen's fever had broken, and soon she regained consciousness and began talking. Not that her wits came back to her so quickly. She'd hardly spoken the name of Robert Dudley since the time she and he had parted ways following the sudden death of his wife; now in her delirium, she confessed her love for him, and made her ministers promise that when she died he would succeed her. The ministers, of course, promised anything to their queen, whom they still believed to be dying.

The others withdrew to the other side of the room to discuss the monarch's strange 'last' wishes, but Richard remained kneeling on one knee beside her, her priest and confessor there to comfort her. Elizabeth opened her eyes and for a moment gazed up at him blankly, as though not seeing him. Then in a whisper she said, 'How is it, dear friend, that you are always here when needed? What strange force guides you so?'

He smiled back at her without saying anything, for fear his words might be overheard.

'Richard,' she said, all formality gone in the levelling state of illness, 'am I going to live?'

Richard reached gently for her hand and said, 'Oh yes, my queen, you shall get well!' Glancing at the gaggle of advisors on the other side of the room, he whispered, 'But you must save your strength for now, and speak not. When you are better, send for me as you would your priest for confession, and then I shall explain what has been said, in the event others mislead you.' He lifted his eyes heavenward. 'Praise be to God for sparing His child!' He squeezed her hand and she smiled, then closed her eyes.

20

Elizabeth did recover, so fully that no one dared even bring up her bizarre deathbed confession, and in time she would commence another round of flanking movements with her cousin the Scottish queen. In the meantime, though, she showed her gratitude to Dr. Burcot for persuading the others that she could be saved by granting him a valuable parcel of land. As a personal touch, she also gave him a pair of golden spurs that had belonged to her grandfather, Henry VII. But she did not make him her Court physician, nor did she ever even see him again, for his very presence reminded her of the frightening days of her illness.

Richard brought Agnes and Hellene the glad news, which only added to their joy at seeing young William spared. But soon the two women began to wonder aloud whether or not the family should move outside the city for the sake of the children's health and well-being. Richard argued against this, for such a move would upset all their lives greatly, and living outside the city was no guarantee against illness. In time he prevailed, and the three adults agreed that the epidemic that had nearly taken the oldest child was but a singular event.

In June of 1563 the Edwardes family would again face tragedy, this time as the genuine event and not a dress rehearsal. On the twenty-ninth of that month a messenger brought word that Richard's brother William, godfather of his son, had died quite suddenly, apparently from a heart attack. Richard and his family immediately took a carriage to the home of his brother, for whom the almost-lost son had been named, to see what they could do for the family in their hour of grief. Elizabeth, the widow, had matters well in hand by the time they reached the house and, though quite obviously stricken with grief, spoke calmly.

'Brother, I know now how you must have felt when my sister died,'

Elizabeth said to Richard. 'You had so little time together! I wished then to make things easier for you if I had only known how, but I reckoned that nothing could lift the burden unless you alone decided that it should be lifted.' She dried an eye. 'William was a wonderful man, a good husband and father, and we shared many years. I can only be grateful for that. And he's left us well cared-for, so there will be no worries there.' She waved a hand at Richard and Hellene, who stood by with concerned looks on their faces. 'You must not concern yourselves. We will get along well - if not wonderfully, at least well. I know that if ever I need you, you will be there to help, and that is a very great comfort indeed.'

The two families continued to dine together on many a weekend, and Richard helped to fill the gap left for William's children by the death of their father. In time he became a hero to them, and he was happy he could be there.

At this time Richard and Hellene had four children besides the three adults living in the apartment at St. James. The married couple had their bedroom, William and Agnes shared a room, and the three little girls bunked together in one chamber, such that any further addition to the family would require changes in the living situation. Soon, however, Hellene discovered that she was pregnant yet again, and because they dared not impose any further on the Crown with the growing numbers of their burgeoning family, Richard and she knew that they would have to make a decision soon.

Two choices presented themselves, and neither looked particularly inviting. Either the family should move out of the palace and into a house with greater space, or Hellene and the children would have to move to the Edwardes' home at North Petherton. They lacked the funds for the former, so it would have to be the latter.

Thus by early fall, Richard waved good-bye to those he loved most dearly in the world. He did so with a burden in his heart, but he knew that he and Hellene had decided wisely. His prognostications about the unlikelihood of another plague sweeping through the city had proven wrong, for once again an epidemic had fallen on London. They dared not risk another child before the sword of the death-angel.

Likewise he knew that a great metropolis like London was no place for small children, who needed clean air and wide spaces to accommodate their boundless energy. At North Petherton, weather permitting, they could play outside all day long and thus expend the energies that might otherwise make them a challenge to their mother and grandmother. And indeed it did not take the children long to settle in at Agnes's home in the country, and William and his sisters found many new and exciting adventures among the forests and pasturelands.

Easy as this transition was for the children, it was not so for their parents. The youngsters would never know even how much their mother missed her beloved husband; less still would they have suspected the depth of the yearning their father had for his bride. Only the strength and depth of their love supported the two in this time of separation, and both consumed their minds with the duties and responsibilities of each day.

In spite of his longing for home - or perhaps because of it, and because of the diversion work offered him - Richard immersed himself in his duties. First there was the training of the children at the Chapel Royal, then there was his role as poet to the queen, and in the latter regard he now put the finishing touches on his newest play, Damon and Pythias. He had composed his own music for it and given extra attention to scenery and costumes, so much so that he believed it to be his finest effort yet, much more grand than anything he had ever done before.

He planned to present it to the queen on Christmas Day 1564 at Hampton Court, her favourite Yuletide venue. Hampton Court was built of red brick with accents of white stone, and had been a favourite residence of Elizabeth's father, who had added to its structure a great deal. Like others of Henry VIII's favourite houses, it had been built by a man who later ran afoul of the king - in this case Cardinal Thomas Wolsey - and offered up as ransom for the monarch's affections. (Henry later confiscated the Cardinal's London home, York House, renaming it Whitehall, and though he very much cherished the properties he'd appropriated from Wolsey, the man himself never regained royal favour, and died on his way to a trial at which he would no doubt have been found guilty.)

The queen was indeed pleased with the play, but not as much as she would be by the poem in her honour that he read after it was over. When he had offered up his tribute, which she better than anyone present knew to be a heartfelt expression of love and not the merely formal paean of a self-serving courtier, she sat almost motionless for a few moments. It might even have seemed that she was displeased, but in fact she was attempting to regain her regal composure enough to say, 'Yours is the greatest gift I shall receive this Christmastide, and I do give thee most earnest thanks, my true and loyal Master of the Children.'

The rest of the day was filled with much laughter, song, and celebration, and there was little time for Richard to think of his home in Somerset. Yet when the day was over, in spite of his triumph before Elizabeth, he could not help but feel the pain of separation from his family. The joy of the season made them seem further away than ever, and in his glum state he could only console himself with the dim possibility that he might spend the next Christmas at North Petherton. If it were to be, however, he knew that the plans must be made far in advance, and at a juncture when the queen's mood appeared most favourable.

In February he produced another play which met with great acclaim, but by then his thoughts were only of the trip home he would make in the first week of the following month in order to be present at the birth of his child. His plans were delayed a bit, but he arrived at North Petherton two days before the child, a boy they christened John Edwardes when he was born on March 15, 1565.

As ever, Richard thought like a poet, and therefore the Ides of March seemed a somewhat infelicitous choice; but the day was only two ahead of the feast to the great Irish patron saint, and that could not be all bad. The new arrival at the Edwardes home was a healthy little fellow, and likewise the mother recovered well from the delivery. She was soon out of bed and supervising the children, for whom the arrival of a baby brother had brought great joy. They all vied to hold him and play with him, but to do so they had to compete with the infant's father, who spent as much time as Hellene would allow holding the child and speaking softly to him.

As was always the case when he visited Somerset and home, the days flew by far too quickly for Richard, and soon the time arrived for his return to London and the duties awaiting him at Court. Before his departure, he arranged for Hellene and John to come visit him in London that summer, and this prospect made parting a little easier.

He threw himself so successfully back into his life at Court that it seemed a mere matter of days until the time for Hellene's visit. Once again he and she shared the apartment at Whitehall Palace, a place now imbued by time with the nostalgic sweetness a young couple feels toward their first humble nest. Their suite had remained unchanged as if she had never been gone, and though Richard had continued there without her, the place seemed to come alive with her once again in its chambers.

Hellene had often gone here in her mind during the long, lonely nights in North Petherton, and she relished the time spent with her husband. Before coming to London, she'd resolved that she would not let her thoughts wander back to Somerset, and though she missed the children, she knew they were in capable hands with Agnes.

Less than a week later, they went to visit the queen and present to her the newest addition to the family. Elizabeth had designated a time in the afternoon when they might have tea in her private sitting room, beyond the scrutiny of Court, and there they spoke to one another like old friends. The queen thought John quite handsome, and remarked that he resembled his mother more than he did Richard. Hellene, always one to speak her mind even with Her Majesty, insisted that his resemblance to Richard could also be found in the child's Welsh features, and this gentle advocacy of her husband greatly impressed the queen.

Soon afterward came the time when Hellene had to return to North Petherton and the children. By now Richard knew that Elizabeth would not cheerfully release him to go away for Christmas, and he dared not tax the queen's good will when he might need to prevail on it for some more significant cause. But Elizabeth herself had suggested that Hellene might return for the holidays without John or any of the other children, to enjoy a vacation with her husband amidst the festivities of Court.

Hellene should plan to come a month early, the queen explained, and it would be a particularly good season to come, because in November the Earl of Bedford's daughter, Lady Anne Russell, would wed Lord Ambrose, the Earl of Warwick. Most of the nobility of the land would attend the wedding at Bedford House, one of London's finest old manors, along with much of the royalty of Europe. Clearly it would be the crowning event of the social season, and Hellene would not want to miss it.

But Hellene's interests had changed greatly since her days as a lady-in-waiting, and she would gladly have traded a quiet Christmas with Richard and the rest of the family in Somerset for all the glittering fetes the royal calendar had to offer. Yet she could not help but think how pleasant it would be to have Richard all to herself at night; likewise she had to admit that she did find herself a bit intrigued with the idea of the splendid wedding and all the parties that would surround the occasion. One could certainly think of worse ways to spend the holidays.

So Hellene left for Somerset with the pleasant contemplation of her return some months hence. She brought with her small gifts for each of the children, and a new bonnet for Agnes which she had been assured was the latest fashion from Paris. For Hellene, their joy in the summertime was but a foretaste of Christmas to come.

21

Richard was ever aware of occasions when he might provide entertainment and amusement for Elizabeth and her Court, and the approaching wedding seemed an event worthy of his attention. In late August Princess Cecilia of Baden came to visit at Bedford House, and Elizabeth was invited by the earl to be there when she arrived. While the queen was away, Richard persuaded four knights of the realm that the wedding would provide an excellent opportunity for a tournament, with jousting and barriers. Having gained the knights' consent, he arranged for one of the finest saddle horses in the royal stable to be brought to him, and rode to Bedford house to seek the queen's approval in person.

He wore a new cape and a jaunty hat for the occasion, and had his best riding boots and spurs highly polished in advance. Even without this splendid apparel he made a handsome figure of a man, and with it he appeared as dashing as any noble who'd ever paid court to a monarch of England. The butler at Bedford House announced him grandly to the ladies in the beautifully appointed drawing room, and Richard entered in a flurry, then with a most elegant bow before the queen proposed the entertainment to her.

He'd taken a chance by coming here, for the queen might disapprove of his interrupting her visit to the earl. But it seemed the appropriate flourish with which to announce the chivalric events, and her response proved that he'd judged rightly. Elizabeth, thanking Richard for his kind and thoughtful act, gave her enthusiastic approval.

As the social season progressed that fall, the occasion of the wedding became the impetus for several grand balls and parties, a number of which Hellene was able to attend upon her return to London in November. The entire city was spruced up and prepared for a holiday season the likes of which it only rarely saw, but Richard, ever anxious to plan events that would delight the queen (and hoping to make Hellene's visit as spectacular as he could), proposed to Elizabeth a 'grande masque bal' with the theme *Great Figures From History.*

Richard's proposal pleased the queen, and it was determined the ball would be staged on the first Saturday in November in the great hall of Whitehall Palace. The latter was chosen because it provided the largest space for such an event, and though already the most handsomely furnished ballroom in the land, it was freshened with paint and polished to perfection for the great upcoming event.

The social season of 1565 had already proven one of the most festive and exciting anyone could remember, and the ball further intensified the excitement that snapped in the air. All of the Court and much of London thrilled with anticipation as time drew nearer the date.

The queen declared that she could only attend attired as a queen, but she kept the exact nature of her costume secret from all save Hellene. Glad to have her former lady-in-waiting back for a time and happy to turn her attention from the genuine drama involving her cousin Mary to the play-act of the costume ball, she confessed to Hellene that she planned to appear as Cleopatra, Queen of the Nile.

Hellene had an idea of her own for her husband's costume, but she first described it to the queen so that the latter would not take offense when her poet and courtier arrived as an emperor himself - and one who had wooed Cleopatra at that. Elizabeth thought the notion a splendid one when she heard it, so Hellene began to outfit Richard as Julius Caesar.

Richard, at Hellene's insistence, decided that he would go as Julius Caesar. She made him a costume of pure white linen heavily embroidered with threads of gold around its borders, and commissioned the queen's cobbler to make sandals heavily adorned in gold. For the crowning touch, she made a laurel wreath of gold for his head and fixed his hair to resemble illustrations she had seen of statues from Rome.

If he was to be Caesar, Richard proclaimed, Hellene must go as her namesake, Helen of Troy. Her long black hair plaited with chains of gold in the Grecian style - not to mention her beauty - would make her ideal for the role, and she sewed herself a gown of whitest linen resembling Richard's toga. The robe, which would fit quite loosely, she lined with cloth of gold, and on her feet she wore gold sandals as well.

The evening finally arrived and the whole palace was in a frantic stir of preparation. Since Richard had a commanding voice and the skills of a fine actor, he'd been chosen to announce the guests by their historic names as they entered the great hall, so he was the first to arrive that night.

Very soon afterward, the guests began to appear, a magnificent array of figures from the Bible and the antique eras, from Greece and Rome, from Medieval times and recent European history. Each courtier and lady of the Court had vied to outdo all others, and never had Her Majesty's ballroom ever shone more resplendently than tonight.

Elizabeth had elected to be last to arrive, and so had remained in her private apartments until she received the message that all guests were awaiting her entrance to begin the first dance of the evening. Suddenly two men dressed as Nubian slaves pulled back the curtains from the great entrance, and the Court gasped at what they beheld: Queen Cleopatra seated on a golden throne and borne on a litter draped in red velvet and cloth of gold, carried by four 'slaves.'

Everything about her glittered with regal magnificence. She wore a golden pharaonic crown, a gown of solid gold, and jewels more lavish than anyone had ever seen. Her make-up, expertly done, was in the true Egyptian style, and it was difficult for the witnesses to comprehend that this gorgeous Egyptian queen - who appeared to have stepped straight off a Nile barge, where she'd no doubt been feeding grapes to Mark Antony - was their own monarch.

The whole court burst into cheers, with many 'God save the Queen's'. The litter moved slowly and ceremoniously through the great hall, the whole Court continuing to applaud. Once the queen had stepped down from the litter, she raised her hand to silence them, and then after a long pause announced, 'If Queen Cleopatra is to open the ball with the first dance, I think it only fitting that her partner should be the very handsome Julius Caesar, first great man of Rome to fall victim to her charms.'

The Court burst into approving applause, for Master Richard was a respected friend to many there. He bowed deeply, proceeding toward the queen, and just as he took Elizabeth's hand the orchestra struck up the music for one of her favourite quadrilles. With that the unlikely-looking couple began to dance, and soon the other guests began to join them on the floor.

At intermission, huge banquet tables were spread with pastries and rich foods, and wine flowed with profusion. The queen scarcely sat out a dance, and each courtier vied to be her partner. Elizabeth was in high spirits, and she revelled in the attention bestowed by all, which appeared for once to come not so much from a desire to flatter as from genuine admiration for her beauty and splendour. It was indeed *her* party, and she was the most elegant hostess the palace and Court had ever seen.

Richard and Hellene received their fair share of the limelight, and were told repeatedly they were by far the fairest couple present. He could tell that his wife was having a wonderful time, and could see on her face that she recognised and appreciated the adoration of old friends.

The ball went on and on, and it seemed that neither the dancers nor the musicians would ever tire. Then finally came an intermission, and in the resulting quiet the clusters of partygoers lowered their voices. Suddenly the great clock in the hall struck three, and to her shock the queen became aware of the time. She'd been enjoying herself so much, and the evening had slipped by so quickly, that she'd not even had a moment to grow tired. She permitted one more round of dances and then excused herself to retire for the evening - a clear signal that the ball had come to an end and all must soon follow the queen's lead.

As Richard and Hellene made their rounds to observe that the work of the servants in closing down the great hall was proceeding as it should, for the first time they both realised just how weary they were. But before they kissed good-night, they agreed that their party had been the supreme event of the decade.

Soon afterward came the day of the great wedding. When the planned contests were ready to begin, Richard arrived on the scene amidst the trumpeting of large horns and addressed Queen Elizabeth, prominently seated in the gallery. If it pleased the queen, he announced, the knights would come forth and perform their endeavours for her amusement. She nodded her consent, and the tournament proceeded. The crowd, already inspired by the excitement of the day, was ecstatic over the entertainment, and both the knights and the man who had arranged their performance received hearty acclamations.

From the time of the wedding on through the Christmas holidays, London society remained in the most festive mood anyone could remember, and scarcely a week went by without a major social event. Hellene found complete acceptance as the elegantly beautiful wife of England's great poet, soon recognised by everyone of prominence in the city. Watching Richard entertain the most powerful men and women of the realm, she often thought how handsome he looked, and how exciting it had been for her to leave the pastoral life in Somerset for a time and once again play among the aristocracy.

Soon she would have to return to the children, but she ended up staying a bit longer than originally planned - long enough, in fact, to become pregnant again. She hesitated a bit before informing Richard of this, but decided it wouldn't be fair to wait and write him from the country, and when she told him he was delighted.

Yet he saw no reason at this early date to inform the queen. Looking toward their interview with as much hesitation as Hellene had in anticipation of telling him, he wondered what Her Majesty's reaction would be. Finally the two decided that he would make an appointment after Hellene had returned to Somerset.

When he and the queen finally talked, Elizabeth fell silent at the news. Richard studied her face for some discernable reaction to what she'd been told, but seeing none, he felt concern. Perhaps she would say that he must choose between being a family man or a courtier, in which case he knew how he would choose.

But her thoughts had nothing to do with him, and her concerns were only for Hellene. Though the young wife was a strong woman, Elizabeth said to herself, how much strength did she have? When she spoke, she said, 'Would the Master of the Children have to prove that he alone can populate the realm? Perhaps your visits with your dear wife should be a bit less frequent, if she is to live to see her children grown!'

For the very first time in his life - certainly in his relationship with the queen - Richard found himself embarrassed and, for the moment at least, without words.

The queen could see that her jest (at least it was partially a jest) had been taken too seriously, and now she spoke more gently. 'Dear friend, I did not mean to cause thee embarrassment - I spoke only in good humour. Pray tell me that the offense is not taken to heart?'

Of course Richard told her it was not, and then he smiled wryly. 'Perhaps the royal quip bore too much of truth. I can only hope and pray that the good Lord who has so richly blessed us has granted Hellene the strength that will be required of her.' His tone becoming more serious again, he added in a far-off voice, 'Without her, you know, all else would be for naught. Never did such a beautiful soul marry herself to one so undeserving, and I doubt I should ever again find one such as she, were I to lose her.'

Elizabeth considered his words thoughtfully, then she replied, 'My poet waxes much too plaintive and poor in spirit. You deserve that and a great deal more, Master Richard. Hellene is indeed a rare jewel, but she doth not shine more brightly than her husband.'

Richard thoughtfully replied, 'I thank thee, but your poet is merely a poet, one who makes pretty phrases with words. Though he may have the lineage of a king, if I may but poorly quote the words of my queen, there is only one in this room or the realm with the stomach to rule, to say nothing of the strength, unselfishness, and wisdom to do it well. A poet may speak of stars and, if he be ever so fortunate, touch them from time to time, but only the noblest may dwell among them and shine as brightly. And your name and destiny, noble queen, was written in the stars which dazzle us from on high, but shine not brighter nor more fair than thee.'

'The poet does this queen too much honour,' she said with a soft smile, 'but I know the heart that inspires the words, and I would never question their sincerity for one moment. I give thee thanks and more. I know not how Fortune has blessed me so well, not just for your words, but more for you; I give thanks to One far wiser than I. Go now before more words do spoil the perfection of this time.'

And so he left, stirred in his heart with love for his queen, who he treasured more highly than any other woman on earth save his wife and his mother.

22

As queen of England, Elizabeth had much that demanded her care, but perhaps the biggest cross she had to bear was the Cross of St. Andrew, symbol of Scotland. Negotiations with Queen Mary had broken down with the outbreak of civil war in France, actually a series of skirmishes between Protestants and Catholics that history would remember as the 'Wars of Religion.' In this, one of the great conflicts of the Reformation, Phillip II joined Catherine de Medici, who actually ruled France through her weak son Charles IX, and the powerful Catholic families of that country, including the Guises, against the Huguenots, supported by England and various German states. For Elizabeth, it amounted to a proxy war with her cousin Mary, or rather with the powerful forces behind Mary, who wanted to gain Scotland to Catholic advantage.

But the venture had so far not paid off for the English. England had performed the unlikely service for France of uniting its various nobility in national and religious fervour against the anti-Papist forces from the isle of Britain. When the French called for withdrawal of the English troops, Elizabeth had to request additional money for the beleaguered Protestant forces from a hastily assembled session of Parliament.

The latter seized the opportunity to attack once more the unpleasant matter of succession, but Elizabeth managed to dazzle them with a shimmering golden cloud of words. Thus she got her money while postponing yet again the sticky question of who would follow her to the throne.

Then the English venture in France took another, quite unexpected, blow: a sudden outbreak of the plague among the troops. With so many men dying from it, additional reinforcements were sent, and these too became sick and died as well. Elizabeth finally took her losses squarely and recalled her soldiers, who returned to London and promptly infected the city with their illness; 21,000 people died in the capital alone, and untold thousands more in the countryside.

The First Religious War ended in March 1563 with a nominal victory for the Protestants, but by now Elizabeth had learned her lesson about foreign wars. Never again would she indulge in such reckless forays, nor again would she go to the aid of others for religious reasons.

Turning her attention closer to home, she found a disgruntled Lord Cecil. It was not good to have so wise and powerful a man disaffected, and his grievances were several. First of all, she had rewarded others for their services in the diplomatic flanking-action with Mary that had taken place over recent years, but not him.

Second, she still seemed to toy with the subject of marriage and suitors, never deciding on any one but never publicly declaring that she refused to ever marry. Cecil wished to make an advantageous marriage for her, and certainly she had no shortage of kingdoms being offered. For awhile she'd even considered a union with Charles of France, but that would have created more problems than it solved. At other times she received proposals from the kings of both Denmark and Sweden, and even from Ivan IV, known as Ivan The Terrible, of Russia.

Cecil must have felt as frustrated with his queen as had the French ambassador, whom she exasperated by stalling her reply to his monarch's proposal for eighty days. When the man pointed out that God had taken only six to create the world, the coy queen had observed that He was far wiser than she. Clearly no one would rush Elizabeth to a decision - or sway her once she'd made one.

Thus the third of Cecil's complaints, her continued infatuation with Robert Dudley. In spite of their separation in recent years, she had made her true feelings quite apparent in her deathbed delirium, when she'd promised Dudley the succession to the throne. Of course such would be impossible: though of course Cecil didn't know it, Richard Edwardes had far more right to succeed her than Dudley, and there was not a shadow of a hope that even he would take her place, much less the Gypsy.

But then in 1564 Elizabeth had hit on a fanciful and imaginative idea that must have pleased Cecil very much. She'd thought for some time that it would be ideal to see her cousin Mary wed to a loyal Englishman who would prevent her from doing anything rash in her bid for the English throne. Now she realised that the man should be Robert Dudley!

Thus not only would she thereby disavow any claims on him for herself, but she would show her desire for amity with Mary by proffering something which she very much treasured for herself. (As for Dudley's feelings at the prospect of being put up for trade like a farmer's daughter, he was not much questioned. In any case, he would have said he'd suffer anything for Elizabeth - and there could be worse fates than marriage to a pretty Scottish queen.) Without naming the gentleman in question, Elizabeth sent her ambassador to Edinburgh to bandy the idea about, and Mary expressed only mild interest.

At that time the Queen of Scotland was attempting to negotiate a marriage with Don Carlos, son of Philip. Though Don Carlos was no prize, it would be a brilliant political arrangement very advantageous to the Queen of Scots, and she pursued it until her talks with the Spanish court ran their course. Then Mary sent word to Elizabeth that she wanted to learn more of her offer.

Elizabeth bestowed the title 'Earl of Leicester' on Dudley to increase his appeal, then announced the man's identity to Mary. When Mary learned that the gentleman proposed was Elizabeth's cast-off suitor, she was not the least amused. Once again the two cousins were back to searching for common terms of discussion.

Next it was Mary's turn to make an overture. In the early fall of 1565, she sent her trusted emissary, Sir James Melville, to visit her 'dearest cousin, the Queen of England.' Though as ever suspicious of Mary, Elizabeth's curiosity about her had always been ardent, and she was glad to learn what she could of her from Melville.

Therefore the unfortunate man was subjected to a barrage of questions concerning his queen. At one point, Elizabeth asked him quite pointedly which of the two he judged to be the fairer. It was a cruel demand, seeming to offer no good answer: did he say Mary, and thus offend his hostess, or Elizabeth, and thus brand himself a traitor to his own queen? But with a wisdom and politesse that proved the wisdom of Mary's trust in him, he replied, 'Your Majesty is the fairest queen in England, and my queen the fairest in Scotland.'

This, however, did not quite satisfy Elizabeth, who then inquired which of them was taller. This time he responded quite factually that Mary was the taller of the two. At this Elizabeth retorted, 'Then Mary is too high, for the Queen of England is neither too high nor too low, but rather the exact and appropriate height for a queen.'

'It is as Your Majesty says,' Melville replied, and if her words amused him, he did not let it show.

Persisting in her inquiry, Elizabeth demanded to know what type of exercises Mary enjoyed. Lord Melville replied that his queen loved to hunt, and that sometimes she recreated herself by playing upon the lute and virginals. But she played only 'reasonably for a queen,' he said, and at this the Scotsman's hostess smiled ever so slightly, as though to herself.

Later that day and after dinner, Lord Hunsdon drew Melville to a quiet gallery in the palace. There he heard sweet music emanating from another chamber, and was told that it was the queen playing upon the virginals.

He had not listened long when he pushed aside the tapestry that hung before the door, and could see Her Majesty seated with her back toward him. He tiptoed into the room, staying at a discreet distance from her, and listened raptly. But then with a start the queen quit playing and wheeled around to see who had intruded on her solitude.

From her appearance, at least, she seemed surprised to see that it was Lord Melville, and she jumped up and strode quickly toward him as though to strike him. But instead she sat down abruptly on a low cushion, and the startled diplomat knelt beside her. Then in the most offhand voice, she inquired whether his queen or she played best.

'My gracious Queen Elizabeth,' gushed the enamoured Melville, 'my queen is but a student by comparison to you. The reports do not do justice, I fear, to your mastery of the art.'

Thus having won her victory, the queen was quite pleasant to Melville for the rest of his visit, and did not mention Mary again while he was there. Melville became further impressed with the Elizabeth's skill as a diplomat and the quality of people she'd placed around her at Court, and he returned to Scotland with glowing details on all he had witnessed. He considered himself most fortunate, he announced to his sovereign, to be a friend of the English queen, and he felt indeed sorry for anyone who became her foe. Therefore he advised Queen Mary to be very circumspect in her dealings with England, for Queen Elizabeth ruled more capably than any king ever had.

Elizabeth hadn't yet given up on her idea concerning Dudley and Mary, and Lord Cecil suggested a good candidate to conduct the negotiations on his behalf with the Scots queen. Henry Stuart, Lord Darnley, was Mary's cousin, like her descended from Henry VII. He was tall, athletic, delicately good-looking, and commanded enormous confidence from those around him - considerably more than his nineteen years would seem to merit.

But instead of wooing her for another man, Darnley won Mary for himself. Or rather Mary, his senior by three years and much the more mature by virtue of her widowhood and station, won him. In any case, they married in July 1565 against the wishes of nearly everyone on the island of Britain, including Elizabeth.

Whether Darnley was a man of low character or intellect was hard to say, for he appeared lacking in both areas, and to say that he was boorish in his role as royal consort is a gentle way of putting it. He had himself declared joint ruler of Scotland, and offended Mary's entire court with his presumptions to rulership and his rakish, spendthrift ways.

Mary's mad affection soon turned to hatred, and as carousing husbands often do, Darnley began to suspect her of adultery. He blamed her secretary and confidant, David Rizzio, an Italian Catholic, and so managed to stir up the nationalistic and anti-Papist fervour of the restless Scots noblemen that together they signed a pledge to murder Rizzio and uphold Darnley as the rightful heir to the Scottish throne.

Cecil learned of the plot in early March 1566, but events happened too fast for Elizabeth to prevent these treasonous goings-on. Three nights later, Darnley and a group of assassins entered a room where Mary and Rizzio and others were having supper, grabbed the queen, and dragged Rizzio out and stabbed him to death - stabbed him, in fact, fifty-six times. Mary fled into the arms of the Earl of Bothwell, and though she returned to Darnley for a time, their marriage never recovered.

It was against this background that on June 19, 1566, Mary gave birth to a son, James. Darnley would claim the child to be Rizzio's, but in any case he was surely Mary's, and Elizabeth consented to become the godmother. She had to send the Earl of Bedford in her stead to the christening, for she'd already begun one of her annual progresses around the English countryside. The circumstance made for a fitting contrast between the tragic Scots queen and her triumphant English cousin: while the one fought for her life against hostile nobles and a conniving husband, the other turned her attention to the serious - and very political - business of pleasure.

23

It cost a veritable fortune to maintain the royal household and Court, and when Elizabeth ascended to the throne of England, she found a treasury nearly depleted by the extravagances of her predecessors. So it became her custom to leave her own palace with an enormous entourage, usually in the summer, and go on long 'progresses' throughout the land visiting her lords. These men, many of them far wealthier than she, would of course be compelled to make an honoured guest of the queen and her entire retinue, and what is more, any earl or marquess considered himself in competition with all others to make her stay at his estate the greatest of the trip.

The progresses, conceived with characteristic shrewdness by Her Majesty, served many purposes. They allowed the queen to show herself to her subjects as she passed through the countryside, the common people being more inclined toward loyalty to a visible queen than one who stayed always in London; likewise her visits had a similar effect on the much more powerful occupants of the local manor house in each shire. Moreover - and this was one of the principal purposes of these trips - they relieved her of the financial burden of feeding and keeping up her own household. Instead, her hosts would consider it an honour to provide food and lodging for the entire Court, with their more than 300 cartloads of baggage. Given that this was no ordinary visit, the long tables of the estate would be laid with the finest delights that part of the country had to offer, and after the royal party had eaten their fill, they would expect entertainment fit for a monarch.

Just as there would be no question of serving them cold mutton, so for entertainment a serenade played by a handful of itinerant musicians pulled in from all parts of the county would not suffice. Elizabeth expected to be honoured whenever she travelled, not only with banquets but with gifts and pageantry. Thus whoever sought to please her had to somehow work in a flattering allegory illustrating her magnificence and beneficence, and allegories came no more cheaply than sumptuous feasts: one noble thus graced by a visit from his queen complained that a single evening's entertainment and food had cost him seven hundred pounds.

Therein lay by far the cleverest facet of the progresses, a tribute if ever there was one to the wisdom of Her Majesty Queen Elizabeth. Courtiers vying for her favour would practically bankrupt themselves trying to outdo one another, and thus the queen kept these potentially dangerous men from accumulating too much wealth and prestige even as she obtained for herself and her household a night's or a week's or a month's worth of free room and board.

With the new year 1566 Elizabeth began to form plans for two of her great progresses through the realm. The first would take place in early summer, when the weather in London began to get humid, and would take her northward. She would stop first at Kenilworth, the estate of her perennial favourite, Robert Dudley, now the Earl of Leicester; and from there she would journey to the Earl of Warwick's castle. Then in late summer she and her court would go through part of the Midlands, returning from Oxford by the first of September.

By informing her hosts well in advance, which she did at the time of the Grand Masque Bal, she knew that the two would take extra pains to outdo one another, thus assuring her of great entertainment and gifts. Both earls, well aware of Richard's talents and his abilities for staging events to the queen's liking, separately sought him out in secret to assist in the planning of their respective entertainments.

Meanwhile, preparations for the early summer progress continued at Court, and on the first of June the enormous retinue of 300 carts, hundreds of servants, and scores of courtiers began winding its way out of London. Everyone was in high spirits, anticipating the events and stops that lay ahead, and it was such a gloriously beautiful day that the queen ordered a picnic in the countryside at noonday.

For reasons of nostalgia on the part of Her Majesty, they spent their first night at Hatfield House. Though this property belonged to the queen herself and thus did not constitute a visit to someone else's house, she had not been there since her coronation, and wanted to see it once more. Besides that, it presented a convenient spot easily reached on that first day of travel.

Soon they arrived at Kenilworth. Elizabeth as yet had no idea that Leicester, with Richard's assistance, was going to stage some of the most elaborate entertainments she would ever see, but perhaps she would have expected no less from two of her most favourite men in the world.

The theme of the extravaganza would come from Greek and Roman mythology. Among the highlights of the pageant were an eighteen-foot-long mermaid and an artificial dolphin, from whose back the Greek mythological figure Arion would appear.

Arion of Methymna in Lesbos, a poet and musician who flourished about 600 B.C., is one of those figures who emerge somewhere from the muddle between myth and historical fact. He is believed to have invented the dithyramb, a hymn originally in honour of Bacchus, composed in an elevated and wildly enthusiastic style, and the name Cycleus given to his father indicates the connection of his son with the 'cyclic' or circular chorus of the dithyramb. Arion played in the court of Periander, the tyrant of Corinth, who loved his court musician like a brother. Therefore when Arion wished to go to Sicily and compete in a contest of musicians, Periander tried to dissuade him out of fear for his life. But Arion went anyway, won the prize, and was on his way back across the Aegean on a Corinthian vessel when the sight of his treasure aroused the cupidity of the sailors aboard the ship. They resolved to possess themselves of it by putting the musician to death, for if he lived they knew he would tell Periander.

Arion, as a last favour, begged permission to sing a parting song, and the sailors, desirous of hearing so famous a musician, consented. So the poet, standing on the deck of the ship fully dressed in minstrel's attire, sang a dirge accompanied by his lyre, then threw himself overboard.

But instead of perishing, he was miraculously borne up to safety by a dolphin who he'd bewitched with his music. The creature carried him to the shores of Corinth, from whence he made his way to the palace of his protector. After Periander learned what had happened, he bid Arion hide himself until the sailors arrived, and when they did, he asked the whereabouts of Arion. They replied that they'd left him back in the city of Tarentum, whereupon Arion showed himself to the terrified pirates. Periander would have had them executed, but Arion wanted not their blood, and so they were banished; some legends say that later his lyre and dolphin were translated to the stars.

The idea was Richard's, and Leicester, well aware of the queen's interest in the myths of the ancients, considered it a splendid one. Watching his queen's eyes as she observed the epic entertainment that night at Kenilworth, he knew that he - and Richard, of course - had done well. The latter had written most of the pageant, including a heroic speech for the actor playing Arion to give while standing on the giant dolphin's back, but this part was not to go as planned.

The poor actor, unaccustomed to the Court and overawed at the queen's presence, spoke only a few of his lines, then suddenly pulled off his mask and proclaimed that he was not really Arion at all, but only 'the plain Harry Goldingham.' The queen was hysterical with laughter, and later said it was the best part of the whole pageant.

And indeed it must have been, for she seemed to notice little else that night, including the colossal mermaid. Turning to Richard, she said, ' 'Tis a pity that your efforts were marred by the simple actor, but in truth his honest fumbling did eclipse your genius, I fear.'

Ever gracious, Richard said, 'Had I thought the queen would be so amused, I should have written the scene that way. In any case, my goal is achieved.'

Elizabeth smiled and nodded at him with a sideways glance, as though to show that she was impressed. 'The poet is too modest, in spite of possessing the agility of an acrobat in accepting the turn of events.'

Soon after this, it appeared that all Leicester's grand efforts were nonetheless in vain, for Elizabeth's visit to Kenilworth was nearly spoiled by an unfortunate rumour concerning Dudley himself. Lord Leicester, she was told, was engaging in a flirtation with her cousin Lettice Knollys. This made the queen furious, not only because she resented any attempts by courtiers to conceal their trysts from her, but also because of her jealousy and continued affection for Leicester. Therefore she announced her intention to cut short her visit.

Leicester was in a panic, and quickly sought Richard's assistance to assuage the queen's anger. When Elizabeth emerged from the house to go hunting, she was met along the way by 'Sylvanus,' who represented all the inhabitants of the forest. The woodland creatures, he told her, were heartbroken to learn that she had thoughts of leaving so soon. His pleas were followed by music, then another figure came forth and introduced himself as 'Deep Desire.' The latter, begging her forgiveness, professed his enduring fondness for the greatest queen of all time. All this, a product of Richard's imagination as much as Leicester's desperation, served both to amuse Her Majesty and soften her heart, so she consented to stay.

But a time would come when they would have to leave Kenilworth on the queen's bidding, and sooner than later. Permanent homes had permanent privies, but here among the tents that housed the royal party and the servants, the only available facilities were those dug by labourers. Elizabeth had a very highly developed sense of smell, and the sensation created by so many bodies, both human and animal, in such close proximity was nearly unbearable.

Besides, she was ready to move on to Warwick Castle, where the earl had made elaborate plans to outdo Leicester and thus win favour with the queen. Often referred to as 'the King Maker,' Warwick possessed an enormous fortune, with land holdings in many shires throughout England. He was known to have in his employ the finest French chef in England, and he spared nothing in putting on a series of feasts Her Majesty would not soon forget; likewise, knowing the queen's love of music and dancing, he staged a great ball and several evenings of entertainment.

Warwick knew yet another device to please his queen, and after she'd been at his castle for some time and had proclaimed her intention to depart soon, Warwick announced that the next day he had planned a special event in her honour. Whatever it was - and he would not say - it had never been done for her before, and following this event would be the most elaborate feast the Court had ever seen.

This excited Elizabeth's curiosity, and though she knew Richard had helped Warwick concoct it (whatever it was), she did not pull him aside and demand to know the secret, for she loved surprises - so long as she knew them to be pleasant ones. When all had gathered following lunch, the earl announced that there would be a series of races on horseback: two groups of twelve would compete, and the winners from each would race one another in the grand finale, the prize to be a beautifully tooled saddle of the finest leather.

Though it was not uncommon for horsemen to challenge each other to prove whose horse was the fastest, never before had such a contest been planned on this scale. The queen was quite pleased, especially when she learned that the Earl of Leicester, who still held the title 'Keeper of the Horse', would make a surprise appearance in the first race, and that Richard was an entrant in the second with one of the finest stallions from the royal stables.

Warwick had selected a site not too distant from the castle, where spectators might have a fair view of most of the race. It would take place over a two-mile run, and the crowd would wait at the starting and finishing line.

The first group of racers was soon in place, and with a blow of the bugle the competition began. By now many of the courtiers had immersed themselves into the spirit of the event, and placed bets on one or another of the riders - particularly on Lord Leicester. Those who supported him judged well, for though the results were close, Leicester proved the winner.

After a short period of time for the crowd to calm down a bit and the first contestants to clear the area, the riders and horses for the second race assumed their places. Again the horn sounded, and they were off. This time even greater wagers were made, and to the dismay of quite a few, not as many of them as had bet on Leicester bet on Richard - and he came in first.

It being deemed only proper to allow the winner of the second race and his horse time to recover, Warwick had seen to it that refreshments were brought in from the castle for the spectators. During this intermission the queen, with flushed face and a giddy tone of voice, appeared as animated as anyone could remember. For her the race had taken on much greater significance than she would have guessed at its commencement: her horse would run against Leicester's, and the two men she loved most dearly would compete with one another to honour her.

It occurred to her to wonder why no one had ever thought of such an event as this until Richard suggested it to Warwick. She had the finest horses in England - why should they not stretch their mighty legs and run to her glory and amusement? Ever the businesswoman, she reckoned too that there could be money made for the treasury from it. Once again, Master Edwardes had exercised wisdom in his choosing.

The betting went on with increased vigour, and the intensity of the crowd's interest had worked up to feverish levels by the time Richard indicated that he and his mount were ready to take on the Earl of Leicester.

The horn blew and the two competitors were off and running in a thunder of hooves that drowned out the sounds of cheering and animated speculation. It appeared from all vantage points that the two horses were quite equally matched, and that the contest would be a close one. And indeed Richard was a fine horseman, though in truth few men in the kingdom could rival the Keeper of the Horse. But as they neared the finish line, it appeared that the queen's stallion had taken the lead by a head.

What had happened was the result as much of Leicester's shrewdness as of Richard's horsemanship. Holding a slight lead over Richard a moment before, the thought had suddenly flashed through Leicester's mind that if he won this race (which he wanted very badly to do for his own reputation), he might further displease a queen still smarting from the rumours at Kenilworth. Instead, since Richard already had a slight lead, he could allow Edwardes and the queen to win without diminishing his own quiet knowledge that he could have taken the victory had he wished. And so Richard on the stallion raced across the finish-line a full length ahead of Leicester.

Elizabeth was ecstatic - she had beaten Leicester, and now she wanted to see for herself how the preening Gypsy would react to defeat. The queen made her way toward the stallion and Richard, calling, 'Master Richard, you are a genius indeed. Your queen salutes and thanks you!'

By this time Leicester had brought his horse around to concede defeat to Richard and the queen. 'My Lord Leicester,' she said triumphantly to him, 'how does it feel to be only the second-best horseman in England?'

'Your Majesty,' he said with a flamboyant bow almost as defiant as her taunt, 'never have I, your humble servant, entertained doubts as to who rules England in all areas. I am proud to be first after the queen!'

'The Lord Leicester is chivalrous, indeed,' said the queen, giving him her hand, 'and surpasses the queen's expectations in humility. I must admit that I am rather proud of you, and consider that those who speak not well of you might take a lesson from thee!'

Leicester, realising that he had been the true victor of the day in more ways than one, was at least as pleased as the queen herself. Later, when they had returned their horses to the stable-boys and were walking back to the main house, Richard said to Leicester, 'Begging your pardon, my lord, but why did you let me win the race?'

'I am sure,' said Leicester, looking down at his gloves with a private smile as he took them off, finger by finger, 'that if Master Richard will give it more thought, he can divine that answer for himself.' With that he excused himself and went to meet a retinue of admirers gathered to congratulate him on his fine showing.

The Court, freshly attired and perfumed, assembled that evening for a sumptuous feast, one with which Warwick quite exceeded all prior expectations of his hospitality. The queen wore a gown of black velvet overlaid with pearls and silver, and her hairdresser had adorned each of her curls with a large pearl.

But Warwick had more to offer her: at the height of the evening's festivities, the earl presented his queen with a strand of pearls so gorgeous and so valuable they might truly have served as a king's ransom. Awed by the gift, Elizabeth was most effusive in her gratitude, and it was clear that this had sealed Warwick as the winner of the prize for the better progress.

Leicester, among the revellers that night, stared philosophically into his glass. He knew - and Elizabeth had confessed as much to Warwick - that the absence of unpleasant rumour here had contributed mightily to her pleasure. If by losing the race Leicester regained a place in his queen's favour, this mattered most.

The partygoers feasted and drank well into the night, celebrating what all knew would long be remembered as one of the greatest progresses ever. But at some point in the late hours of the evening, the abstemious Elizabeth and the homesick Richard both found themselves apart from the revelry.

A soft breeze stirred, and the stillness beckoned quiet and contemplative souls to stroll beneath the star-studded canopy of the heavens. After only a few steps they had quite left behind them the noise of the banquet hall. Before them lay the majesty of a kingdom far greater than Elizabeth's, the jewelry of the heavenly hosts arrayed on the purple sky, and the two drank in the magnificence of it in silence.

Elizabeth was the first to speak. 'Seldom can I talk with my brother as I wish, and I fear that I do not express how I feel toward you often enough. With you it is as family, family that I never knew before; with you the queen can lay down the crown, the jewels, and the pretences of state, and be simply Elizabeth Tudor, sister and friend. In being so, all is understood.'

'It is the same for me, dear Elizabeth,' said Richard as they walked quietly under the dark sky. 'Though we two be a great deal alike, we must play different roles when others are about, so that none glimpses this bond between us or suspects its source. Sometimes I regret the burdens I bring on myself by choosing to live in London while my wife and children remain in Somerset, and then I remember that only in such a disguised state can I best serve my sister and queen. I must confess that sometimes I wish it were not so, but then when I consider the admiration I have for you, it seems a mere pittance to pay.'

'I know not what I might have done without you, Richard,' the queen replied with emotion in her voice. 'You give me strength by your own strength, and from your love I receive something I have never had before, and which I may never know from any other man.' She turned to him in the moonlight. 'You know that I am as desirous as any lady of the realm to know the love of a good man, not for reasons of favour or position, but for myself alone. And yet such is denied me, in part for the welfare of my people - my children, as it were. And so when I feel lonely, I content myself with having your presence near.'

They fell silent for a while, then Richard said, 'England is fortunate, indeed, and yet methinks how ironic it is that our father wished for a male heir when now his daughter holds the reins of state more firmly, and steers the course far better, than any king e'er did. I am sure 'tis proud he would be of such an heir as thee.' He smiled at her, and she smiled back gently, then he went on speaking. 'As for the king's issue for years to come, that too is hidden from the world, but in being so disguised they may accomplish more than the fetters of position and fame might allow.'

'And indeed it gives me comfort that the legacy goes on, even if those living who know of it are few and must remain so,' she said earnestly. She went on in a wistful voice while Richard listened in silence.

'Sometimes, dear brother, it is with envy that I view your life. I remember full well the pain of having been raised a motherless child, with a father who cared for all else above his own daughter. I learned early to rely on no one save myself, and though 'twas a lesson well learned for one who would aspire to the throne, never was it to my liking.

'To my loneliness was added the knowledge that always I must appear as other than I might feel myself to be, ever putting on the mask of the royal personage when I am but flesh-and-blood woman like the rest!' She chuckled without humour. 'I find it ever a mild jest that many call acting a low trade, for if so, then we of the monarchy purvey the lowest of vocations. We are actors all, playing roles assigned to us at birth by the issue of royal blood. Though our palaces be of stone, in truth they are of glass, that others may see in on us at all times.

'And because we live our lives on a stage, we are expected not to feel emotions, but only to portray them - and then only as appropriate to our station. Most times we cannot afford even to seem as though we feel, and thus we are ruled by our position as much as we appear to reign over the kingdom. The Holy Writ informs us that from those who are mightily blessed, much is expected, and yet I wonder myself betimes whether this destiny be truly a blessing or a sentence passed by the tribunals of custom.'

She stopped and thought a moment, then stood straighter as though in resolve, and said, 'But I wax too plaintive - whether blessing or sentence, I have ever been well-prepared to meet that which is asked of me, and it was this to which I was born and for which my mother sacrificed herself.'

Turning toward Richard for a moment before walking on, she said, 'I have digressed mightily from that which I set out to say, which was only that knowing you as my brother has made a great difference for me. The love and true friendship we have shared makes me more content at the prospect of never sharing more with another.' And then she stiffened, as though preparing to assume yet again her formal role of queen with subject, and concluded: 'You have served your family, your queen, your sister, and your country with great excellence, and I do humbly thank thee.'

Richard shook his head and smiled. They had come now to a stop for a moment under an oak tree, its green leaves shimmering gently in the evening breeze. 'Mine was, as your task before you has been, that which I was meant to do. Though I knew not our father even as well as you, I believe I understood his wishes, and that I have honoured them. I thank my sister and queen for helping me to respect those wishes, and if I have served thee well, then I am pleased and content.'

From the well-lit house they heard sounds of laughter and music, which jarred him back to the moment. 'And now, begging your pardon, we must go back to our respective roles. May God continue to bless you and give you the strength and wisdom you must have, and may you always know in your heart of hearts that Richard loves thee and will always be there to help in whatever way is needed.'

These soothing and true words now spoken, brother and sister left one another with dear feelings in their hearts, and returned to the stage to enact the roles which destiny demanded of them.

24

Richard did not travel with the Court on the progress, but proceeded directly to Oxford to prepare there for the queen's arrival on the last leg of her journey. He had written a new play, *Palamon and Arcite*, which he knew to be the finest he'd ever composed, and he would stage it in two parts for Her Majesty upon her return; but between now and then, he had much work to do.

While Elizabeth and her Court enjoyed the beauty of the Midlands, Richard laboured feverishly for the perfection he demanded from this, his finest work. He had a new stage built, and the hall at Oxford was meticulously refurbished, including extensive gilding of the ceiling and walls to make them resplendent and sparkling for the queen's visit. By the end of August, the place hardly resembled its former self, having become like a woman who puts on makeup and jewelry to beautify herself.

He also brought in the children of the Chapel Royal Choir, many of them players in the new drama, for they needed to rehearse in the setting where they would perform for the queen. To them, it was a fine treat indeed to be freed from their duties in stuffy old London and sent to the country with Master Edwardes.

When the royal caravan reached the city, Richard came out to meet them. The queen had a retinue of guards and footmen around her carriage, but when she spied Richard, she beckoned him come closer.

'Your Majesty,' he said, doffing his hat grandly, 'your humble servant is pleased to announce that the theatre awaits the queen's pleasure.'

Elizabeth looked him up and down with a maternal eye. 'Methinks my poet has grown thin. We hope he has not paid too dear a price for the queen's amusement!' Glancing ahead down the road, she said tiredly, 'It has been too long since the queen has looked upon her poet and friend, and I thank you for your efforts. I hope that we may visit soon, but for now the queen must find a bed that does not move.'

The royal procession went on to an open field where tents and pavilions had been raised, resembling a small city, for the Court's accommodations. Meanwhile Richard ran quickly to the hall to see to the last details.

The next morning, the first day of September, he again visited the queen. She appeared a bit pale, and joked ruefully that the progress had been too pleasurable, and extended over too long a time. But she was pleased to see Richard, she said, and she had much to tell him of the Court's experiences over the past few weeks.

As fatigued as she seemed, Elizabeth teased Richard slightly: 'It would seem that my poet's renown has quite spread throughout the kingdom. My lords and ladies were disappointed that you were not in our company, for they hoped to be entertained by you. But I assured them that they would see you on the next visit - perhaps in the spring.'

'And I pledge that I shall be there,' said Richard.

That evening the players presented a work entitled *Marcus Geminus* for the queen. Though this entertained Her Highness, she was disappointed it was not one of Richard's originals, and commented on that as she left that evening. Richard reassured her that the play had only been chosen to give the cast a chance to become accustomed to the stage before they performed in his own drama the next evening.

Everyone at Oxford, perhaps more anxious to see the queen than the play, had turned out for the evening, and the enormous crowd greatly taxed the facilities of the hall. At one point Richard thought he could hear the floor joists groaning from the weight placed on them, but he dismissed the fear as evidence only of his exhaustion.

But the throng grew even larger the next night. Every area which would accommodate a human body was taken - even a staircase leading to the balcony that overlooked the hall. As they waited for the queen to arrive and the drama to begin, the people talked noisily among themselves, and there was a palpable sense of excitement building in the place.

Suddenly the staircase collapsed with a heavy groan, pulling a section of wall behind it and on top of the people who only a moment before had been waiting with expectation for the play to begin. Playgoers in the other areas rushed toward the doors, but when it became clear that the whole building was not about to cave in, this stampede subsided, and Richard and others began working hurriedly to clear the wreckage.

The death toll was not nearly as bad as it could have been - two Oxford fellows crushed under the debris - and Richard guiltily found himself thinking more about making the area presentable before Elizabeth arrived than about the men who'd died. He had worked hard for this moment, he thought, and he didn't want anything to mar his queen's enjoyment of it.

Just as the hastily assembled crew was removing the last of the debris from the fallen section of wall, a trumpet announced the arrival of the queen.

She was soon seated, and the audience quieted for the beginning of the play as though nothing had happened. Soon they were all so enthralled by the drama that no one thought either of things that had happened before or indeed of anything but the events on stage.

And then the curtain came down, ending Part One of *Palamon and Arcite.* The queen and commoners stood in a rousing ovation to the players and to Richard, who could only think that if the first half pleased them, they would be thrilled by the second half.

But before that could happen, on the next day, word arrived from the queen that she was not feeling well and could not attend. Therefore, she said, the play should go on without her, and she would see it another time. But Richard, determined as Jacob wrestling the angel, was not to be defeated; therefore he announced that the second half of the play would be performed an evening later, so that the queen might attend.

It was a daring step, for it disappointed the crowd and did not at all ensure the presence of Her Majesty. He knew that if she refused his offer he would have to take her at her word, but instead she came as requested, and the delay only enhanced the anticipation of the audience to see the completion of the drama. Now they sat spellbound as the climax and the denouement of *Palamon and Arcite* unfolded before them.

When the curtain finally fell, the entire hall was silent for one long, thunderous moment - long enough for Richard to wonder if he'd failed miserably. And then the crowd jumped to its feet in a spontaneous explosion of applause and resounding bravos.

Richard had accomplished his dream: he had written and staged what he knew to be the finest work within him, and he had pleased the audience mightily - not to mention his queen. As she was leaving, he approached and with great ceremony knelt before her. 'I am very proud of you, my poet friend,' she said with a proud smile. 'In London you shall find a reward that I think will be much to your liking.'

Richard answered that to have pleased her was reward enough. Then, because he had to rush off to congratulate the players himself, he promptly forgot her promise.

The following morning the queen attended St. Mary's Church for disputations. As she was leaving, Richard suddenly appeared at her side along with Professor Etheridge, his former teacher of music at Oxford. Etheridge had a newly acquired book of Greek verses that he wished to present as a gift to the queen, and this pleased her greatly, for even now she kept up her Greek in what few quiet moments she had to herself.

In introducing them, Richard told the queen that Professor Etheridge had been his master at Oxford.

'He was your Master, you say,' she said with a mischievous smile. 'Then certainly he did not give thee whipping enough.' She joked this way lest she seem too flattering toward her poet, causing others to wonder at their relation to one another; in that joking lay a bond of camaraderie, as though they were only a boy and a girl, brother and sister.

25

The first two weeks back in London were busy with settling back into normal routines of life after the disruption of the two progresses. During this time, Richard saw little of the queen, and when he did, she seemed preoccupied. But he dismissed this observation with a silent rebuke to himself for not taking her circumstances properly into account: Queen Elizabeth had a great many demands upon her time, matters of state that weighed heavily on her, and could hardly be expected to devote all her attention to him.

But the news of Richard's triumph in drama had preceded him to London, and had he known what the other courtiers knew, he would have realised that his queen was even more pleased than he at the success of his play. For some time, she'd been planning to honour him, and now seemed a fitting opportunity; certainly all agreed that few in the realm could be found so deserving as Master Richard Edwardes.

One day the queen sent word to him of an upcoming occasion at Court she wished him to attend, after which he would report his observations to her. Such requests were not unusual, but her reticence as to the exact nature of the event itself was. A somewhat puzzled Richard sent back a message that of course he would do anything his queen wished, and he promised to appear before her at the appointed hour.

When Richard entered the throne room, he became suddenly aware of the large number of courtiers present. In fact the entire Court, attired in their finery, had assembled. But before he could take full stock of this, the queen stood up and said in a stern voice, 'Master Richard Edwardes, it is the queen's pleasure that you come kneel before her!'

Everything seemed odd, and as he walked forward he wondered what wrong he could have done to earn such a haughty address from Her Majesty. But he did as he was told, and as he knelt down, the queen turned to Lord Leicester and bade him bring her the sword of state.

It seemed unbelievable to Richard that he should be punished, yet he could hardly think himself deserving of any honour.

But then Queen Elizabeth, speaking still in that imperious tone that now revealed itself as the solemnity reserved for a great occasion, said, 'I dub thee Knight of the Realm.' She lowered the sword first to one shoulder and then the other, then ordered: 'Arise, Sir Richard, and let the Court note that he is thenceforth to be addressed as Sir Richard, and Master Richard no more!'

For the first time Richard raised his eyes toward the queen. He felt a trace of a tear in them, but in no other way did he betray the emotions that swirled within him. Elizabeth met his gaze for an instant, and in her look he saw that she was as moved as he.

'Her Majesty does do her humble servant great honour,' he said when he could speak. 'May her servant ever prove his worth for the honour she has bestowed on him today.' Then in a louder voice he said, 'God bless Elizabeth! God bless the queen!'

At these words the Court burst into loud applause, which did not subside until the queen raised her hand to speak, announcing that they would forthwith celebrate the knighting of Sir Richard Edwardes with wine and pastries.

For the next few hours, Richard was surrounded by well wishers, but during this time he received a note from the queen inviting him to a quiet supper in her private chambers. Immediately afterward she excused herself, as always a clear signal that others should follow, and Richard soon made his way to her quarters.

The queen met him with a warm smile. 'There is more than I dared speak of before the Court,' she said, beckoning him to sit down. 'What I plan to do further is none of their concern, though in truth 'tis no more than I have done for others. But still, I wished that no suspicion of motive should be borne of it.'

She turned toward Richard and, sounding as though she were describing the joys that awaited at Christmastime, said, 'There is a large estate in south Wales, which from what I hear rivals Whitehall, and it has returned to the Crown. The place is called Edwards Hall, named long ago after Edward III, and with it goes the entitlement of baron.' Richard nodded slowly. He knew the place well, and he remembered what he'd said to Hellene as they rode past it: 'I feel strangely drawn...' Elizabeth waved a hand.

'Now, this is not so great a rank, I know, but in any case when time has elapsed and arrangements have been made in secret, Edwards Hall shall belong to you and your heirs.'

She paused grandly, and Richard thought he should speak, but he didn't know quite what to say. 'Your Majesty...'

'You interrupt, and your queen has not finished. Now, as you may recall, one behest we in England received from Edward III was the Order of the Garter, and in the spring when next there is an installation of men to the Order, you shall be among them. Think not that this comes from aught other than your talents, or is other than the just reward for your efforts.'

'And,' she went on, not allowing him a moment's comment, 'as a further token of my esteem for you and not mine alone but all England's I have had a banner made which shall hang in Westminster Abbey after you receive the Garter. It bears your arms, Sir Richard.' And with that the queen summoned a lady-in-waiting to hold up a richly embroidered piece of heraldic tapestry for Richard to see.

Richard recognised it immediately as the ancient arms of the Edwardes family, showing a lion rampant azure on a field of ermine. The upper left hand corner contained a canton with a golden double headed eagle on a field of crimson, the Blewitt family arms. But atop the shield was something new to him, and he didn't know what to make of it.

Elizabeth supplied more than enough words for both of them: 'It was my intention that nothing about the arms should imply the truth of your birth; however, it would not be appropriate without at least some subtle recognition whose meaning only you would know. Since your mother's family came originally from Normandy, I chose to have the mantling done in a French style, resembling a gold frame, into which are woven six Tudor roses. No one will notice the symbol in such ornate mantling, and thus the arms itself remains unmarred.'

Richard, having finally regained his composure, knelt and said, 'I am overwhelmed by your kindness and generosity, Your Majesty. The words 'thank you' seem inadequate would that you might truly know what is in my heart!'

'Now, now, my poet has knelt enough for one day,' she said, laughing, and then more seriously: 'Worry not, Sir Richard. The queen has always known the things you could not say. And all this is but little I have done. If it pleases you, and I can see that it does, then that is all the queen need know.'

'Perhaps some day I may.'

She held up a hand. 'No more, Sir Richard. You have earned this and much more. Speak not of it again, lest you make the queen displeased that she did not do more.'

'Yes, your Majesty, as you wish.' Richard returned to his suite at Whitehall with joy in his heart but no one with whom to share it. His only regret in the midst of all this had been the absence of Hellene. He dared not write her with all that the queen had told him, for someone in the palace post might read the letter. And so he had to celebrate in solitude, and in the midst of such great joy he felt an enormous sorrow and longing for his wife and children and mother far away.

Elizabeth knew of Richard's desire to return to Somersetshire to be with Hellene for the birth of his sixth child, and in the weeks that followed she toyed with him a bit about his wanting to leave the Court again so soon. Then just when he'd about given up hope, she informed him that she would like to go in late October to the royal hunting lodge at Huntworth in Somerset. Teasing yet more, she asked if he thought he might be able to take himself away from his husbandly duties for a time to accompany her on the hunt.

Richard, of course, was delighted at the news, and immediately wrote Hellene of his intended visit. Time flew by quickly as he prepared for an early Christmas with his family, for he knew that by taking his leave from the hunt, another holiday absence would not be possible nor would he have wanted Hellene to travel to London so soon after giving birth.

The queen, still mindful of her weariness at the conclusion of the recent progress, had elected to take a royal sailing ship around the coast, thus saving a goodly amount of time and difficult travel. The royal party sailed from London on the last day of October and, the weather being fair, rounded the southern coast of Britain within a few days and soon made Somerset. The latter lay across from Cardiff, Wales, on the great bay formed by the Bristol Channel, and the slowed pace as they entered the bay only heightened Richard's anticipation.

As soon as they landed, he made ready to leave for his home while Elizabeth and the rest travelled directly to Huntworth. He would have to return to the royal lodge on the morning of the fourth day, when the hunt would begin, so every second between now and then was like a grain of gold in an hourglass of diamonds.

Stopping at a stable near the port, he had been let a horse, a handsome gray named Sebastian. Richard had always been kind to animals, knowing them to be placed under man's care by the Almighty, but now he dug his heels into the creature's side and slapped its ample rump from time to time, urging it on. In a cloud of dust and a clatter of hooves they raced over green hillocks, through impossibly narrow hedgerows, fording icy streams whose water the galloping beast splashed up as high as Richard's waist. Soon Sebastian, snorting and blowing, was charging up the hill before Halswell Hall, to the sweet little cottage behind it.

When Richard got down from his steed, he found five little people absolutely ecstatic at the appearance of their father, so much so that Hellene and Agnes could only stand back and smile and watch as the children gathered around him. At the evening meal, when all were seated around the family table, Richard told them of his triumph at Oxford and about the gifts from the queen. The whole family rejoiced, but none more profoundly or with deeper gratitude than Hellene. From the house in Somerset on a clear day they could see the coast of south Wales: soon they would move there and to a palace at that!

Hellene knew how richly her husband deserved the rewards he'd received from his queen, and yet the abundance of it brought to her mind a question she'd long held in abeyance. Even in her days as a lady-in-waiting, she had come to guess that the two had more between then than only the admiration of queen and poet. She felt no jealousy, sensing that such had no place, and besides she had a suspicion she knew the bond between them. Perhaps, she thought, she would ask him someday, but not now; there would be plenty more years to speak of this and a thousand other questions, and for this evening she wanted only to savour the happiness of the moment.

The next three days sped by at a full gallop. Richard husband, father, son, friend was home, and the family needed nothing more than what they now shared. On the last evening, before the children were tucked in bed for the night, he told them a story. In fact it was a shortened version of the next play he planned to write, of which he had only a few lines composed; the rest remained a vision in his mind. Yet he knew that his youthful audience would tell him truthfully if it were a great tale or only middling, and from their rapt expressions, he knew he'd not fallen short of the mark.

At about two in the morning, Hellene wakened Richard to tell him that the time had come for the birth of their child. He wasted not a moment in rushing for the midwife, and was soon back with her. He had scarcely settled down in the kitchen with a cup of hot milk when the cry of a newborn split the stillness of the night. When he was allowed in to stand at his wife's side and see the child, he saw it was a fine healthy boy. Hellene, beaming up at him even more overjoyed than she was exhausted said she'd made up her mind firmly that the infant's name should be that of his father. To this Richard conceded without much persuasion.

Dawn came quite quickly after the child, and with the crowing of the cock a weary Richard knew he must leave his family now. Every longing still held him to them, like the heavy bonds of slumber that would have dragged him down to his pillow if he'd paused for a moment of this long morning. But he knew his duty to the queen, so he fondly kissed Hellene, who had fallen asleep, and then walked gently down the stairs.

Although he lost not a moment in preparing for the hunt, by the time he'd saddled his favourite horse, mounted, and begun riding toward Huntworth, he was an hour later than he'd planned to be.

The queen and her party had risen at dawn and prepared for the long awaited hunt. The cooks had been alerted, and a large English breakfast had been prepared, for the sport might well last until late in the day. When they had done with breakfast, the horses were brought round, and the Earl of Leicester (who had joined the royal party this year, along with Lord Hunsdon) chatted animatedly with Elizabeth as they awaited the arrival of Richard Edwardes. Off to the side stood the rest of the party, phalanxes of noblemen and courtiers and servants, and a battalion of baying hounds.

'And so I said to the duke,' Leicester was saying to a bemused queen, 'begging Your Majesty's pardon, it being an old turn of speech from the country roundabout' Suddenly he stopped in mid sentence, irritated to have his witticism interrupted.

'What is it, Master Bartram?' Thus the queen in a sharp voice addressed an insolent looking courtier who had approached the two of them on horseback.

'Your Majesty,' said the lad, trying to appear contrite, 'my apologies for the intrusion, but I must inform you that the hounds are becoming restless. Lord Hunsdon,' he said, pointing toward the impassive figure on horseback a great distance away, who stared ahead of him without expression, 'says they're at their best for the hunt right now, and we would do well to begin ere long.'

Elizabeth turned a sarcastic eye in the direction of the loud dogs, ignoring Hunsdon himself, then said to the young man, 'Your queen thanks you for this wisdom.'

Here in the country and on the hunt, the ordinary rules of Court life were loosened somewhat, and certainly the lad would never have dared to so intrude on a private conversation of the Queen's if they were in London. But even so, she was displeased with him, and she let it be known from the look she gave him. The boy rode away and, when he thought the queen couldn't hear him, shouted to Hunsdon, 'We must wait yet longer, my lord.'

Rather than using the roads, Richard had upon leaving the Edwardes home started out across open country. It was much shorter to reach Huntworth that way, and he was anxious not to delay the hunting party any more than he needed to. Again the horse, which had rested up with the other animals in the stable behind Halswell Hall and taken his fill of hay and oats, found himself pushed to gallop at full speed. The queen could not be kept waiting.

Meanwhile Hunsdon, clearly irritated at having to wait (and for Richard Edwardes, of all people!), challenged Bartram and others to compete in an archery contest. So the courtiers began shooting arrows at a target from a short range, a diversion that brought much laughter and merriment from both the lads and the earl himself.

But still the young men longed for the real hunt, and Bartram cursed Richard for taking so long. Realising Lord Hunsdon had heard him, he looked up with an apologetic expression, but the earl put up a hand as though to say no apology was needed. Scanning the horizon, Hunsdon exclaimed that he saw a deer among the trees. Quickly Bartram, eager to please, drew his bow, and a moment later an arrow went flying in the direction of the creature that he too had sighted.

Just then Richard emerged from the forest at the edge of the clearing, waving to the Queen when suddenly he was struck through the chest by the ill fated arrow. He reeled for a moment, still mounted on the horse named Sebastian, and then fell to the ground.

26

Elizabeth's keen eye had missed nothing. In an instant, she had mounted her horse and, soon followed by Leicester, rode quickly to where the young courtier stood, his bow still in his hand. 'Stupid fool!' she snarled. 'God may forgive you, but as He is my witness, never shall I.' The young man stared up at her, stunned at what his excess of choler had wrought. He looked toward Hunsdon, but the latter had lowered his eyes. 'Your days at Court, perhaps even England itself, are finished!' the queen went on. 'If Sir Richard is mortally wounded, your rashness will cost you your head.' She cast a rueful glance over the miscreant. 'Not that such would be a great loss.'

Other hunters in the group had mounted their steeds and joined Elizabeth and Leicester as they rode in haste to Richard's side. He seemed to be reviving a bit, and he was bleeding only lightly, not gushing: clearly the arrow had missed his heart. In fact the weapon had made a clean penetration, and its head poked out menacingly through his back. She rushed instantly to Richard, then turned around and began giving orders. 'We must get him quickly into the lodge and summon the physician!' she said in a panicked tone.

Leicester, who had his wits more about him at the moment, said, 'Your Majesty, we must first remove the shaft. 'tis plain to see that for the best part his vitals have been missed, and the head of the arrow is still intact. That's good, and we must now quickly rid him of the shaft and pray that the bleeding subsides anon.'

Elizabeth stepped back and let Leicester, who moved with the speed of a seasoned soldier and surgeon, begin to work. First he gently broke off the sharp head, careful not to move the shaft that pierced Richard's body. 'This may hurt a bit, Sir Richard, but I shall be quick about it,' he said gently to the patient, who lay on the ground breathing in gasps. 'Are you ready?'

Richard, too weak for words, only nodded. Leicester gripped the shaft from the tail end and, with every ounce of strength he possessed, pulled it swiftly and surely out. The shaft, soaked in blood, came free with the first try, and though its removal must have hurt like the worst tortures in the Tower of London, Richard gave no evidence of it with word or look.

'We must get him into the lodge,' said Leicester.

'No!' Richard said, struggling to breathe and talk, each syllable a distinct exertion. 'I must be taken to my home. My wife has given birth this morn, to a boy she's named Richard. I must be there. She needs me now.'

Elizabeth pulled Leicester aside and said in a muted voice, 'He is as stubborn as ever any Welshman has been. If he says he must go home, go home he will, with or without our help.' She leaned closer and whispered fiercely, 'Robert, you know how best to do it. Be about preparing the way, there is no other hope. He may not live, but come what may, we can't deny a man the right to see his wife and children at a time such as this.'

While Leicester rushed to do her bidding, Elizabeth returned to Richard's side and began to make small talk in hopes of diverting his thoughts. Richard, though he was the one in mortal pain, hastened to assure her that things would turn out right, that she must not worry or in any way blame herself. Soon Leicester returned with haste, bringing with him a large wagon filled with hay over which soft linens had been spread. 'The hay will soften the jolting a bit,' he explained to the queen. 'It was the best I could think of in the moment.'

Elizabeth squeezed his hand. 'You are ever worthy of all my trust, Robert. Now go, whilst I return to the lodge and take on more suitable attire before I follow you there.' Leicester turned to go, but she called him back. 'Take care of your cargo, my lord,' she said, her eyes gleaming. ' 'Tis more precious to me than gold.'

Leicester mounted the seat by the driver, and four of the young courtiers climbed in and sat at the corners of the large wagon. Just as they were about to leave, another man ran alongside. It was Lord Hunsdon, and he had tears in his eyes. He had never cared much more for Leicester than for Richard, but in the shock and sorrow of the moment (for he had never guessed that the 'deer' he'd spotted was a man), all that was forgotten. 'Robert, may I come and give my assistance as well?' he asked. Leicester nodded, and Hunsdon, as he had once joined Richard and Dr. Burcot on the night they saved the queen's life, climbed onto the makeshift ambulance.

Slowly they began to move. Hunsdon looked back with concern at the patient, but by now Richard was unconscious. It took so long for the slow moving wagon to reach the Edwardes home that Elizabeth had time to change, and on a fast horse she raced ahead of them and reached the house some minutes before the patient. Word had been sent ahead, and a room had been prepared adjacent to Richard's and Hellene's bedroom. The local doctor was there, and Hellene lay abed in the adjoining room with the door open, listening fearfully to every word spoken.

Hunsdon insisted on taking the place of one of the courtiers, so he and three other men carried Richard on a makeshift litter from the wagon to the room. Once the patient had been placed on the bed, the surgeon moved quickly, cleaning the wound and applying dressings, all the while giving instructions to Agnes, who stood by with a worried look on her face.

Once he had done all else he could, the doctor pulled a small vial of smelling salts from his bag and moved it gently beneath Richard's nose. Richard responded slowly and weakly, but soon became alert. The doctor instructed him that he must not move at all for the next few hours lest he cause further bleeding. Clearly the physician was optimistic, and indicated that in the absence of ill fate, Richard's chances were quite good.

Soon the doctor had driven everyone (even the queen) from the house, and Agnes brought in to Richard a cup of herb tea sweetened with honey, an old remedy often used to soothe and induce drowsiness. She was about to leave when she saw that Hellene had got out of bed, put on her robe, and moved toward Richard. Though her daughter-in-law had no call to get up so soon after her delivery, Agnes knew it would be foolish to try to stop her, so instead she stopped and watched them in silence.

Hellene slipped quietly to the other side of the bed and held Richard's hand in her own, pressed tightly to her cheek. Thus she sat for a long time, until Agnes quietly slipped out the door.

When next Richard awoke, it was to the face of his beloved, his courageous wife. 'Dear Hellene,' he said, 'should you be out of bed so soon?' She did not reply, but only placed her small and delicate fingers to his lips as she had once done so long ago. Then it had been to stop his torrent of words and emotions on first confessing his love; this time it was only to tell him to lie very still and think of nothing but his body's healing.

The next day Richard seemed to be improving, and he ate some broth Agnes prepared for him. He asked his mother for paper and a pen, for he had been dreaming, and a poem had come to him that he had to write down while it was fresh in his mind. Though many lines long, he wrote it quickly and without pausing long to search for the right words.

Soul's Knell

O Lord that rulest both land and sea, even by thy heavenly power,
grant I may pass these raging seas, now in this happy hour;
For as the deer that seeth the dart his death doth dread full sore
so do I fear the winds, the sea, and too the drenching shower.

But if thou wilt my course to fade amidst the drenching waves,
I yield my spirit to thee, O Lord, that all the world saves
And to the fish I give my flesh, a worthy food to be,
and rue the time that happens thus, my country for to flee

For lo, even now my ears do hear how these same waves do roar
that shall forth drive my drenched corpse unto the sounding shore
And there some man shall see me lie upon the shining sands
and thus shall pray unto the lord with lifting up his hands

O Lord, my friends and children all guide with thy holy hand,
and grant they flee the raging seas and die upon the land;
For so even here I see one lie while he this race did run
amidst the cruel seas he caught his end, alas, too soon

It is, alas, a rueful thing to see this woeful sight
make thou, O Lord, his silly soul partaker of thy light
And I to show the fervent love I bear to Christian blood
here will I take the corpse unknown and wind it in a shroud

And bring it to the holy church, the Christian rites to have
and so within the hallowed ground will put him in a grave
Upon his grave shall stand a stone as witness of his case
and shall forbid all such as sail to attempt that dreadful place

Thus shall I die, thus shall I lie, this is my destiny
but woe is me that shall give cause each one the seas to flee
and rue the man that framed the ship whereby we cut the seas
to see the countries far apart, our fancies for to please

But woe is me yet once again that thus shall lie unknown
and shall not place my wretched course under some English stone.
O Lord, why dost thou take me now amidst the drowning seas
and shorten thus my springing youth and so my pleasant days?

But now, O Lord, but now I say begins my youthly prime;
take me in age and let me live as yet a longer time,
That I may wail my wicked ways and too my wanton will
and learn to hate all earthly joys of which I had my fill

But woe is me, I pray in vain, even clean against thy will;
for in my sins and wickedness, O Lord thou wilt me kill.
Thy will be done in land and sea, to die myself I bend;
O death come now, for God my Lord appointed me this end

O death, how sharp art thou to such as are in tender age
which by repentance think at length, their sins for to assuage.
But die I must undoubtedly, what need I further talk,
and in the salt sea flood my corpse unto the shore shall walk

I yield my spirit into thy hands that died upon the rood
for thou hast bought me, God of truth, even with thy precious blood.
I am beset with sin, alas, I am the child of ire
keep thou, O Lord, my silly soul from everlasting fire

In thee I trust, O Lord, thy blood, thy blood I crave
forget my sin and grant my spirit the heavenly joys to have
Lo now I sink, lo now I drown, and drink the mortal flood
O Christ, O, Christ take thou my spirit that trusteth in thy blood

The lines, which seemed to come not from within him but from the Holy Ghost guiding his pen, recalled to him One far greater than he who had prayed for His cup to be removed before He went and 'died upon the rood.' Yet He had been sinless, and Richard as a mere man was not; even one who had lived his life conducting himself always in Christian love, as he had ever striven to do, found pause at the knowledge that he might soon pass through the gates of death.

When he had finished, he asked his mother to dress the wound, and when she did she remarked at how small it really was. It was not inflamed, and had sealed itself, for there had been little more bleeding. Richard assured both Agnes and Hellene, who was now up and about, that he was feeling better and knew that in a few days he would be as good as new. He asked for a cup of his mother's herb tea so that he might rest again, and Hellene brought it to him. He sipped on it for a time, and then gently drifted off to sleep.

The children had been told what had happened, and that their father was doing very well, but that they must remain very quiet these next few days so that he could rest and heal. They responded admirably, for they perceived from the confidence their mother and grandmother conveyed that all would soon be as it had been before the accident.

For several days Richard continued to improve, and soon was sitting up, bolstered with pillows, for part of each day. But he was still weak, and dared not try to stand. Hellene had politely suggested that the queen not visit, as her regular appearances would only cause Richard alarm, and Elizabeth saw the wisdom of this, so instead a messenger came from Huntworth twice each day and took reports back to her.

After a week, everything seemed to indicate that Richard would soon recover. That evening, October 31, 1566, he and Hellene were alone, Richard sitting up and sipping his tea, Hellene beside him on the edge of the bed. He told her he was getting drowsy, but he wanted her to stay, for there was something he wanted to tell her.

'Can it not wait for morning, my love?' she asked gently. 'Should you not rest now?'

'Nay, what I must tell you has already waited far too long,' said Richard, motioning for her to lie down beside him. When she did, he took her hand in his and laid them both upon his chest, which rose and fell gently with his breathing. Then he proceeded to tell her the secret of his Tudor heritage from beginning to end from that fateful night in Huntworth Lodge when King Henry had his way with Agnes Blewitt to the honours recently bestowed on him by his half sister, Queen Elizabeth. He concluded by telling her she must inform no one, not even the children, and she promised they would never hear it from her lips.

Then he said, 'I had to tell you so that you would understand the importance to me of that which I now request.'

She nodded her assent.

'Truly I believe that the worst of the injury is now through, and soon I shall proceed to London with the queen, and yet there is something I must ask of you, something of which we may never speak again.'

Again Hellene promised that she would do whatever he asked.

'Then when it comes my time to die,' he said softly, 'I do not wish to be buried in London in any place of honour. The price of our secret has been dearly paid, and I would not have it known at my death. A crypt of great prominence might cause some to wonder, and in wondering, perhaps they might divine the truth. You must promise me that if I go first, that will not happen; bury me instead in a quiet place, here in this country I love, among these emerald hills and not too far from the thrashing sea. There I will quietly sleep through the ages till Gabriel's trump is blown.'

'A promise is not truly required, my love,' she protested, 'for I would sooner die than betray your trust.' He started to say something, but she anticipated his words: 'Still, a promise you shall have, if it gives thee peace.' She smiled up at her husband, then nestled her head beside his shoulder.

'Wherever I am buried,' he continued, speaking in very serious tones, 'there must be room also for you. I know that we will be together in spirit after death, but I want our remains to rest in the same place as well.'

'It shall be exactly as you ask, my love.'

'And this I have thought of much in these past few days,' Richard said, 'though I did not want to speak thus, as it might have made you sad.' He paused as though searching for the right words. 'My dear Hellene,' he went on, 'I feel that our love is so strong that not even death can separate us. I know in some mystic fashion I can always convey to you when I am pleased even from over there, in the land without shadow and by the same means I may know that all is well with you. There will be some kind of sign I know it. And yet I know not how I know it. Somehow I always feel that I will be as close to you as your own breath, and you will sense that I am with you.' He stopped, wondering if his words sounded different to other ears than they did to his own. 'Does this seem terribly strange?'

'No,' she hastened to say, her eyes glistening with tears, 'it does not sound strange at all. Indeed, I have had almost the very same thoughts myself. You and I are more fortunate than most, for our hearts and souls are so completely one that truly they are inseparable. This surpasses all I ever dreamed or thought possible at all.'

She held his hand firmly and looked into his eyes with longing, but she knew that for his health she had best let him sleep. 'You have spent quite enough energy now, my dear,' she said, suddenly changing her tone to that of a nurse, 'and you must have your rest to heal. If truly we can speak to one another across the veil of death, then sleep should pose no barrier. Please rest so you can be well very soon, my love.'

Richard, still holding her hand firmly, dropped off to sleep, and before she knew it the inky balm of slumber swept over her as well.

She was awakened some time later she knew not how long by a tingling in her arm and in the hand that Richard still held to his chest. But his chest did not any longer rise and fall. Slowly the realisation came over her that Richard had stopped breathing, and she realised too that his hands were cold. Then the stabbing painful truth swept over her: her beloved no longer lived.

The tears flowed shamelessly for a long, long while as she gathered her thoughts, and then came to realise what she must do. The children could not know for the moment. William was only five, the others younger still, and what could a child understand about death? She slipped out of the bed, dressed quickly, and stepped down the hall to Agnes's room. Pushing the door quietly, she found her mother-in-law fully clothed and standing before the window, looking out with an expression of calm on her face.

Agnes did not turn around, but held her place in silence. At last she spoke in a soft but controlled voice. 'Hellene, you need not tell me the message you bring I have known it for several hours now.' Then she turned and with firmness and tenderness said, 'I will send Christopher to tell the rector what must be done, and neither the children nor the parish will be alerted. There can be a memorial service later on, and the parish may attend then.' She stopped, as though thinking of something else. 'Have you thought of the christening for your baby?'

'Yes,' said Hellene, 'but that, too, is for the family alone. I could not face the one without the hope of the other.'

'Someone must tell the queen,' said Agnes.

'Yes,' Hellene replied, 'but she cannot attend. We must not attract notice not now.'

And so the rector performed both services, and to his dying day hoped fervently he would never again be called upon to perform both a funeral and a christening for the same family on the same day. God was merciful, for it never happened again as long as that man lived.

The two women stood through it all with tears, of course, but with composure and dignity as well. Both seemed to the rector to possess such inner strength in this time of great emotion that they must have some royal strain in them.

27

Many days and weeks and months went by for Hellene, their passage an unbroken succession of bleak moments that slowly, terribly slowly, she thought, would bring her to the hour of her own death, when she would join Richard again. In the meantime, though, she remained numb, as unfeeling as a ceramic doll, and at odd times when she missed him most she would feel a sudden surge of blinding anger: at God for allowing his death, at Richard for dying and leaving her with six children to raise, at her own self for feeling her loss so deeply. She cried herself to sleep many a night, and on others she lay awake, reconstructing their moments together and sometimes in panic realising that the very memory of his face was beginning to fade from her.

She learned that there was nothing more deafening than the silence that had once been filled by his voice, nothing so empty as the vast gulf on the other side of her bed, nothing as hollow as the heart that once thrilled at the mere touch of his hand.

Fortunately for her, Agnes took on the burden of the children in this time as she had once done for Richard long, long ago when there was only William. The youngsters saw little of their mother, and this spared them the knowledge of her deep and abiding grief.

But just as the fact of change, death, worst of all is the Almighty's worst curse, it is among His greatest blessings, and at the end of the winter there came a morning when she woke up strangely renewed. It was as though suddenly she became aware of the six young lives very near to her, and the rich joy she had before her in these gifts from her late husband.

He had said in his last words to her that he would ever be as close as her own breath, and in that as all things, Richard had spoken truly. To her happy amazement, she found now that the images of him and their life together, which had before grown dim, now returned to focus; and she could remember the sound of his voice, the way he walked, the feel of his arms about her.

Without being told, the children had sensed their mother's pain, and now again without needing any words, they responded to her re-emergence with their laughter, which had not been heard in the little cottage for many months now.

With the return of clarity and joy, Hellene recalled Richard's mention of the promise Queen Elizabeth had given him, a grant of an estate in south Wales. If the queen's offer still held, the property and its tenants would provide a means for Hellene and her family to live with dignity. Yes, her children had inherited the legacy of the Tudors, but one could not eat a royal name, and princely blood would not warm the bones on a cold night. Now Hellene had the firm sense of mission: she must go to London and beseech the queen on her family's behalf. She would grovel at Her Majesty's feet if such were required, but Richard's children must not be denied their rightful inheritance.

She went to Agnes to report her intentions, but her husband's mother was wiser than she: with a quiet smile, the gentle woman said, 'Welcome home, my dear child. Perhaps you might send ahead a letter to London to inform the queen of your visit.'

'Oh, Mother Agnes,' said Hellene with tears in her eyes. 'Whatever would have become of us all without you?'

'I suspect you would have done no differently, but then you would not have had me to reassure you, so I suppose an old lady's worth is not truly wanting, is it?'

Soon Hellene left for the capital, and on her journey she saw a countryside that seemed entirely new to her. Before this she'd had Richard's eyes to see for her, pointing out all the sights along the way; now she saw it as though he were within her, looking out through her twin windows and exulting at the beauty in every hill and dale along the way, praising God for His loving mercy and tenderness. The people she met at the inns and towns on her travel treated her with kindness and deference, seemingly knowing her mission, and when she had gone on, many remarked at the glow on her face and the fire in her eyes.

Upon receiving Hellene's letter, Elizabeth had sent word that she must plan to stay in Richard's apartment at Whitehall Palace, and when her coach arrived, the guard welcomed her home as an old friend. Then the carriage bumped along the cobblestone courtyard, to the very entrance where she and Richard had gone in many a time. The guard at the door, too, smiled and welcomed her, then led her by the light of a candle down the hallway to the chamber she knew so well.

She had kept herself from thinking how she might feel when she opened the door to that enchanted place, and when the guard was gone she looked around in silence. Richard's few possessions had remained exactly as they were, and for a moment she could almost believe that he might suddenly walk in and doff his cap, bringing the latest gossip from Court and reports of the queen's activities that day. She stood motionless for a long time, then she opened her eyes and moved about the room, looking at and touching things he had touched. She did not weep; again she felt a strange joy, as though he were there somehow.

That night, she scarcely slept, and she left a candle burning so that its dim light might help her store up in memory every detail of the place. She was up at dawn the next day, dressed quickly, and went for a walk through the courtyard and the grounds about the palace. Then she had a coach take her to St. Paul's Cathedral so she might see it, perhaps for the last time, for she knew not what course her life might take from here. When she had touched with her eyes many places she and Richard had known together, she returned to Whitehall and prepared for the audience with the queen.

In her suite she found fresh flowers and a note from Her Majesty saying that she would see her at noontime, when they would share a private lunch in Elizabeth's rooms. Hellene selected a deep blue velvet dress that Richard had loved, and put on a locket he'd given her for the last Christmas they had shared. Then she took a carriage to Whitehall.

There she was greeted with the recognition befitting the wife of England's greatest poet, and a footman showed her into the queen's private parlour. Elizabeth soon arrived, and after the servants were sent away, she embraced her old friend and beckoned her to sit down.

'I cannot tell you how sorry I am for your loss, dear child,' said the queen. 'These things seem not fair, but then who are we to reckon the ways of the Almighty?'

Hellene raised her eyes and looked intently but kindly into her queen's eyes. 'Be not sorry for me, Your Majesty. I am the richest woman in all Christendom - I was Richard Edwardes' wife, the mother of his children, and his eternal and undying love is still with me. I was weak and sorry for myself at first, but no more, for he is still here in my heart.'

Elizabeth smiled, and did not speak for a long time, caught up in her own thoughts of the dear friend that had passed. After some moments, she began to speak again, asking news of the children and Agnes, then she drew herself up and said, 'We have talked of many things already, but I suspect your visit is not simply for such. Is there a way in which I may help an old friend?'

'Your Highness is ever as gracious as her servant recalls,' said Hellene with a smile. She got up from her chair and walked to the window, hoping that her queen would not notice how her hands trembled. 'What I have come to ask is most difficult for me, and were it not for the well-being of my children, I should not have the courage at all.'

'Then it is a thing best quickly spoken,' said the queen gently.

Hellene turned to face her monarch. 'On his last night, Richard told me the secret your family has kept so long.' She blushed. 'His words only confirmed what I had already guessed long ago, for perhaps Your Majesty recalls the time when I once near caused offense by delving too deeply into it.' She drew a deep breath. 'I do not come asking for anything for myself; it is the children who are my concern - they are almost all that I have of him now.' Having said that, she fell to her knees before the queen.

Elizabeth got up from where she was seated and took a step toward Hellene. 'My dear child, I cannot permit you further torture. You must wonder of the promise I made to Richard concerning the estate in south Wales. Concern yourself no more: Edwards Hall is yours and your children's forever. I waited only so I might speak of it when you were beyond the first grief. Unfortunately,' she added in a rueful tone, 'an arrow fired in foolish haste has prevented the fulfilment of the rest of the promises, but at least Sir Richard knew my intent. So do rise to your feet, my child, for you have not to beg the queen for what is rightfully yours.'

'Oh, Your Majesty,' said Hellene, tears now welling up, 'what may I do to show you how grateful I am?'

'I do not require such to know what is in your heart,' said Elizabeth gently, extending her hand to help Hellene to her feet.

'And there is another thing I can and will do for you,' she added with a sly smile, 'a thing of which you know not. It has come to my attention that your brother has been appointed guardian of the children, a fitting and brotherly thing, but as a queen who has had to make her way among kings, I wish also to give you more control than some might think fitting a 'mere woman.' You shall be executor of the estate, and may handle its disposition as you see fit for the benefit of all your children. What's more, you shall not have to conform to English law, which states that the oldest son inherits all, but may if you so choose place the estate under the Welsh law, in which it is the youngest who receives the largest portion. Therefore if this is to your liking, I shall see that it is made binding in the Canterbury courts.'

'Yes, Your Majesty, and I thank you again - England is ever fortunate to have so gracious a queen.'

Elizabeth waved a hand. 'My dear Hellene, 'tis pitifully little I do for dear Richard, who asked naught for himself. Had he been of the mind, he might have proclaimed his secret, raised an army, and ascended to the throne; but he wished only to do that which his heart told him he must do. In that he proved the royal strain of his blood, and when I consider the rich blessings he enjoyed of home and family while I have consigned myself to live ever alone I wonder who was the wiser of us.'

'It is my privilege to do these things for his family, for he proved himself most worthy. Our father would have never guessed how we would prove ourselves, for he believed not that a woman could be a king, and yet each in our own way, Richard and I have done the king proud.' She chuckled. 'In my youth, there were those who questioned my right to call myself the king's daughter, yet I will ever be known as such, whereas Richard he was grateful enough to be but a poet and the son of a yeoman from Somerset.

'And now, my dear child,' she concluded, 'your queen must leave you, but you will never be far from my thoughts.' From a table beside her she withdrew a simple ring of gold and placed it in Hellene's hand. 'If ever you are in need, only send this ring to your friend Elizabeth, and I shall be there for you. Now I wish you safe journey and godspeed.'

Hellene bowed her head, then Elizabeth said, 'One thing I near forgot: when you reach your new home, you will find it quite ready for you, and will even see a surprise placed there for Richard.' Her eyes twinkled. 'It is a bit of Somerset in Wales, and I will let you find it for yourself. Perhaps when you gaze upon it, you may think fondly of his home, of the secret, and of me. And now good-bye until we meet again.'

Elizabeth smiled fondly at her for a moment, then she turned and left the room in her by now characteristic measured stride, an outward manifestation of Richard's effect on her life. Hellene stood there for a time, wanting to remember every detail clearly. He had seen that palace on their honeymoon, she thought, and said he felt drawn to it: could it be Destiny that drew him? With these thoughts in her mind, she made ready to return to Somerset, carrying with her in spirit not only Richard but the woman who had called herself 'your friend Elizabeth.'

28

The driver of the coach had been alerted to blow the horn as a signal when Hellene approached, just as Richard's arrival had been heralded so many times before. Soon the children, followed by their grandmother, spilled out the door, and each in his turn threw his arms around Hellene's neck and kissed her. Agnes was the last to greet her. 'I can see that you bring good news, Hellene,' she said, 'but then I never doubted it. Our queen is a great lady, and ever mindful of' - she said the last words in a whisper - 'her family.'

The next days flew by with wings. Soon all that was to be taken to their new home was packed and ready, and a day came when their carriage and cart were passing by the churchyard of St. Mary's on their way out of Somerset. Hellene took a lingering look at the cemetery, and for a moment the sadness she hadn't felt in a long while rose up in her.

William, seated next to her, suddenly tugged at her sleeve. 'Mother,' he said softly, 'will we be coming back soon to take Father to our new home?'

It took her a moment to gather her wits about her. 'Yes, William, we will come back for him.'

'I did not mean to make you sad, Mother,' said the boy, seeing tears in her eyes, 'but I knew that would be what he would want.'

'Dear, dear William,' she said, clutching the child close to her. 'How wise you are for such a little man. You are very, very much like him, are you not?'

The trip across the bay took longer than they had thought it would, and it was dusk when at last they saw the towers of their new home. For a moment the excitement that had been building for all seemed to die: the place looked as gloomy and uninviting as a dungeon.

This great hall had been built in the late eleventh century, during the days when knights clad in heavy armour plate fought great battles to defend castles which were themselves mighty fortresses against invasion. The Norman noble who had built this place, Sir Godefrey de Pomerio, had not had comfort in mind, but rather security, and its gloomy gray walls with their single uninviting gate presented an impenetrable facade to the eight weary travellers who now approached it. Over time this place had passed through various families until it reverted to the Crown, and the more than four hundred years it had stood thus had taken their toll: one of the towers was crumbling, a sure sign of more work to be done on the inside.

The men with them moved quickly to empty the carts and bring their few possessions into the entry hall, and one of them lowered the great chandelier so that Hellene could light the dusty candles.

Once this was done, and the fire that had been laid in anticipation of their arrival was lit, the place began to appear more cheery, less like a fortress and more like a home.

Hellene had worried that the yawning emptiness of Edwards Hall would swallow up their meagre chairs and beds, but now she saw how much care her queen had taken in seeing that the place was made ready. Lovely paintings and tapestries hung from the walls, the windows were covered with luxuriant drapes, and in every room there were elegant items of furniture placed with care.

Agnes had brought all their pots and pans along with flour and salted meat, but she found the kitchen already stocked with enough food to last them a month. Forthwith she began preparing a meal for the family, and over Hellene's protests bade her go with the children and explore the labyrinthine second and third stories of the house.

Each bedroom, of which there were many more than enough, had its own fireplace with a fire prepared; these were lit, and the coverlets (already placed on the bed) were turned back in preparation for the night. Returning to the downstairs, flushed with the joy of all she'd found, Hellene paid the men and invited them to stay and sup with them.

After the men had left, Hellene suddenly remembered Elizabeth's words of a surprise from Somerset to be found in the courtyard, and taking William with her, she went in search of it. By now the rain had begun again, and the wind was gusting, so she wrapped the lad in a muffler that had been Richard's, a gift she'd given him shortly after they were married. They looked for awhile, but after becoming drenched, she judged it wiser to wait for the morrow, when they would begin their search anew. Once back inside the great hall, Hellene realised that the scarf, in spite of her efforts to secure it, had been blown away by the wind. But by now she'd turned her attention to making sure that William warmed and dried himself in front of the fire before going to bed.

After the children were tucked in, Hellene and Agnes collapsed into their beds; several hours later, though, Hellene awoke with a start. The sky outside had the faintest hint of gray at the edges, and she knew that morning could not be far off. The rain had stopped, and all was silent in the great expanse of Edwards Hall, but she was sure she'd heard a noise. It was almost as though someone were near.

The feeling did not frighten her, but rather gave her comfort, and instinctively she reached toward the other side of the bed. This presence she felt, whatever it was, seemed to be telling her that she was home, and that she and her family would always be safe, in the words of the Psalmist, both from 'the terror by night' and 'the arrow that flieth by day.'

She could not go back to sleep and, remembering the muffler, decided to go retrieve it. She dressed quickly and tiptoed down the grand creaking staircase into the heart of the great hall, where she took up her cape from the hall tree where she had hung it to dry the night before. Pushing open the huge oak door, she stepped into the courtyard.

She worked her way around the perimeter of the courtyard, walking slowly and studying the area as she went, more concerned about exploring her new yard than about finding the missing shawl. Just as she approached the door to the chapel, suddenly she spied the scarf, which had been caught on a bush beside the door. She reached down to free it, and as she did she saw that the shrub had bloomed sometime during the night.

It was the gift Elizabeth had spoken of: a Glastonbury thorn bush. It was much too early for the flowers that normally bloom in spring, but this tree came into flower on a schedule all its own. Richard had told her that when he was sure all was well, there would be a sign - and here it was.

Careful not to touch the thorns, she wrested the scarf free and pulled one bloom from the bush. She held it gently in her hands for a long time, until she heard the sounds of children's laughter from within. By now it was morning, and she entered the great hall to find them all awake.

The children thrilled at the sight of the thorny bush, only half understanding its meaning, and in the days and weeks that followed, there was much more for them to discover. The rest of 1567 passed quickly for them, and soon it was autumn: hunting season, a year since Richard's death.

Late one cold and windy evening, after they'd tucked the children into their bed, Hellene and Agnes heard an unexpected rap on the great oaken door. The two women looked at one another in fear, wondering who might be calling at such an hour. A caretaker lived in a cottage nearby, but he would be in bed, and there was no other man to protect them.

Beside the door they kept a great cane of oak wood, and though she had often joked that she wouldn't be able to use it if she were in danger (for it weighed so much she could barely lift it), Hellene retrieved it and motioned for Agnes to answer the door while she waited behind her with her weapon at the ready.

The older woman slid back a small door at eye level and whispered, 'Who is it?'

A figure in a great cowl covering the face stood before the door, and for a moment the two ladies of the house were stricken with terror. Could it be a ghost? But suddenly Hellene felt great peace, for she remembered a bit of advice her mother had given her as a girl: 'always show kindness to strangers who come to your door, for you never know but what it is an angel.'

Still, she kept her club in her hand.

But the words that came, in a muffled voice, from under the hood shocked her almost as much as a visit from Michael himself. 'It is your friend Elizabeth, come to see you from London.'

With a thrill, Hellene raced to help Agnes lift the great crossbar that blocked the door. When the door swung open, their visitor entered and lifted off her cape to reveal that she was indeed the Queen of England.

'Your Majesty,' said Hellene with a deep curtsy, 'you do great honour to such a humble dwelling as Edwards Hall.'

'Humble dwelling, forsooth!' said the queen with a twinkle in her eyes. 'Please, dear ladies, stand up.' Agnes had also curtsied, though not as deeply, for the years had stiffened her bones. 'It is your friend Elizabeth, and not the queen who visits. Come give me an embrace to warm these cold bones.'

'Had we known you were coming, we would have...'

But Elizabeth stopped their words. 'I could scarcely alert the countryside with a royal visit, so I had a boat bring me across after dark, and wore this confoundedly heavy cloak. I came only with two guards, who wait before the door. Now, if you would be so kind, I would like a cup of tea and a seat before your fire.'

When Agnes returned from the kitchen, finding the two other women sitting in front of the gentle blaze and talking as old friends, she brought with her not only tea but a special treat she'd made for the queen in days past, when her son dwelled at Whitehall Palace. The queen's eyes lit up when she saw it: fresh fruit generously covered in thick, sweet cream.

'My dear,' she said, 'you should not have gone to such trouble, but I am delighted that you did!'

'It was no trouble at all, Your Majesty, merely a trifle.'

'I have always wondered what to call this confection,' Elizabeth said, taking the fork Agnes gave her. 'Now I know, and a trifle it shall be henceforth.'

When she had eaten, the queen thanked Agnes again and said, 'I had to see for myself that my dear friends were as comfortably housed as you said in your many kind letters. It is one thing to read from afar, another to come and see.'

'Indeed, Your Majesty, it is true,' said Hellene with a glow that came not merely from the fire before her. 'We are as happy as ever any family can be, thanks to your thoughtfulness and generosity.' After that she gave a complete report of everything, from finding the wonderful surprise to the present moment.

'And you are happy, my dear?' asked the queen in a serious tone. 'Should you not think of marrying again so that the children might grow up having a father?'

Hellene was silent for a short while, studying her hands and trying to find the right words. 'No, Your Majesty,' she said at long last, 'marriage again is not possible for me, though I think nothing wrong in it for most widows. Richard was the finest man I shall ever know, and I could never love another as I loved him - indeed, it would not be fair to that other man.'

'Yes,' said Elizabeth kindly after another long pause, 'but Richard is...' She did not finish her sentence.

'Begging your pardon, Your Majesty,' said Hellene, blushing, 'but I feel him to be with me still, in spirit, dwelling in the love that he and I shared, which still lives. I am content with this, and I think that to do otherwise would be wrong both for the children and for me.'

Elizabeth smiled gently at her, and Hellene went on: 'I believe that Your Majesty understands the decision I have made, for she has made a similar choice for her own children, the people of England. This is for you, as mine is for me, your destiny - that for which God placed you here. Am I not right, Your Majesty? Forgive me if I speak brashly, for such seems to be my habit.'

Elizabeth patted her hand. 'No, my dear, you speak not brashly, but truly. There is but one life and one duty for Elizabeth Tudor, and if I were to marry at all, it would take away from that which I must do.' She sighed. 'Can any queen ever be sure it is for love of herself that her hand is sought? I could not run the risk, even though there was one I loved deeply...' She stared into the fire a moment and then, seeming to come to herself, she concluded: 'You are quite right, Hellene. We both have our destinies laid out for us, and to do otherwise would never be proper either in the eyes of God or ourselves. How wise you are, my dear, and how I miss your presence at Court!'

The conversation trailed off, and the three women stared reflectively into the fire until finally Elizabeth rose. ' 'Twas the most pleasant hour I've spent in a long, long time, but I fear it has ended.'

'Your Majesty,' said Agnes, 'would you not stay with us?'

'Thank you,' said the queen, 'but I must be gone. Others await me, and I must ever return to 'my children'.' This last she said with a smile to Hellene, who went into the other room to fetch her cloak for her.

They chatted for a few minutes more, and then Elizabeth, the Queen of England, disappeared once again in the great cape which served as her disguise. For a long time, Hellene and Agnes stood before the great open door of Edwards Hall, the forbidding wind whipping about them, and watched as her figure (and those of the guards who flanked her) became smaller and smaller in the distance. As she shut the door, the young widow said to herself that she knew Richard would have been happy. But then she smiled at herself: he saw it all from above, and he was happy.

Epilogue

The voice of a lady-in-waiting brought the aging queen back to the present: 'Your Majesty, shall I not help you to dress for the ambassador from Spain?' The man had come at King Philip's bidding to bring the queen gifts, and she must look her best. Hurriedly Elizabeth returned the poem and the letter from Lord Leicester to the casket for yet another time, then turned with full composure and summoned the other ladies to help her dress.

They placed a favourite red wig, richly adorned with pearls, on the queen's head, and others brought the jewel-studded gown that had been selected for the occasion. Soon every finger of the royal hands was adorned with rings, and she fairly sparkled in the candlelight of her rooms.

The elderly sovereign, now transformed completely, drew herself to her full height and walked out of her chamber with the measured stride Richard Edwardes had taught her so many years ago. Jewelled and gowned as she was, and with the wig the colour her hair had been in her youth, one could hardly discern from a distance the ravages of the years. She was Elizabeth still, the Virgin Queen, the earthly goddess and the greatest leader her kingdom had ever known.

She had become legendary in her own lifetime, and had prepared her people and her country to become the world's greatest empire. When her cousin Mary's son James assumed the throne upon her passing, he would find he'd been left a great inheritance indeed. Yet she had lost much too, in the form of those many friends and acquaintances - even enemies - who had already passed through the veil of death. Leicester was dead, Hunsdon and Cecil too; Mary of Scotland had gone in a gruesome way, executed for treason against her, the Queen of England. Even Philip, whose son Philip III now ruled over Spain, was long in his grave. She knew that ere long she would join them, with many to mourn her but no one to carry on, for she would die as she had lived, the Virgin Queen.

Her father had sought to sire a legitimate son through half a dozen women, but it had all come to naught, and he had died drowning in his own frustration even as his body had given up its blood on the streets of Windsor. Her sister Mary, too, had longed as passionately for a child as she had for her husband, and death had left her with neither. But the Tudor lineage had continued nonetheless, like the water of a river always seeking a way around obstructions on its path to the sea.

Humbly he had lived, and with little less humility had Richard Edwardes gone to his grave. Always he had kept the secret of his birth, always served in quiet faithfulness, until the day the arrow found its mark on his breast. While she had her many victories, both in the days when he lived and in the almost four decades that had passed since he died, he had walked beside her in silence, first as a man and then as a spirit in the shadow of the throne, his wise words always ready but never given out of turn.

There had been no fanfare on the day his first child had entered this earth, but instead a death and much sorrow. But on that day, and on the five subsequent days when Henry's other grandchildren were born, all the Tudors throughout the ages rejoiced to see that though their name had died, their legacy did not.

Elizabeth, Queen of England, had appeared as a comet on the skies, and had shone with a brilliance seldom equalled. Her illumination would echo down through countless centuries, and when she was no more, she would be remembered throughout eternity. But what was the light quietly trailing the comet, that ineffable brilliance from heaven? It was he, too often unsung, too frequently unseen, and his silent triumph would stand through a hundred generations.

'But the rose remembers
The dust from which it came.'
Edna St. Vincent Millay